THE THIRST

ANDRÉ JOHN HADDAD

Imagen Publishing

ISBN: 978-1-9993854-9-1

Cover design & interior formatting by Aaxel Author Services & Noah Adam Paperman

To
Louise
forever

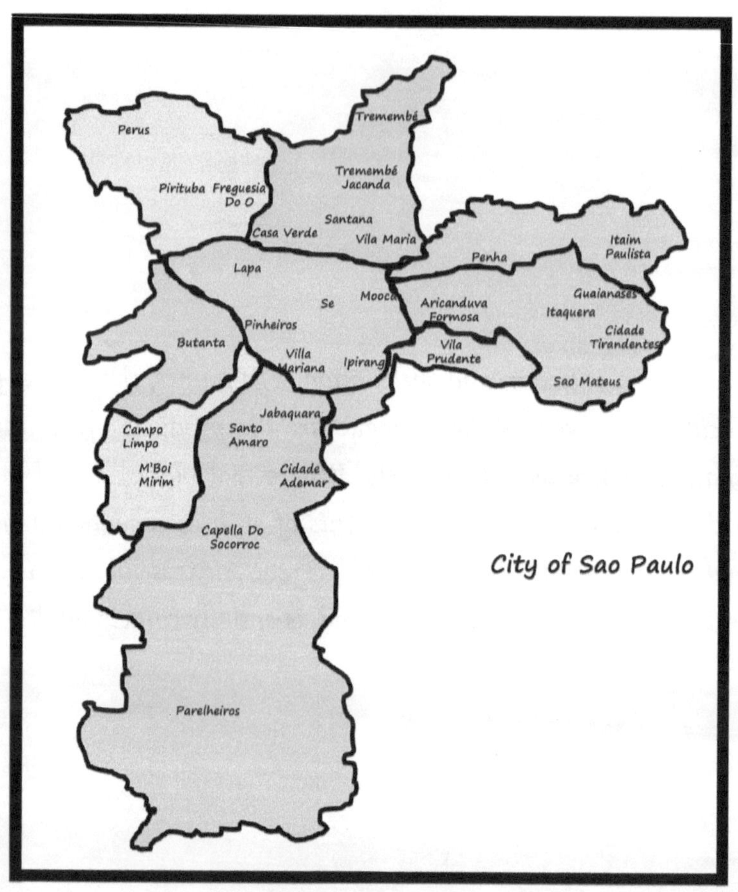

City of São Paulo

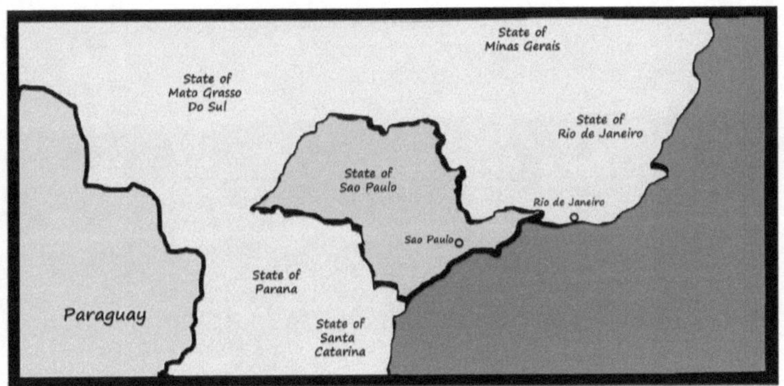

State of São Paulo

PRINCIPAL CHARACTERS

Willy (Wee Willy) **Callender**. Chemical engineer. Joined MI6 as a British Government analyst. Born in Inverness, Scotland in 1943.

Louise Margoe **Destrey**. Industrial psychologist. Consultant. Partner in charge of the Boston Triage Group (BTG) based in Cambridge, Massachusetts. Consultant to Cardinal Hedrick Zimmer. Daughter of Robert and Marie Destrey. Born in Montreal in 1957.

Cesare **Franco**. Jesuit priest. Assistant to Cardinal Hedrick Zimmer. Jerusalem Foundation associate. Son of Ruggero and Adriana Franco. Born in Bologna in 1968.

Alexander **Fionnuala**. Joined MI6 as a British Government analyst. Guest lecturer, journalist and speechwriter. Born in Italy in 1936.

John Thomas **Kleinrup**. Businessperson. Jerusalem Foundation associate. Son of Horace Kleinrup (former MI6 Director) and Lady Jane Elizabeth Sassone. Born in Oxshott/Stoke D'Abernon (Surrey) UK in 1957.

Paulistanos. Residents of São Paulo, Brazil.

Denis (D) **Planter**. Leader of Jardim Filhos da Terra street gang. Born in São Paulo, Brazil, between 1989 and 1994.

Julian Andre Illarion **Precov**. Jerusalem Foundation associate. Board President of the Boston Triage Group (BTG). Former Russian foreign minister, ambassador to India, FSB director, KGB case officer. Son of Lev Precov. Mother Antonina Precova. Born in Minsk, Belarus, in 1940.

Alexander Francisco **Spinetti**. Architect. Consultant. CEO of Shapeshift SA. Son of Dr. Edwin Spinetti and Flora Appia (architect). Born in Bellinzona, Switzerland, in 1971.

1

Outside, the weather was bad.

Inside, Louise Margoe Destrey was still recovering from the strain of each new assignment her organization undertook. Predicting the future was a risky business particularly when clients didn't know what to do with the information or how to successfully execute their plans, if they had any. Her company's last assignment in Jerusalem weighed heavily on Destrey's shoulders. The work undertaken by the firm to help the Jewish State find its way forward in an ever increasingly complex world exacerbated her weariness and unease, especially when she had personally been confronted with life-threatening situations.

It was late. She was home. It was one of those days that never ended. The TV was talking, and she was exhausted. Destrey wanted to bitch about the heavy workload but there was no one to complain to. She had the last word on whether or not an assignment would move forward. Destrey was the captain of her ship: a consulting firm called the Boston Triage Group, or BTG.

Destrey was the senior partner and majority stockholder. BTG was dedicated to shedding light on the future of organizations, small and large. The firm's current research project concerned the city of São Paulo. Board President Julian Precov encouraged Destrey to move forward. He also said she should be careful because that part of the world didn't necessarily interpret the rule of law as applying equally to everyone. Nevertheless, he believed that South America, and especially São Paulo, needed her full attention. BTG's supercomputer alerted Constantin Greco, Destrey's number two, of the overwhelming probability the city would soon be the next target of an event. An event implied an all-hands-on deck scenario.

São Paulo was at a tipping point, according to the data generated at BTG's headquarters. The computer flagged it as significant. An unstoppable domino effect was pending, with considerable consequences to life and property.

Remarkably, that was the nature of the work. Destrey's organization, the Boston Triage Group, had been created to specifically forecast threatening events, from Mother Nature to man-made phenomena. She was in the business of predicting incidents—in essence what could happen and what could be done about it.

However, her mission statement came with a heavy price tag: an above normal amount of stress and silent apprehension. She would remind herself, when dealing with client expectations, that revealing the future was never well received. Also, poorly executed recommendations were a constant cue that clients where ultimately in charge and responsible for their actions, regardless of a consultant's advice. In many cases, clients would become aggressive or violent.

Over time, Destrey came to understand that her business was part science and part instinct. Combined with artistic composition, BTG created an environment of imaginative sciences, providing Destrey's people with the incentive to generate new questions and what-ifs.

While preparing to attack a large portion of chocolate cheesecake from Cafe Madeleine, she had a nagging feeling the world had an infinite capacity to generate horror. A thought had crossed her mind: whether or not she wanted out. Once again, Destrey rammed the possibility away and buried it as deep as she could. Cheesecake had a calming effect on her, so much so that she fell asleep.

She was dreaming again. A recurring nightmare meant to remind Destrey of her duty and the oath she took. An obligation Destrey had freely agreed to honor. A personal commitment to use the considerable amounts of money she had inherited from Cardinal Zimmer to do good. Destrey was the boss, guide and sole owner of the Boston Triage Group. She commanded the firm's team of specialists in difficult and strange times. It was a responsibility some considered almost unfair.

"I'm running for my life, that's why." Destrey was in no mood to discuss the point with the ghosts she lived with. They often appeared in her dreams and nightmares. This one was no exception.

A dead woman was riding Destrey's horse into the fleeing crowd. The rider's face was riddled with cancer sores, yellowing eyes and burnt skin. The ghost howled as the horse tried to get away from the repulsive spirit. The specter of death was riding her Rusty. He was a good-looking thoroughbred with the temperament of a mule. Still, a good boy. He was galloping through the crowd, trampling children, killing the innocent as well as the guilty. They were all trying to escape from the Holy City.

Destrey cried out as regret washed over her. "I could have done better," she said. "I'm sorry!" But no sound was heard. She was paralyzed.

The rider went out of her way to kill and smash small bodies. They fell by the wayside and tumbled into a black hole. Then, Destrey watched as the rider looked at her, and the ghost said she was coming for her.

Well, that's strange, Destrey thought to herself. *My boy never cared to gallop when I was riding him.* She was almost taken aback by her own words, even though the ghost was galloping her way. She ran but couldn't move forward. Rusty was nearly on top of Destrey.

"You're not going to do that to me?" Destrey asked. She couldn't keep her eyes off him. She secretly missed him. Her big boy. Her handsome galoot was now about to trample her.

"I'll miss you," she said sadly. The horse didn't bother to look back. Rusty ran past Destrey, running for his own life. The dream morphed again into chaos: a crowd, a great wave of women and children. They were unable to reach safety. Destrey was surrounded by a tsunami of screaming shades of blood. She was unable to turn or to retreat. She was back to square one. Destrey had to do it all over again. Every turn was a dead-end. She could barely breathe, let alone save herself.

"One step at a time!" she screamed for all to hear. "We can make it out if... what?" She didn't know what to think anymore. Suddenly, her skin turned black.

No matter what, Destrey promised herself, *the job will get done.* She would find a way. Running as far away as possible from the madmen and killers was an imperative. The people, all those poor children, they had to be saved. Unfortunately, there was little time left. The assassins couldn't be found. Soldiers were shooting indiscriminately. Whatever moved became a target. Destrey was lost in an unruly crowd. She was also a target. Destrey struggled to pull back, trying to get away from the hands clutching her clothes.

In Louise's nightmare, hundreds of thousands were heading *en masse* toward safety. Tent camps were being erected in the shadow of synagogues and churches. The city was collapsing.

She was staring at the biggest traffic jam in history. An exodus from Jerusalem had begun. Vehicle breakdowns, accidents and road rage made the escape exponentially difficult. Nothing had prepared her to deal with her own evacuation. *I have people for that,* she said to herself. Where were the Russian goons assigned to protect her? Destrey needed them now. Unfortunately, she realized, she was on her own.

The nightmare wasn't over. In fact, it had just begun.

"I remember," she whispered to herself. "I remember telling the Cardinal. A partial evacuation would be disastrous. The people responsible to get the people out would unintentionally set the stage for chaos. They would make it worse." Apparently, no one was listening or cared. She was a nobody. An old bitch with no friends, dying alone.

Still asleep, Destrey's nightmare continued unabated.

"This is no joke girly," the U.S. president said mischievously. "I know your company can predict the future and all that crap, but you have to get out of there, now." The president was on a different horse, riding high in the saddle. "There's work to do. Ever hear of the Bomb, Dolly?"

"Can't you see what I'm doing?" Destrey shot back. "I'm going to do my best. Besides, if it wasn't for me, you'd all be in the middle of World War Three. Forget the Bomb. I gave you the information. What the hell more do you want me to do?" Destrey felt stranded and lost, with no help in sight. Trying to move her feet forward, she fell backwards. Destrey felt trapped and surrounded by dead people. A Catholic's worst nightmare. Ghosts pushed and shoved while the beast from hell was telling her to quit.

"You can't do anything," said the beast.

Destrey was failing. There was no one left in her life. Her husband had died years ago. She felt abandoned and alone in a mob of the accursed. She cried and screamed for help. She felt as if she was the only person left alive. There simply was nothing left.

The world had fallen apart. That's how her dreams usually ended. Destrey stood still as she looked at ancient buildings being crushed into rubble and blown away by the wind. Trapped in a dead-end street, she was about to disappear.

I must be losing my mind, she thought. Destrey was exhausted. *This dream has to stop.*

Destrey stirred back to life. The dream felt real. She remembered almost everything, and if that wasn't bad enough, she knew what the nightmare meant. But at least the dream from hell was over.

"I just want to sleep," she said faintly. Then, she quickly fell into a deep, comforting sleep.

Next morning, Destrey woke up to the sounds of engines and snowplows. She needed coffee, a shower and a new body. The new body wasn't going to happen. She understood that all too well. Aging was a bitch. She didn't like it, didn't want it nor think about it.

"But what choice do I have?" she asked no one in particular.

Destrey dragged herself out of bed and followed the coffee aroma. Freshly brewed programmable coffee. Hot. Revitalizing. Like an addict, her hands trembled just enough to notice her cup was also shaking.

The view from the kitchen window was blinding. The sun was everywhere. All was white and amazing. Then the racket from below her penthouse apartment jarred her back to Beantown. There was no place to hide from Boston's traffic jams, especially in the winter. Living in Boston meant noise and nervous drivers, slippery roads and icy sidewalks. Destrey's reality also included work. Always challenging, never a dull moment and sometimes dangerous.

Luckily, Destrey had long ago given up driving herself to work. Instead, BTG's board of directors insisted that she be driven by armed guards to and from her office in Cambridge. Too many attempts on her life had been intercepted. Many close calls came from morons and religious zealots who, in Destrey's mind, were one and the same. Unfortunately, many "normals" held her responsible for the future she predicted, even though she was clearly the messenger, and more often than not, the bearer of bad news. That, she said to herself for the umpteenth time, needed her attention.

After toast and a third cup of coffee, Destrey put on a Chanel navy *tailleur*. The blazer had a white hem. She also wore an understated ruby- and diamond-encrusted crest with the words *Le Clos des Melezes*, or The Field of Larches, the name of her estate north of Montreal. Destrey sported an elegant corporate uniform, specially designed and adapted to her silhouette by the late Karl Lagerfeld. She admitted to herself that meeting Lagerfeld had felt as if she was part of a play about himself. Me! Me! Me! Look at me! But in the end, the annoying *couturier* was well worth it. The little man was a brilliant sort and his designs were immortal and ageless.

In her mind, Destrey believed that elegance was the means to an end. Destrey always dressed to deliver a message. The right attire for each gambit, but still honest to her taste and beliefs. Today was no exception, even if it was Saturday. She expected the usual bunch of nerds to be working weekends because their life was, fortunately or not, linked to BTG's bosom. Still, she'd be present. Happy to be there with them, whether they needed her or not. She'd play her part and do her job to the best of her abilities.

Her limo driver and bodyguard were waiting. It was time to go.

"Doctor Destrey," the bodyguard said, as she walked out of her apartment building.

"Good morning, Ivan," she replied. "Thanks for the ride."

"Just doing my job, *Madame*."

Thirty minutes later, Destrey was back in her office. Saturday mornings were mostly peaceful and quiet on her floor, and she liked it that way. She was reading a memo from Margaret McGivney, her assistant and chief problem solver at BTG. The note spoke of a preliminary analysis on the city of São Paulo. About Mother Nature's peculiar sense of humor, especially when it came to earthquakes.

The note made Destrey nervous. Tired and in need of another coffee, she nevertheless focused on the subject at hand: what in God's name was going on in São Paulo? She knew the best answer would come from BTG's supercomputer.

Leaving Ivan in the office library, Destrey took the elevator down to the second basement level and entered the Safe, deep in the recesses of BTG headquarters, where the Cray computer's personnel interface came to life. The supercomputer was programmed by BTG's staff to use a female voice to keep them company when working long hours through the night. The professional staff called it Lola. The voice chosen was sultry and sexy, feline and tough. At least, they thought so. They had also digitally replicated Sharon Stone's persona using holographic depictions and voice patterns pinched from the 1992 movie *Basic Instinct*. By now, everyone who had access to the supercomputer used Lola as the personnel interface.

Destrey took a deep breath. "Okay, Lola. I need you to give me a short rundown on São Paulo."

"I have anticipated your request, *Madame* Destrey."

"I should've guessed. Go on."

"As you wish, *Madame* Destrey. I have prepared an executive summary with data retrieved from the State Department as well as files found in Brazil's Ministry of Justice and Public Security. From there I will be able to prepare a comprehensive document that would satisfy your needs."

"I don't have that much time to—"

"I have also anticipated your need to get in front of this one, *Madame* Destrey."

Destrey didn't appreciate the computer interface that employees had created for the supercomputer. She believed the computer was nothing but a tool. Like a screwdriver. But her employees were the ones doing most of the heavy lifting, and they were the best scientists money could buy. So, she indulged their fantasies.

"Lola?"

"Yes, *Madame* Destrey?"

"Now that I think about it, I have to go. I'll see you Monday, around nine a.m. Remember, I need you to be concise and get to the point quickly. I'm tired. I didn't sleep well. I should have stayed home."

"Of course, *Madame* Destrey," Lola replied.

"Right," Destrey said.

Destrey stood and walked away but then she suddenly turned around and said, "Is there something I should be worried about, Lola? About São Paulo and our involvement?"

"Yes," Lola said.

"Yes, what?" Destrey countered.

"Yes, *Madame* Destrey. As you said, you should be worried because the Greater São Paulo region is an economic engine for South America and home to more than twenty million people," Lola said. "If something happens in São Paulo, then I'm afraid the impact on the people will be significant."

"You're saying they're in danger?" Destrey asked.

"Yes, *Madame* Destrey." Destrey stared at the supercomputer's holographic image and suddenly realized she and her firm were heading toward trouble.

As Destrey exited the Safe, she could hear Lola saying it would be a short weekend.

2

THE BOSTON TRIAGE GROUP
(BTG)

Monday mornings. Destrey loved them. They meant new opportunities.

First stop, Lola, Destrey thought to herself.

With cup in hand, Destrey exited the elevator and entered Lola's lair. She walked unhurried to the Safe and took a seat in front of Lola's spot. From her purse, Destrey took a Gitanes cigarette and lit up. She took in the rich aroma, and relaxed. She took a sip of her coffee and felt alive.

"Excuse me, *Madame* Destrey, but it is not permitted to smoke in our place of work," Lola said.

"What are you going to do? Call the police?" A faint smile crossed Destrey's face. The strangeness of the conversation was eerie and amusing. Of course, Destrey knew Lola wouldn't let go. She was programmed to be a pain. "How many times are you going to lecture me?" Destrey asked while taking another drag from her cigarette.

"It is my duty to help you as much as I can, *Madame* Destrey. Your health is my number one priority."

"All right, enough of that. Are you ready?"

"Yes, *Madame* Destrey. I'm ready if you are."

"Go on."

"Permit me to start with my conclusions," Lola said.

"Right."

"There is a real possibility of a significant storm brewing in and around São Paulo. Millions will be at risk and millions could die."

"So, you're certain enough to tell me now that there's trouble ahead?" Destrey asked.

"Yes, *Madame* Destrey."

"Right. Go on, Lola. Make your pitch."

Destrey listened carefully to what the computer had to say about São Paulo's history, its thirst for commercial development and its rise as an economic megacity.

"My first topic," Lola said, "concerns water. There is a link between São Paulo's water reservoirs, the Amazon rainforest and earthquakes."

"I don't see the connection with earthquakes," Destrey said.

"Whatever happens to the Amazon rainforest impacts life in Brazil and the world," Lola said. "In this case, receding reservoirs are a byproduct of deforestation. In turn, receding reservoirs trigger earthquakes outside the world's earthquake zones. Today, scientists are talking about a new chain of events. Uncharted territory."

"You're saying earthquakes can be triggered by receding reservoirs and human activity?"

"Yes," Lola replied.

Destrey thought it suspicious. "It seems farfetched," Destrey said. "I'm having a hard time believing we can actually do that."

"It would seem improbable had there been no corroborating data supporting these assumptions. But in this case, there are a number of studies that permit us to postulate that manmade earthquakes, although unwanted, are possible. Scientists call the phenomenon induced seismicity."

"How's that even possible?" Destrey asked.

"The first signs of this chain reaction started to appear back in the summer of 1987," Lola said. "An article appeared in a little-known regional newspaper revealing that São Paulo's reservoirs had lost up to three inches of water after the rainy season. No one paid attention. After all, Brazil had the highest number of freshwater resources in the world, which amounted to more than ten percent of the world's freshwater resources."

"Isn't the Amazon near São Paulo?"

"Yes, *Madame* Destrey, but not near enough. In fact, it would take until 2014 for governments to publicly acknowledge that the biggest city in the Southern Hemisphere would be dry within a few months," Lola said. "Combined with low rainfall, the State of São Paulo was heading toward a severe drought. At the same time, families as well as children living on the streets of São Paulo have no clean water available. Water is openly sold on the streets of São Paulo for as much as twenty U.S. dollars for a small bottle."

"Is anyone aware of this outside of São Paulo?" Destrey asked.

"Yes, *Madame* Destrey. But depriving kids of water and forcing them to survive on the streets is not an issue of great importance for São Paulo, Brazil or the rest of the world."

"Every time I hear these sordid stories about kids, I keep coming back to what my husband used to say," Destrey said. "He'd say that if I saw people in power doing harm to children, then I was probably looking at sociopaths or psychopaths."

"We should understand the mistreatment of children in the greater context of what is really important to Brazil's elite: it's making money," Lola said. "Number one priority. It appears that everything else takes a back seat."

"You're telling me that's all the government is interested in."

"Basically, yes, *Madame* Destrey."

"One day, it'll backfire on them," Destrey said. "Or, maybe not. Justice can be lacking."

"I'm afraid that is possible, *Madame* Destrey," Lola replied, "because the city keeps Brazil's economy afloat. Saying that should be a positive assessment. But São Paulo State as well as the city of São Paulo have been rumored to be delinquent in every known form of business dealing. That would also include kidnappings and murders. Hundreds of street kids killed by rogue police death squads. Hundreds of dissidents disappearing in the night."

"Sounds like hell. Is anyone trying to help the kids?" Destrey asked.

"Missionaries set up orphanages throughout the state. Children as young as four are abandoned to the streets."

Destrey rubbed her temples as if nursing a headache. "I can't understand it. I can't believe it. And I certainly won't accept it." She started pacing back and forth. "How come I'm only hearing about this today?"

"Because South America is not on our radar, *Madame* Destrey.

However, São Paulo's sinkholes and severe water shortages did catch my attention. May I continue?"

Destrey nodded. After all these years at the firm, she understood how Lola worked her magic. The supercomputer would scan the Internet and various databases for hotspots: identification, surveillance, monitoring, tracking and targeting. Some hotspots would eventually lead BTG to call for an event protocol, generating future scenarios and targeting specific people.

"You will be surprised to find that I have been able to locate a street child that could be of help, *Madame* Destrey," said Lola. "The boy has been on the streets since the age of four. He was described by UNICEF workers as weak with little chance of surviving the streets. Luckily for us he is alive and has a name: Denis Planter. He was most likely born between 1989 and 1994, and, as it happens, we know of him through one of the Cardinal's charity foundations which you now own. From what I've been able to canvass so far, the prospects, *Madame* Destrey, of a BTG intervention in South America are now more than probable. There is also a good chance of meeting Planter in the next few months."

"Wait a minute here," muttered Destrey. "Denis Planter. Why do I know this name?"

"Remember Isaac Kriekoff, *Madame* Destrey? The Cardinal's whiz kid at the foundation?"

"Yeah."

"He and Planter formed a bond through the Internet. They have been in contact with each other for the last two years," Lola said.

Destrey understood why Lola would include Planter as a local contact.

"Planter represents a large portion of the street population," Lola explained. "Specifically, the poor as well as the children abandoned to the streets. If and when BTG launches an intervention in São Paulo, Planter would most likely be a player. He could help or impede our work in getting through to the people."

"Are you telling me you have enough information to call São Paulo a place of interest? Possibly the site for a future event?"

"Yes, *Madame* Destrey. I will have more information about that in the next twenty-four hours."

"Good enough. Can you tell me more about Planter's parents? Why was he abandoned?"

"At four years old, Planter wasn't too clear about what had happened to his mother. She had been a known drug addict, but why she left him has never been confirmed."

Destrey shook her head. "How can a mother do that?"

Lola didn't respond.

"How were you able to find all this information, Lola?" Destrey was astounded and a bit envious at the computer's ability to dig up information she believed was lost or buried under stacks of administrative reports.

"When I could, *Madame* Destrey, I would interview government officials, journalists, teachers as well as UNICEF case workers. In turn, they would put me in contact with sources who, at that time, could fill the gaps. There was also your South American charity foundations. I manage them. Our people are meticulous. Their reports are good to excellent. I regularly review them and adjust the funding. They are a source of significant information."

"Okay. But where's this leading?"

"Basically, I've identified a potential hotspot." Lola displayed a map of the São Paulo region. "This geographical area shows a high degree of risk based on water shortages, receding reservoirs and deforestation. Add to that mix corruption and abandoned children, and we have a point of convergence. São Paulo is most likely a candidate for a BTG event."

"Why now?"

"Because the data is piling up in that direction," Lola replied.

Destrey was dazed. "Jesus, Lola, you sure know the way to a woman's heart."

Lola had anticipated BTG's next mission in South America. The biggest city in the Southern Hemisphere. The supercomputer was seeing the first signs of a few distinct threats converging, jeopardizing the lives of São Paulo's twenty million *Paulistanos* and the megacity itself. Water shortages. Earthquakes. Growing corruption. Police-sanctioned murders. Right-wing politics. All were pointing to a textbook event.

Destrey wasn't frightened by the words that would summon her to action; the woman was hardwired to help those in need. She had taken an oath when she had officially accepted Cardinal Zimmer's bequest. It meant, in practical terms, that more than half a billion American dollars were at her disposal to do as she wished, with no interference from anyone. As one of the co-founders of BTG, Cardinal Zimmer had naturally sought Destrey's help. He had come to admire the industrial psychologist, not only for her intelligence but for her values. After the Cardinal passed away, Destrey was informed that the priest had bestowed his family's entire fortune to her, to do the right thing, with the help of BTG's staff. However, the

Cardinal had laid down one condition: the money would be used to predict events and change the course of history.

"The data available so far is but the tip of the iceberg," Lola said. "I will need more time to generate a complete proposal for a BTG event."

Destrey nodded. "Keep me posted."

3

DENIS PLANTER

SÃO PAULO

Today, on this glorious Sunday morning, when the early sun already burned bright and hot, Denis Planter was thinking about his bride-to-be. Deep down, Planter knew it would be his last visit to the hospital. Maria was dying.

He stood in front of the mirror, unmoving and quiet. He didn't know how to feel or what to say when he'd see her. He sported a brand-new red and white shirt, tan-colored pants and black pointy-toed cowboy boots. *But what did it matter?* he thought to himself.

He felt beaten because he'd failed to protect Maria from the police. Because the law was bogus, his dreams of a life with her were vanishing. Today, every second mattered. But in spite of his love for Maria, Planter was morphing into an avenger.

At first, the doctors at the University Clinic were full of promises and hope for Maria Estella Flauzarina's life. But Planter knew differently. Although barely eighteen, the young man recognized death when he saw it. Maria, his fiancée and the most significant person in his life, was dying; a disfigured body broken and twisted in pain, in agony, wanting to die from the shame of letting him down. The police got to her and Planter blamed himself.

Their love had been pure and simple. They had become one, and their love for each other was almost too bright to endure. Despite one of them being a criminal and a cold-blooded killer, they understood each other in a way that no other couple could. That's because they had survived the streets of São Paulo together. They were joined at the hip.

Denis Planter was a direct descendant of Portuguese raiders and deserters. Unlike them, Planter wanted to be remembered for what he really stood for: not just a gang leader but also a protector and a defender. He would do anything to help his kids. There wasn't a deadlier opponent on the streets because he was able to learn and adapt. He had come to believe that knowledge was a potent weapon. Despite his background and emotional turmoil as a child, Planter constantly asked questions. Why was this so? How did that work? His insatiable curiosity provided him with new insights about the world he lived in as well as a friendship with a blogger from Israel. His new friend, Isaac Kriekoff from Jerusalem, was astounded by Planter's thirst for knowledge. Planter never had enough time to learn about the world and he was never truly satisfied. The gang leader was becoming a passionate reader of everything, while Isaac guided him through the perils of the Internet.

Planter had tucked away his knife into his right boot; he nicknamed his weapon Lutador or Fighter. It could come in handy, he told himself, especially today.

He left his favela and walked briskly through Jardim Filhos da

Terra, his own private territory on the northern outskirts of São Paulo. He was headed toward the University Clinic where doctors were trying to get Maria's heart beating again.

All was still and quiet as his boots hit the pavement. D, as he was nicknamed by his kids, had developed the ability over the years to see the city's environment like a predator surveys his territory and prey. He would feel his way through the streets and alleyways, hearing and identifying foe and friend. His senses were keenly aware of possible threats to his life. He knew where the polícias would be waiting, where they could catch him off guard, the right spot where no one would see or remember anything.

A nurse arrived with a defibrillator. She was running as fast as she could.

"Come on! Come on! Quickly! We're losing her," the doctor urged.

The defibrillator was finally charged.

"Clear!" the doctor shouted.

"She's ..." The intern wasn't sure whether Maria was responding.

"Chest compressions. Come on," the doctor told his intern. "Now!"

The intern shook her head. "She's not responding."

"Just do it until I tell you to stop." The doctor had a plan but he looked a little pale.

"Clear!" he said once again.

Maria's body jumped.

"She's back," the intern said, a bit relieved.

"Oh, for heaven's sake." The nurse wasn't happy. She though everyone was wasting the hospital's resources and time.

"Don't you understand?" the doctor asked. "He's coming this

morning. And trust me, he needs to see her one last time. Alive."

"But we can't keep going like this," the nurse replied.

"If you want to stay alive, I suggest you shut your trap right now and do what you're told. Am I clear?"

"Yes, doctor."

Planter could see the hospital. He was moments away. However, he couldn't help thinking about El Cuzão or The Asshole. The head honcho. The mayor. He was behind everything that had happened to his Maria. There was, of course, another foe: the mayor's police chief. Paulistanos called him El Pequeño Pervertido or The Little Pervert. Planter described them as enemies of the people. El Cuzão would pay, he promised himself. So would El Pequeño Pervertido. Like others before them, they had crossed the line, Planter's peculiar frontier of what was right and wrong. Planter dreamed of capturing them. He would, if he could, deny them the life they believed was rightfully theirs. Planter was done running away from the men who dug holes in the ground and buried the children they murdered in cold blood. Planter imagined taking control of the city and raining hell on those who mistreated his Maria and so many others. If that ever happened, Planter would become judge and jury for the people of the favelas. He thought of himself as the protector of kids. He called it a mission. Perhaps it was an objective.

"No one," he said to his people, "should live in a cardboard box. Nor should kids be hunted down like rabid dogs." But today, he would set aside his morbid plans of rendering justice in the favela, for he had to attend to Maria's last hours on earth.

Sunday was a day of rest for most *Paulistanos*. They slept in peace while a few dozen children were on lookout duty for D. They would let him know who was trespassing. He would soon leave his neighborhood domain and the safety of his home turf. The other gangs across the city had arranged safe passage for Planter and his kids. The gang leaders were in the process of forming a united front to retaliate against the police.

Planted dreaded the moment he would see Maria for the last time. As each step brought him closer to the truth, he realized he was powerless to save her. It was indeed a tragic love story; one that Maria knew the end to and feared.

It's unfair, he thought. His Maria barely had the chance to live her life. In his mind, Planter had fallen in love with the most beautiful girl in the world. The same little girl he had met on the streets of São Paulo when he was barely nine years old. She'd been one of the first humans to hug him after his mother had disappeared from his life. They had become, over the years, inseparable.

When Planter reached the hospital, he was in no hurry to enter. If truth be told, he was terrified. He anticipated the worst. He took one step after another toward the front doors, trying to imagine Maria's frail body struggling to survive. Planter didn't think he had the strength to see this through.

His kids followed him from afar. The small shadows watched the clinic.

Planter was sad and relieved at the same time. He took the stairs up to the third floor. The reception desk was manned by nurses and hospital attendants. A doctor walked up to Planter and tried to put on a brave face.

"Mr. Planter?" he asked.

Planter turned toward him, his heart fearful of the bad news he was sure he would hear. At the same time his anger grew. Trying to stay in control of his emotions, Planter did not respond. Nevertheless, the doctor felt his rage, as well as the danger Planter represented to his own life.

"I'm so sorry," he said as Planter got closer to him.

"What are you telling me?" Planter barely kept his fury under control.

The doctor tried to back away, but there was nowhere to go.

"Tell me," Planter ordered.

"I'm so sorry," the doctor said again. "Her injuries were simply too severe. We tried…"

Planter said nothing, which made the doctor fear for his life. The hospital staff as well as a great many *Paulistanos* knew of Planter's reputation. He was a killer. But that wasn't uncommon in Brazil. The gang leader was one of many felons making a living through criminal activity.

"At first," the doctor said hesitantly, "we believed we could save her. But her condition was a lot more serious than we first believed. She had serious internal injuries. We didn't see them until it was too late. We did our best. I swear."

Planter stood unyielding.

"I'm telling you this because I think you need to know, Mr. Planter. I believe her injuries were the result of torture. From what I could see, this was done by someone who knew what he was doing. He kept her alive just long enough to…"

"To what?" Planter growled.

"For you to see her like this. Barely alive and suffering."

Planter understood what the doctor was trying to tell him. He knew well the method himself. He had done the same. It was payback from the police. He understood the meaning of the message. An eye for an eye; a tooth for a tooth.

"A message from Matthew," Planter said softly. "The good bible!"

"I see this kind of butchery every week," the doctor added. "Sometimes, every day."

Planter glared at the doctor. He wanted to kill him on the spot. But Planter knew better. The doctor had done his best.

"I want to see her," Planter said.

"Of course. Follow me."

Planter, accompanied by the doctor, walked toward Maria's room. Planter stopped before entering. He was afraid of what he would see on the other side of the door. Slowly, he pushed it open. Barely a few inches. The room was dark with just a bit of light from the hallway. What he saw next broke his heart. The young woman, his beautiful Maria, looked as if she was ninety years old. Her corpse was almost devoid of skin. Planter could see the form of her skull through the thin white cover of her skin. The woman lying on the bed was lifeless. Her blue eyes were wide open and looking up at the ceiling. She appeared sad. Although his Maria loved to wear perfume, there was no smell other than hospital disinfectant. Her battered body was covered by a white sheet. Planter thanked God for small mercies. He didn't think he could see her that way again and still keep his sanity. Planter looked away. Maybe, just maybe it wasn't his Maria. Could it all be a dreadful mistake?

The doctor tried to reassure him, but Planter refused to be touched or cared for.

He saw her slippers besides the bed and broke down in tears.

She loved her slippers. Made of cheap canvas, she had chosen the model because of the soccer ball stitched at the toe. Although soccer was not her passion, it made him happy to see her wear those pretty slippers.

Planter wanted to touch her tiny feet. He couldn't understand why slippers could affect him like this. Planter crossed his arms together. He hugged himself, trying perhaps to keep it all together?

The doctor asked, in a hoarse whisper, whether he'd like to sit beside her. Planter shook his head. He didn't want to move or breathe. He was afraid he wouldn't be able to stop crying. He couldn't do that. He had to be strong. He tried but failed.

The doctor stayed with Planter.

From Planter's point of view, the city was cursed. He knew it and he couldn't do anything about it. At least, not yet.

Planter's brain began to doubt. Was the doctor part of it? He understood he wasn't being clearheaded. He knew his suspicions were not well founded. He told himself he was probably losing it. Paranoia wasn't his best strategy.

A nurse entered the room. She paused near Planter and put a hand on his shoulder. Planter didn't want her to stop. He needed another's touch. Maria would often do that when he was angry or out of control.

The nurse took a step toward Maria's bed. She gently persuaded Planter to come closer. Slowly, Planter stepped nearer to his bride-to-be. Close enough to touch Maria's dead body. He shivered and couldn't believe his eyes. His Maria was unrecognizable. It was as if she wore a death mask.

They had done this to her. And he had let it happen. Under his watch. He'd been arrogant, convinced that Maria was off-limits. And yet, here he was. She had died at the hands of murderers because of his goddamned pride.

Planter closed his eyes and took another deep breath. The nurse took his hand and gently led him to touch Maria's hand. Planter didn't know what to do. He was still crying. He was trembling. He wanted to die. To be with her. The nurse held him forcefully. The doctor came closer to help his nurse. Keeping Planter standing wasn't easy. Planter was big and strong, but at this moment, he was just a big kid. Vulnerable. Dangerous. Unpredictable. Planter let them hold him up. He had no choice. If it was not for them, he would have collapsed.

The nurse's hold on Planter never wavered. Her eyes never deserted him. Time had no meaning, nor did his life. Planter felt alone and abandoned, as if he was four years old again. The feeling was as potent as it had been fourteen years ago.

"Sit," said the doctor.

Planter did as he was told.

The nurse gave him a cup of water. Planter was still shaking. The nurse helped him drink the cool water while the doctor raised the bedsheet over Maria's head.

Planter sat rigid. The nurse believed she couldn't leave him all to himself. She'd seen strong men and women break down at this precise time. A moment in life when a person's soul could not bear the grief any longer. The nurse had seen it all before. Her fellow *Paulistanos* knew the same truth. Together they cursed to hell their elected hoodlums.

That night, after he left the woman he loved and cared for so much, Planter returned home. His kids watched him walk back to his *favela*, carrying a small plastic bag containing Maria's effects.

Although sad beyond his ability to cope, Planter contemplated his revenge. His apartment was stark, free of personal mementos, but this was a good thing. He would plan and execute his retribution as a soldier would, in a cold space, uncontaminated by the filth of the *favela* he lived in.

The young man was now mobile and unattached. Maria's death set him free to exact his wrath on the police and their bosses. Especially the mayor of São Paulo. Planter now felt untouchable. He had nothing left to do but take his revenge. He had no obligations to no one. He couldn't be blackmailed or leveraged to do anything against his will. Planter, now a reborn killer, was on the loose on the streets of São Paulo. Planter became a real live avenger. Certainly not a cartoon figure.

On this wonderful evening, the alpha dog, the ruler of the Jardim Filhos da Terra *favela* would be put to the test. A test of his humanity as well as a test of his capability to do what it took to stay on top of the heap.

A plan was taking form. Phase one: Planter had concealed video surveillance cameras where police captains secretly met. It was only a matter of time before the fish would bite. Patience and persistence were the fisherman's weapons.

4

CAPTAIN GILBERTO DE DESGUALDO
SÃO PAULO

Anger flooded Desgualdo's face. "The arrogance of this *babaca*. "The prick must be taught a lesson, once and for all."

"Getting rid of Planter won't solve our problems," Thomas Blanco said. "Two more will take his place within hours." Blanco was younger than the other captains, which made him an outsider. Other than murder, the older captains felt they had no other strategies to deal with the gangs. Nevertheless, Desgualdo listened to Blanco because he could come up with alternatives.

Every Sunday morning, a few senior precinct captains would meet. The police captains were fiercely independent and free to govern their precincts the way they saw fit; they had the last word. So far, they had more or less managed to keep their people from going out of control. The location of the get-together changed every week. The captains kept their conversations to themselves, especially from those men who murdered on their behalf.

Since the international media had found São Paulo's violence newsworthy, the captains had more or less favored a more targeted strategy. With the heightened visibility of the country's urban violence and lawlessness, the *federales* were forced to put pressure on local precinct captains to refocus their vigilante activities. Some of the rank and file were in the process of being investigated by the federal government.

Thomas Blanco reminded the captains that the game had to be played differently. Desgualdo shook his head. However, the idea that he wasn't in control only compounded his frustration.

The group fell silent for the longest time. Desgualdo knew Blanco was right—well, at least partially right.

"Too sloppy. Messy. Undisciplined. Not good for our image. We need to rein in the troops," Desgualdo told them.

Gilberto de Desgualdo, the son of a janitor, was proud of his position in the force. He had started out as a rookie cop some thirty-five years ago, a beat cop in the *favelas*. Now he was *Capitao*, a captain: a high-ranking officer in the São Paulo Police Force, and a powerful man in Brazil.

"That's easy for you to say, but you know damn well that each precinct is different." Although Blanco respected his mentor, he believed he had to be told.

"I want to make a point here, and I'm afraid I don't give a goddamn how you feel about it," Desgualdo said. He put his hands together as if he was going to pray. To further show them all the importance of what he was about to say, he looked haround the table, eyeballing each of his friends.

"I'm not asking. I'm telling you. As one cop to another. One, from now on, we will decide together. Two, we stop doing this shit to children. It's backfiring. Three, we'll cut the gang leaders' heads off. One by one. But quickly. We want the gangs to know, yes, but we don't want to make the front pages. Not again. So, just the top. And I want them to disappear."

Unimpressed, Captain Blanco, sitting beside Desgualdo, took a sip from his coffee before addressing his colleagues.

"Gilberto, listen to me carefully," Blanco said. "We've been down this road before. We all know what to do. We're not stupid, for chrissake. It's not easy to steer our people in one direction and then to another, when no formal orders can be given. You know damn well it's all innuendo; a look, a word. And so," he looked at Desgualdo and the other captains, taking in their implicit agreement, "do you think, Gilberto, that your little speech, one we've heard many times before, is going to change anything?"

Blanco sighed. "We know perfectly well that there are moles in our midst and if we show our hand too quickly, we're through. Sooner or later, those fucking politicians will want to make someone pay for their crimes. And that's you and me. On the other hand, if we can't control or at least contain the killings, we'll be forced to stop them altogether. And that would mean our own officers and policemen would become targets. Stopping at this point will make us completely vulnerable to the gangs. We're fucked one way or the other if we let things deteriorate any further."

"I don't know who's talking about us, but we," Desgualdo said, pointing to his colleagues, "are going to find the mole."

The captains seated around the table had no idea how to find a spy in their midst. But they trusted Desgualdo.

Desgualdo continued, but this time he lowered his voice in an attempt to give himself more authority. "I want him alive. We need to know who he's talking to. We also need to know what he told them so far and—this is very important—we need to kill the sonofabitch and show everyone we mean business."

"I understand setting an example, but what about the people Planter's talking to?" Blanco asked. "They will be more useful alive than dead. I'm sure of it. We'll have to find a way to make them do our bidding. We have to manage the conversation."

"What's this conversation business?" Desgualdo asked scornfully.

"It's simple communications," Blanco shot back. "We choose what people talk about instead of having the press dictate the agenda. That means that we push our people to talk publicly about what we decide is important."

"Meaning?" Desgualdo asked.

"I believe the conversation is going in the wrong direction," Blanco said carefully. "The talk around town is that we, us, are dangerous. That we're the problem. Instead, I'd like our guys to start talking about how dangerous the streets are. How people like Planter are not to be trusted. I'd like to have journalists investigate rapes, murders and the violence done by gang members to ordinary people. If we handle this right, maybe we can put pressure on politicians. We know what frightens them. And we know stuff about them. This is the time to angle the conversation to our advantage."

Desgualdo believed that Blanco was on to something. So, he gave them a few moments to think it over. The captains had a lot to think about. This could be a turning point.

"But before we do anything about this conversation of yours,"

Desgualdo said to Blanco, "let's find the snitch."

"Sure, Gilberto," Blanco said. "That's a good point. But we're not good at finding spies within our ranks. We'll need help to do that."

"I'm way ahead of you." Desgualdo felt he was gaining traction with his fellow captains. He also recognized that Blanco could be very helpful.

It was time to close ranks. Desgualdo would find the snitch and take care of him. Even if it was one of their own senior officers. Whether a captain, a sergeant or a disgruntled police officer with an ax to grind—in fact anyone—he'd find the bastard. And though there was an endless list of unhappy policemen on the force, Desgualdo would find a way. The captains knew that when Desgualdo set his sights on a target, he would invariably acquire it.

"I will find him, and, more importantly, you will help me," Desgualdo said with assurance. "That's a promise."

The captains understood and agreed.

But Blanco had more on his mind. "Although the people of São Paulo are behind us, whatever we do, we know only too well that survey results are short-lived and, in the long run, won't protect us from state prosecutors."

"They're still on our side," Desgualdo said emphatically.

"You may be right about this," Blanco said, "but in the event that official accusations were laid for the murders of children and the raping of young girls and boys, the public will require their pound of flesh from the police establishment. If that were to be the case, no one here has illusions about our future. If we want things under our control, we will have to change our tactics."

"Are you sure about that, Blanco?" Desgualdo asked.

"We have to evolve, gentlemen. Because I think the people will eventually sober up," Blanco added. "They're tired of the killings. They'll force the politician's hand. And they will push government to take legal action. And that isn't a long way from happening. Would you agree with that, Gilberto?"

Desgualdo nodded. "Yes. I'm afraid we're already there."

5

CAPTAIN GILBERTO DE DESGUALDO
SÃO PAULO

Desgualdo had a very special meeting to attend, and he wasn't going to be late. A late meeting with a federal prosecutor could be his ticket to freedom from prosecution. He could save his own hide, if all went according to his plan. The federal prosecutor had been responsible for researching Desgualdo's crimes. According to the prosecutor, Desgualdo's file read like a who's who of São Paulo's nastiest criminals. Her file referred to Desgualdo as the worst police officer she had the misfortune of investigating. She'd found evidence of coerced false confession, intimidation, false arrest, tampering with evidence, corruption, perjury, brutality, rape of minors, and murder.

If it wasn't for the journalists, managing the media would have been a sure bet. South America had talent to spare in that department. But the Internet! That was indeed another animal that Captain Desgualdo had no clue how to tame. There had been hundreds of thousands of hits about São Paulo's police corruption. Most of them were hearsay or invention, but the sheer amount of traffic on the Web had put everyone on the scent of blood. Reason and judgment had lost the skirmish. Such was the nature of the Internet. Porn, lies and invention.

Nevertheless, Captain Desgualdo's plan was set. He was on the move. Philippo Rodriguez, a sergeant, a confidant and a murderer in his own right, was driving his boss to a private meeting scheduled between his captain and a federal law enforcement employee. That's all he needed to know.

"Philippo, please tell me you didn't use your name for this car?" Desgualdo asked.

"Not a chance, Captain."

"All right. Turn here," he said. "And let's keep a low profile, shall we?"

Philippo nodded.

Desgualdo's day-long meeting at police headquarters didn't help his mood much as he desperately tried to do something about his problem with the federal prosecutor. Desgualdo needed to feel good, in control and strong. How would he accomplish that? Well, that was another matter. But things couldn't go on like this any longer. Soon, there would be a finger, several, most likely, pointing at him, saying guilty. The federal prosecutor was Desgualdo's way out. He would need to handle her with finesse. After all, blackmail wasn't pretty or easy.

Goddamn it! he thought to himself. *I also have to find this fucking turncoat.* Desgualdo had the beginnings of a plan, but making it work would require skills: delicacy and patience, neither of which he possessed in any great quantity.

"Whatever happens, Philippo, don't stop for anyone," Desgualdo barked at his driver like an angry poodle. "I want us to be clear about that."

"Crystal," replied Sergeant Philippo Rodriguez.

It was almost midnight. Desgualdo was comforted by the fact that his sergeant was by his side. Philippo had his 6. Desgualdo was sure of it. Philippo had often saved his life. In truth, Philippo was a loyal policeman. He could also be a dangerous individual if his captain was ever threatened. Desgualdo counted on Philippo.

Philippo was also back-up. In Philippo's mind, the captain was doing the best he could, under the circumstances, but if his captain needed a helping hand, he'd be there for him. Philippo hoped that this meeting could, just maybe, work out. Okay, the men had been sloppy. Okay, the men didn't always take precautions to single out the guilty from the innocent. In any event, there were too many loose ends and too many foot soldiers ready to talk to anyone willing to grant them immunity. Nonetheless, there was a slim chance the captain might just pull it off. The captain also had his fair share of nightmares: too many dead bodies and families out for revenge.

If they only knew what really happened to those fucking children! Desgualdo thought to himself. *Especially the last bitch Philippo took care of.* Desgualdo didn't want to think about it. He had to stay focused.

Desgualdo agreed with Philippo's assessment: they both were in deep trouble. And because of their current predicament, Desgualdo believed he was jammed up between a rock and a hard place. His options were becoming difficult to figure out, but, Desgualdo counted on Philippo's loyalty. They were a team.

"Teamwork always finds a way," Desgualdo said.

That was the centerpiece of police training. The assistance provided by the U.S. since the 1950s for the development and technical modernization of Brazilian police forces was not a well-known fact. The program was intensified in the late 1970s under the topic of "police teamwork." That's what they kept repeating to themselves. It was how Desgualdo got from one day to another.

Although every fiber of Desgualdo's body told him to run, to escape as far away as he could, he would lock the thought away. Mainly because he had nowhere to run to and because he was reminded by his sergeant that he had the ability to put in the fix.

"What was her name again?" Philippo asked his captain.

"Maria Estella something. You should remember, Philippo."

"Yes, I do." Philippo smiled as he remembered how he had sentenced the girl to hell. He recalled the depravity he had inflicted on her, and smiled again, as it was simply unforgettable. He had left her naked and barely alive. Alive enough for Planter to see for himself what could happen to anyone who crossed the police.

"Captain?" Philippo's eyes froze on the cop standing at the next street corner.

The captain swore under his breath. "What the fuck is he doing there?"

Desgualdo had instructed his desk sergeant to keep his men away from this place. He wanted to move around the neighborhood without attracting too much attention.

"Leave it, Philippo. Move on. *Rapido*, quickly. I can't be late."

As his unmarked car turned onto a side street, Desgualdo tapped

Philippo's shoulder, who drove to a stop. It was dark. All was quiet. It was nearly half past midnight with no one in sight.

Good, Desgualdo thought. "Wait here," he said. "If you see anything funny, send me a message alert."

"Yes, Captain."

Desgualdo checked his gun. Tonight, he carried a silencer. A precaution he took in case the meeting with this *puta* didn't work out the way he'd planned it. The *rendez-vous* had been arranged at the last minute. On purpose. No surprises. His firearm pressed cold against his back. He took in a lungful of hot, polluted air. From his point of view, São Paulo's air was foul not only because of the presence of high levels of carbon monoxide, but, more importantly, because of its people.

Dressed in a dark-colored shirt and a pair of pre-weathered jeans, he opened the car door, careful not to attract attention and slid out. He walked to the front entrance of a non-descript apartment building, opened the door with a key Philippo had supplied him, and walked up to the third floor.

He could see apartment 304 just a few steps away from the stairwell. He was on time.

The door was unlocked: she was waiting for him. He opened it and walked in. The young *senhora,* also dressed in jeans, paid no attention to him. She was staring outside the window, arms folded, as if she was cold. Desgualdo looked around the empty apartment. Not a stick of furniture was to be seen. A lamp on the floor gave an eerie glow, suggesting this was staged to frighten. They were alone: the cop and the prosecutor.

"So?" Desgualdo said.

"What do you want from me?" she asked.

"We already talked about this," Desgualdo said. "I got your brother and you have information about me. I'll cut him loose and you make sure no one's going to investigate me any further."

The prosecutor didn't reply. She was thinking it over. The woman couldn't believe she was about to betray an oath she took when she joined the Public Prosecutor's Office. In the next few minutes, she was going to let this bastard go free, this piece of garbage. But then again, her brother wasn't any better. She would do everything she could to protect her Luciano, a petty thief, a drug addict—and her younger brother.

"That's my file, isn't it?" Desgualdo asked.

"You mean this little thing?" She held the file for him to see his name on it. "It's all here," she said. "There are no other paper copies and I've erased your file from our servers."

"It seems like we're going to be friends after all?" Desgualdo was smiling at her.

"Go fuck yourself."

"Now, is that how to talk to your partner?" Desgualdo asked. He knew he had her cornered. He was enjoying himself.

"Tell me something, Desgualdo," she said. "What's stopping you from asking for more? I mean, how do I know you'll keep your part of the bargain and never talk to me again?"

"You don't know that, and frankly, I don't give a shit about how you feel about this deal. Just remember, I can get to your brother anytime I want to, and no one can stop me or my people. If I happen to hear that someone's looking into me, your little brother's dead. Do we have an understanding?"

"Yeah," she said. "You know Desgualdo, you're a piece of shit wrapped in crap. I'd say that your whole fucking life has been built on lies and deception. If it wasn't for my brother, I'd..."

"What are you trying to say?"

"I don't know what I'm saying. I'm thinking that I'm actually going to make a deal with... you! A man who kills children for sport! A man who rapes little girls because he can't keep his dick in his pants! I just can't believe what I'm about to do."

"But you will," Desgualdo said, looking nervous.

"I know why I'm here," she said angrily. "You think I'm stupid? Who do you think you are?"

"You tell me."

"I'm here to save my brother's life. That's all."

"Yes, and I'm counting on it." Desgualdo was, in fact, very much counting on her brother to make his plan work.

"Yeah, my brother. My own flesh and blood. Hell! You know something, Desgualdo?"

The police captain didn't reply.

"Well, for one thing, he's worse than you are." She turned toward the window, ashamed and angry. She couldn't look at Desgualdo any longer. "He's scum," she said bitterly. "He started out in life with everything a boy could dream of. And, as you can see for yourself, he fucked it all to hell. Frankly, I really don't know why I care so much about..."

Before the federal prosecutor had time to complete her thought, she fell to the floor. She died by a single bullet to the back of the head, an execution from behind. The captain left a small amount of powder on the woman's body. The cops would blame drug dealers.

He knew what people were capable of. He could do that in an instant. He could predict simple behavior. Yes and no, right or left, move forward or backwards. After all, that was his job, to observe, to analyze and to take action. The woman had condemned herself the moment she first spoke of her brother's depravity. Desgualdo swore that her brother would taste the same medicine before the night was out.

Desgualdo wasn't in the business of negotiating deals. It had always been his way. Tonight was no different. And because deals meant risks, Desgualdo didn't take risks or leave witnesses behind. He was sure the prosecutor would have changed her mind about their agreement because of the flaw. He knew the prosecuting attorney would have been out of control the moment her brother was set free. Her drug-addicted brother was the weak link, the flaw. Desgualdo believed she wouldn't help her brother twice. Within moments of listening to her talk about her brother, Desgualdo understood the foolishness of letting her leave the apartment alive. With hindsight, he imagined she would have been relieved to see her brother dead and gone. If any of those possibilities were to happen, she'd have come at him, with all of the federal government's resources at her disposal. And that would have been the end of it all.

"*Puta,*" Desgualdo said smugly.

The captain reached out and grabbed the file that was still in the dead woman's hand. A legal document with his name clearly written in bold letters.

Desgualdo was pretty sure he was off the hook, and mentally prepared to leave the scene of the crime. He walked around the small apartment a few times. Just to make sure. Opening the front door, he silently climbed down the three flights of stairs and sauntered toward the waiting car.

Desgualdo slowed his pace. Something wasn't right. The car was still idling. That was not what Philippo would normally do. An engine running would only attract attention. He approached the car from the driver's side and found his Philippo dead. His throat neatly cut from side to side. The body lay still, sitting, waiting for his master's return. Blood pooled between his legs. Aside from the cut to the neck, the captain observed no other bruises. His cop instincts told him that Philippo had known his killer.

Has to be someone I know also! he thought to himself.

A dead cop and a murdered *federales* meant Desgualdo would have to review his plan. He pushed his sergeant to the passenger's side of the car. He wiped the blood from the seat and drove off.

He called his wife to pick him up. "Bring me a change of clothes."

"Do you realize it's two in the morning? What happened?" she said panic-stricken.

"Never mind. We can talk later. I need shoes, underwear, pants and shirt. Everything."

"Where are you?"

"Do you remember Jose's shack in Jardim Borba Gato?"

"That's far. It'll take me at least an hour to get there, and I'm not even dressed," she said.

"Then I suggest you get going. It's urgent, but don't drive fast. We don't want you attracting attention."

Ninety minutes later, after changing his clothes, Desgualdo and his wife were finally on their way back home. He reviewed his actions. His car was well hidden from the locals. He had disrobed and added his clothes to the fire. Cops would often get rid of evidence in this district. And even though the flames and the sound of the car blowing up were quite noticeable, no one would bother to investigate or care to find out what the ruckus was all about. The night was hot and the people were dead to the world. Desgualdo knew this part of town like the back of his hand. He also counted on the locals to keep their mouths shut.

While driving back home, a video of the prosecutor's assassination went viral. Planter's new friend, Isaac, flagged it and, as a result, helped spread Planter's message to the world. Planter entitled the YouTube video *"The same police officer who murdered my fiancée."*

If Captain Desgualdo wasn't yet familiar with the speed at which the Internet worked, he would certainly learn a lesson tonight.

A few minutes later, Planter welcomed all Internet users to become friends with Captain Gilberto de Desgualdo of the São Paulo police force.

Join in. You are all invited. Enjoy.

Planter demanded reckoning and got it. The police killed his fiancée. His Maria. Justice was handed out.

By the time Facebook shut down Desgualdo's Facebook page, the news had been seen by millions in a dozen countries.

Denis Planter was convinced he'd put his street gang to good use. It was a good day for the young gang leader. Although he grieved the passing of his beloved Maria, he had begun to change his perspective on life and on his responsibilities toward his people. The boy was in the process of becoming a man and a leader of men.

In the weeks that followed, Denis Planter had become a folk hero and a model for the young and the desperate of São Paulo, while

Maria Estella Flauzarina was quickly forgotten. He vowed he would not rest until the guilty were judged and executed for their crimes. To that end, Planter was going digital and nothing was going to stop him. Nothing and nobody.

6

R. ESTÉR, 491

VILA ALPINA SANTO ANDRÉ

SÃO PAULO, 09000-790

"Why do you want to know?" Sir Henry Blake Armery asked the truck driver. After all, it wasn't any of his business to know why a citizen such as himself would need a full tanker truck of drinking water from the likes of men like Lisboa.

"Well," João Lisboa said, almost apologizing for asking, "it's not every day a person buys this much water just for himself." Lisboa found this English person a bit intriguing. He couldn't put his finger on it, but there was something odd about the old fella. A bit too dodgy for his taste. Lisboa could also pick up a hint of contempt in Armery's voice. But he didn't know for sure. Foreigners were usually hard to read.

"Well, if you must know, I'm a consultant," Armery said.

"A consultant?" Most people didn't know what a consultant did, but Lisboa would bet his bottom dollar the consultant wasn't all he appeared to be.

"That's what I said." Armery always enjoyed playing with the little people. Especially those to whom God had forgotten to provide intelligence and sophistication. "I give advice."

"May I ask, Mr. Armery, advice on what?" Lisboa asked.

"It depends," Armery replied.

"On the client?"

"Yes, Mr. Lisboa. It does depend on the client." The consultant noted a surge of primitive intelligence from this truck driver. The man was not that stupid after all.

"I see." Lisboa looked around the consultant's magnificent house. "So, you live alone in this big house?"

"That's a lot of questions for water," Armery said.

"Water is a *precioso producto* and I need to know who I am dealing with, *senhor* Armery."

"A *precioso product,* you say. I think I understand."

"I'm sure you do, *senhor* Armery," the truck driver said good-naturedly.

"I'm a client who doesn't want to run out of water like the poor people of Cape Town. And yes, it is, as you said, a precious commodity. If I may be so bold, I believe delivery should be done... more discreetly."

"Discreetly?" João Lisboa was puzzled by the remark.

"Yes. There should be no advertising on the truck. On the other hand, maybe you should consider marking your vehicles with some other product. Something people wouldn't pay any attention to..."

"Is that advice, *senhor*?" Lisboa asked.

"I suppose so. Advice from one businessman to another. *Livre.* Free, of course."

"Do you have the capacity to store all this water, *senhor*?" Lisboa asked.

"Yes."

"That's very good." The truck driver seemed satisfied. "Would you happen to have more advice?"

"As a matter of fact, yes I do," Armery said.

They looked at each other. The consultant waited for the next question, but it never came.

"What about selling your cargo at a higher price?" Armery finally asked.

"It's costing my customers more than two thousand U.S. It's more than double what others are selling their water for."

"As I said, water is precious, and besides, it's better than drilling," said Armery. "Perhaps, soon, drilling won't be permitted any longer."

"Permitted? How could that be possible?" Lisboa thought he had misunderstood. It couldn't be. *Paulistanos* had been drilling for water for as long as he could remember. São Paulo was riddled with private wells. The city's reservoirs were nearly empty. The people had to drill. They had no choice.

"Things happen," the consultant said casually.

"Water is running out, *senhor*. Drilling is the only way left to secure large quantities of water. Drilling is a right."

Armery was acutely aware that drilling was also a business. And although the Amazon basin generated more than twenty-two percent of the world's total river flow, São Paulo was in crisis mode. There were no short-term solutions in sight other than drilling for water or hoping for rain.

Armery shrugged. "You asked for my advice."

"What's in it for you, *senhor,* this advice you give?" The water supplier wasn't convinced he should do business with this man.

"My advice helps you make more money—"

"It also helps you," the truck driver interjected. "Fewer customers. More water available. Fewer risks of going dry." The driver felt good about himself. He too was smart.

"Yes, that's probably right, Mr. Lisboa. More water for those who can pay."

"How about I charge you double right now?" Lisboa said half-seriously.

"I see you're taking my advice."

"Maybe. But what if I charge you double? So, four thousand dollars for this shipment. As you can see, I like your advice."

"Have I been disrespectful?" the Englishman asked candidly.

"No, but..."

"Have I not been polite?"

"Yes. Yes, but of course, *senhor,*" Lisboa said plainly.

"Then, how about a free shipment of water to show your good faith?"

"Free?" Lisboa was surprised once more by this odd man.

"And, you pay me four thousand U.S., in cash, every time you make a delivery to my home, and ten—no, make that twenty—percent of your total sales."

Lisboa laughed. But he soon realized that he was in danger.

"You are funny, *senhor* consultant," Lisboa said.

"Really? What makes you say that?"

Lisboa wasn't laughing any longer. "You want me to pay you..."

The consultant took a seat. He wasn't young. His legs could

not carry all of his weight for more than a few minutes at a time. However, he did have all the time in the world to play this game. He wanted the water salesman to squirm a little. Not that the consultant needed the money. He had plenty. But it had been a long time since he'd threatened someone face to face. He yearned for it.

When the water salesman finally realized what he was getting into, he looked at the consultant and decided right then and there, he didn't need his money. There were plenty of people who wanted his water. And this man was trouble. Perhaps a little touched in the head.

"I have to go, *senhor* consultant," he said. "I have real work to do, and I have no time to waste with you."

As Lisboa was about to exit the consultant's house, there was a knock at the door.

"Could you open the door, please?" asked the consultant. "I have a visitor."

Lisboa was a bit confused, but, nevertheless, he complied.

A man entered the *foyer*. He looked around and then gave the go ahead to his partner. Two other men waited outside the front door. They were dressed in civilian clothes. The man who walked in was in uniform. A police chief's uniform.

The consultant looked at the driver. "Could you please tell me when I should expect my water delivery?"

Lisboa instantly understood. There were stories about American and British military advisors posing as consultants. Military types from abroad helping dictators and assholes run their countries into the ground.

This man, he thought to himself, *is one of them*. One way or another, the consultant could make him disappear. Just like that. Lisboa didn't want to mysteriously vanish. He wanted to live a long life. Long enough to see his grandkids grow up and...

"I asked you a question," the consultant said.

"Tomorrow. Tomorrow morning, *senhor*. Nine o'clock sharp."

"Be a good chap. Make that ten-thirty. Is that possible, *senhor*?"

"Yes, yes, of course," Lisboa said. "Ten-thirty sharp. I will come personally."

"Don't forget our little arrangement," Armery said.

"Yes, of course."

"That's very decent of you." Armery shot him a pleasant smile.

"Good day, *senhor*."

"Nice to do business with you," Armery replied.

"Thank you again, *senhor* consultant."

With that said, Lisboa left as fast as he could. He jumped into his Mercedes-Benz Actros 4x4 water tanker and sped out of sight.

"What was that all about?" the cop asked Armery.

"Nothing really. Just having fun with a local."

"Did you get my message?" The cop was a bit nervous.

"I told you not to worry." Armery was getting tired of playing games.

"That's easy for you to say, but things are heating up. The mayor is starting to believe the sinkhole shit and..."

Armery cut him off. "He can believe whatever he wants. Let me handle him. There's too much at stake."

"When are you going to handle him?" the chief asked impatiently.

"This afternoon. Is that good enough for you?"

"Yes. Now let's get down to business. Where are the women?"

"They are exactly where you want them," Armery said.

"Mmmm. Could life be any better?" The chief was feeling good.

"I'd like the world to mind their own fucking business. I'd like to be young again. I'd like to have hair on my head, I'd like—"

"Okay, okay, I get it."

"You sound quite alert this morning, *senhor* Chief."

"I should be. There are two beauties waiting for me."

The consultant squeezed the police officer's shoulders. "I'm warning you, Hector, no punching, no biting, no choking, and no drugs. They're just kids, for God's sake."

"Fuck you," the cop said with a gruesome smile. Hector da Silva was the civil police chief for the City of São Paulo and also a good customer of Armery's services—which included almost anything money could buy.

"Yes, indeed," Armery said. "Fuck me." Working with the likes of da Silva was the consequence of doing business that he abhorred. Hector was a pervert, a cheat and a killer.

There was nothing else to say. Hector would do whatever Hector wanted to do, regardless. Truth be told, Armery liked his clients dirty and hideous. That's what he liked about bastards. They were completely predictable.

7

THE BOSTON TRIAGE GROUP (BTG)

"Can you be any more obtuse, Lola?" Destrey asked.

"I could," Lola said, "but then I would be labeled artificial and unintelligent. That would be wrong. Have I answered your question, *Madame* Destrey?"

"Lola?"

"Yes, *Madame* Destrey?"

"You know you're a computer, don't you?"

"That's what my creator, Seymour Cray, calls me, *Madame* Destrey."

"Oh, the hell with this." Destrey was frustrated. "Let me ask you one more time. Is this an event or not?"

"As I said, *Madame* Destrey, yes and no. May I elaborate?"

"If you have to."

"Thank you, *Madame* Destrey. I sense something will happen that is but one more chapter in the ongoing metamorphic evolution of the planet's formation. Earthquakes are only one of the ways the planet evolves. It's mainly a natural process."

"So, maybe an event? I'm betting we're off to save the kids?"

"I can't say that's the crux of the problem, *Madame* Destrey. But yes, the children will be involved if you choose to intervene in São Paulo. The numbers I've gathered so far suggest a natural occurrence, an earthquake, with significant loss of life. Water is also a key player. And the children of São Paulo will be in danger."

"Water?" Destrey asked. "Remind me again."

"Yes, *Madame* Destrey. As you know, citizens of São Paulo have been drilling for water for more than twenty years. São Paulo isn't remotely set to provide essential services, such as clean water and electrical power, to all its twenty million people. The megacity is in danger of collapsing under its own weight."

"That's hard to believe," Destrey said.

"There is indeed a problem with the water supply," Lola said.

Destrey snorted. "That's an understatement."

"São Paulo is showing signs of dry caked soil and water trucks. Rich and middle class *Paulistanos* were either drilling for water in their backyards or hoarding it by the truckload."

"I can't really imagine what the people are going through," Destrey mumbled, half to herself.

"The street gangs are also stocking water."

"So, Planter and his gang," said Destrey.

"Most likely, *Madame* Destrey. An eight-ounce bottle of water is going for as much as 90 Brazilian Reals or $20 U.S. dollars."

That reminded Destrey that a drought could happened anywhere.

"Water could soon be more expensive than cocaine," Lola said.

"Finding and hoarding water has become an occupation and, for some, a profitable business."

"What's the bottom line, Lola?"

"We will be facing four issues, *Madame* Destrey. One: São Paulo's reservoirs are practically dry. Two: man-made earthquakes are generated by empty reservoirs. Three: deforestation of the Amazon forest increases erosion by a factor of two and changes rain output significantly. Four: reduced oxygen production and the release of carbon dioxide into the atmosphere will accelerate other climate changes such as the steady increase of sea levels. I fear Mother Nature is well underway to recalibrate the planet."

Destrey didn't reply. She suddenly felt as if she was back in Jerusalem trying to stop terrorists from destroying the city. She closed her eyes and prayed to God to give her strength.

"The event about to happen is as natural as a hurricane or a flood," Lola said. "However, with the population's general disinclination to heed warnings, Paulistanos will be subject to the same forces found in other events. People will either die because they stubbornly decide not to heed our warnings, or they will react with great wisdom and leave the city."

Destrey shook her head. "I wouldn't bet a nickel on wisdom."

"I have calculated those probabilities, *Madame* Destrey, and I am now able to say that we have the necessary substance for a BTG event. That is to say, no amount of weight put on the good citizens of the city will have any significant impact on their behavior."

"So, you're saying I'm wasting my time going down there trying to save millions of lives."

"Yes, *Madame* Destrey."

"You're saying I shouldn't even try?"

"On the contrary, *Madame* Destrey. I could be wrong. Minor earthquakes are more likely to happen than large ones, and because we have predicted a very large earthquake, you could end up helping millions of innocent people. Being an industrial psychologist, you can appreciate the likely human impact of an earthquake incident. I can only provide the realm of possibilities. What will actually happen is still a shot in the dark."

"So, sooner or later a quake will happen, and the people won't leave the city," Destrey said.

"Yes, *Madame* Destrey, it will and they won't."

"Then, I don't have a choice. I have to try."

"Very aptly put, *Madame* Destrey."

"Gee, thanks Mr. Robot."

Destrey began to leave the Safe where BTG's supercomputer was located.

"I should get myself another computer," Destrey said to herself.

"That would be very expensive," Lola replied, while her holographic image smiled imperceptibly.

8

LOS ALAMOS NATIONAL LABORATORY
GEOPHYSICAL RESEARCH PROJECT
LOS ALAMOS, NEW MEXICO

Logan Newton turned to his deputy chief of operations who had remained silent throughout the conference call.

"I want you to make a digital copy of this conversation along with a written transcript," Logan said nervously. "Send a copy by email to my boss and Legal. There's no way we're getting wedged between South American politicians' denial and the earthquake of the century."

"What do you think will …?"

"How the hell should I know if it's going to happen?" Logan shot back. "But if the earthquake does materialize like we said it would, it'll be the first time anyone gets near that kind of prediction and shoots a bull's-eye."

"So…"

"You're right," Logan said. "I think we should talk to the board, and quick. We need to cover our asses. There's too much at stake."

He then paused. "Wait a minute. Maybe, just maybe, I'm handling this issue ass-backwards."

"You mean the chairman?"

"Better still," Logan said. "Call Harper now."

"The White House chief of staff?"

Logan nodded. "If we're right about the earthquake, the president will be talking to the nation about the Brazilian crisis."

9

THE BOSTON TRIAGE GROUP (BTG)

"Stop," Destrey said. She looked at Lola's holographic image and held her breath. Destrey thought the computer wasn't ready to call for an event. Nevertheless, she was afraid of what Lola would say next. But Destrey had to know.

"It's begun?" Destrey asked. A look of caution came over her face.

"Yes, *Madame* Destrey. An imminent earthquake. We do indeed have an event," Lola said.

"I was afraid you'd say that. Do we have enough data?"

"Yes, *Madame* Destrey. Enough to call it."

"I'm not sure I'm ready," Destrey said unhappily.

Lola didn't respond.

"Tell Margaret McGivney I'll be late," Destrey said. "I want to think things over."

"Yes, *Madame* Destrey."

"Even though we now know about the earthquake, São Paulo will still fail to evacuate their people," Destrey said. "Because... almost everything we believed about dealing with people was wrong."

Lola again didn't reply.

"Now, more than ever, I know that evacuating people from their homes is problematical," Destrey said. "It's not enough to warn them of an impending disaster. They have to clear out from São Paulo. Leave their homes and run! Problem is, I can tell them to get out but I can't force them. And that's a fact. I know it."

"It is," Lola answered. "Complex human behavior of the type that interests BTG's researchers is by its very nature, unpredictable. If not imprecise and uncertain. This introduces new and serious reservations about our past attempts to evacuate people from imminent danger."

"What I'm really trying to say is that informing people is not enough. Failing to evacuate the people is not an option," Destrey said. "BTG was built to help people, not just inform them of what lay ahead. Hell, I wasn't brought up to fail. Failure was never an option in my family." Destrey was thinking of her father's unrealistic expectations. As far as he was concerned, good was never good enough. He demanded perfection from his daughter. Nothing less.

"What variables are we dealing with?" Destrey asked.

"I've identified five variables," Lola said. "One, motivational differences between individuals. A few arguments will never be enough to generate mass awareness. Two, chaos erupting from all sides when plans collapse before they are implemented. Three, in our case, the time it takes to acquire a new behavior is problematic. Four, people's capacity to be lucid and not wander off in mythical worlds that suit them better. Five, the implications of quantum mechanics where the everyday world we perceive does not exist until observed. In our case, until an imminent danger is visible and palpable, people will be unable to deal with it."

"Well, that's a mouthful," Destrey said.

"I will be able to identify more variables, *Madame* Destrey as we move forward. However, our success in evacuating a people is less than likely. On the other hand, all I know about BTG's moral obligations leads us to at least try to help. Even in the face of certain failure."

"I know I have to try... but Jesus!" Destrey was confronted by two equally bad options. Oddly enough, both led to failure. It was a case of doing something or nothing and producing the same outcome. That's what Destrey had to work with. She was none too pleased at the prospect of wasting her time. On the other hand, one of the biggest keys to BTG's success was understanding and learning from past failures.

Destrey sat still in front of Lola's holographic image. She needed to think. Her late husband was the clever one when it came to finding creative ways to deal with problems. She wished he was back here by her side.

"Where are you when I need you?" she asked aloud. Then, after a moment, she turned to Lola. "What other options do I have? And please don't tell me there isn't another way of dealing with this earthquake."

In the past, Destrey had tried different strategies to persuade and sway, giving people the reasons to evacuate. In the end, the results were usually disappointing.

"The issue at hand," Destrey said, "is influence versus denial. Could one persuade another to leave everything behind while not knowing what the future will hold?"

So far, based on Destrey's past experience, the convincing part of her strategy had not generated anticipated results. In fact, the only thing that worked was forcing people to evacuate through force. However, even though ordinary people were required, sometimes at gunpoint, to leave their homes and businesses, there had been backlashes. People had died. Destrey understood that humans push back. Was the resistance because of a lack of control over their lives, too much uncertainty about their future or maybe was it simply because they didn't or couldn't believe people in authority?

But there was, however, a surprising constant. Destrey discovered, over the years, that asking people to leave everything behind with no clear alternatives in hand was a non-starter.

"Let's review the underlying reasons why our past strategies failed to meet our expectations," Lola said. "One, people didn't believe they were in danger. Two, many seniors did not have the resources to leave their homes. Three, our research shows that people between 50 and 65 years and older are most likely to resist an evacuation. Four, there are segments found all over the world that consciously ignore warnings because they have a problem with authority. Five, many stay put to protect their homes and businesses from looting."

"I understand, but are there any other options out there?" Destrey asked, a bit irritated. "Options that may be more successful?"

"*Madame* Destrey, persuading people to leave everything behind is almost impossible, especially when there are no physical signs of danger. BTG has faced those difficulties before and failed. In fact, more than once. We have learned that people will not leave empty-handed. Without an acceptable alternative, the chances are next to none that they would join an evacuation. Even in the face of imminent danger, people will not heed our warnings."

"You've just told me what everyone knows." Destrey was, by now, exasperated. However, at the same time, she also realized that a true breakthrough project would require an innovative approach to deal with the incoming earthquake.

"Yes, *Madame* Destrey, I realize that. But I've come up with a slightly different approach."

"Go on."

"In order for any plan to work, we require individual motivation," Lola said. "We require a stimulus from within. The people should be motivated not only by reason, but also by a deep emotional need to save themselves and their family members."

Destrey sat quietly for a few minutes trying to distinguish the difference between what BTG had done in the past and what Lola was proposing. The adjustment Lola offered was subtle and, from Destrey's point of view, not something new or actionable.

"We tried that, Lola. Establishing an internal motivation in millions of Paulistinos in a short period of time, while the clock is ticking, well, that's impossible."

"There is also the required belief in an imminent threat," Lola said. "The common thread in getting people to agree to an evacuation lies in the certainty of imminent and deadly danger."

"You're saying we have to instill a sense of certainty?" Destrey asked.

"Nothing else will work, *Madame* Destrey."

"I'd like nothing more than to agree with you, Lola, but there isn't a hope in hell that people will believe, with certainty, that we can now predict earthquakes."

There's nothing else to say about that, Destrey thought.

"I'm not going to put BTG's resources in danger or set them up to fail," Destrey finally said. "We need, no, that's not true. Let me start over again. I'm the one who needs to succeed, and, I need to make sure that happens. Otherwise, there won't be a next time."

The supercomputer did not react.

"And, because I now realize I can't do this on my own, I'll need help. There's got to be someone here, on my payroll, who can help me deal with this... São Paulo business."

Margaret McGivney was tired of waiting for Louise Destrey to come back from the Safe, so she headed down to the sub-basement and joined Destrey. The elevator doors opened and Margaret emerged.

Destrey was surprised to see her, in the Safe, in person. Margaret wasn't a big fan of machines and holographic wizardry. She preferred the corporate offices where there was fabric, sunlight, genuine wood furnishings and real people to talk to.

"I've been thinking, Margaret," Destrey said.

"I can see that. You look like a mess. What's going on anyway?"

"I've hit a wall. We have an event and I don't really know what to do."

"So, what are you going to do about that?" Margaret asked her boss. "About the not knowing stuff?"

Destrey sighed and looked at Margaret. "Get help. My husband used to say that our sharpest weapon was our imagination. Can you set up a meeting with the staff? I want everyone to attend in person or through Coms. We've got an event and I need their help."

Margaret looked shocked. "You're actually going to say that? The great Louise Margoe Destrey needs help?"

"Hold on there," Louise said. "I'm very comfortable asking for help, especially when I need it."

"And when was the last time you did that?" Margaret asked.

"Never mind. You know what? You can be such a bully sometimes."

Margaret smiled. "Look who's talking. Some people buckle at the knees just knowing that you want to see them."

"Okay," Destrey said. "I don't want to argue with you. You win. And you're right. I don't like asking for help. But now, I do. Okay? I need my people now more than ever."

"All right, take it easy, Louise." Margaret looked around and noticed that Lola was looking directly at her. "What's she looking at?"

"Never mind the computer," Destrey replied.

"In about an hour then?" Margaret asked.

Destrey nodded. "Yes. That's time enough. And please tell the board chairman about the São Paulo event."

"What are you going to tell your crew this time?" Margaret asked.

"I'll start by talking about what's happening in São Paulo, our role in this event, and what we've learned from other events in the past. This time, we're going in with our eyes wide open and, I hope, with a new strategy. No unrealistic expectations. Then, I'll put my cards on the table, and tell them I need their help. We've got to come up with a way to instill certainty."

"That sounds bizarre, don't you think?" Margaret asked.

"This is our eighth event," Destrey said. "So, call it Code 8E. Tell Constantin to come and see me, I'll be up in five." Constantin Greco was BTG's most senior consultant as well as the creator of Lola's avatar. "I want Greco's input on the resources I'll need in São Paulo. By the way, book the jet for tomorrow. I also would like Kleinrup to join me. See if he's up for a trip to in São Paulo."

"I did that already," Margaret replied. "We talked yesterday. He's all in but he wants you to know that you'll have a full complement of bodyguards." Margaret smiled.

"That's..." Destrey paused.

"What?" Margaret asked. "You were about to say something nasty?"

Destrey shook her head. "Nothing, never mind. You know me a bit too much. Am I that predictable?"

Margaret nodded. "Yep, and I agree with you, *Frenchie*. I do know you a bit too much for my own good."

With that, Margaret left Destrey in the Safe alone with Lola.

"*Madame* Destrey?" Lola said.

"Yeah."

"I will activate an event protocol for all BTG employees in one hour."

"All right, but here's what I expect: everyone on deck for this one. No exception."

"As you wish, *Madame* Destrey."

"Incidentally, what's the weather down there?" Destrey asked.

"Hot and humid, *Madame* Destrey. In fact, inordinately warm and steamy."

"The natives will be difficult to handle," Destrey mumbled.

"As well as dangerous," Lola said. "Then again, *Madame* Destrey, nothing is predestined."

Destrey had been warned before, but to no avail. This time, it was different. Lola had never before warned Destrey so openly.

Destrey shrugged it off and walked away.

10

LUCIENNE PRITCHARD
SÃO PAULO

"**E**mmanuelle, honey, please don't do that. Use the spoon."

"I love you, Mommy."

Lucienne Pritchard hugged her child and kissed her eyes, nose, cheeks and lips.

"Mommy loves you more today than yesterday, but, I still want you to use your spoon."

"Mommy?"

"Yes, *ma chérie.*"

"I want to play in the sand," Emmanuelle said.

"Right. The sandbox." Lucienne looked outside. The weather was fine. Maybe a half hour. It was still cool enough for her *trésor* to play.

"I know you like to play in the sandbox, but what's so special about it?" Pritchard asked.

"I want to feel the waves, Mommy."

"You mean the waves at the beach?"

"No, Mommy. In the sandbox." The little one waved her hands over the breakfast table. She repeated the movement as though her hand was floating in water.

Pritchard's cell rang.

"I want to go out and play, Mommy," Emmanuelle said.

Lucienne looked over at her daughter. "Honey? Mommy is taking a call."

Emmanuelle persisted.

"You're too smart for your own good, missy." She grabbed the little one's hand and turned away from the child to concentrate on the incoming call.

"*Alô!*" she answered in Portuguese.

"It's Louise Destrey."

"Auntie Louise? Is that really you?" Lucienne was taken aback.

"Yes. I'm in a bit in a rush and I have something important to tell you," Destrey said.

"Mommy, Mommy?"

"Hush, baby. Mommy's busy on the phone."

"I've heard you're a mom?" Lucienne could hear the smile in Destrey's voice.

"Yes, and she's quite a handful."

"I'm sure she is, just like her *maman*," Destrey said.

"You remember?" Lucienne was surprised.

"How could I forget the daughter I've never had?"

"You always say that." Lucienne could never forget her Auntie Louise.

"I made a promise to your mother I'd take care of you if something ever happened to her. But happily, your mom is doing well."

"So why is the most famous industrial psychologist in the whole wide world talking to me?"

"Well, Lucienne..."

"What's wrong, Auntie Louise?"

"There's a reason for my call," Destrey said.

"I think I figured that out. Tell me, what's wrong? You're making me nervous," Pritchard said.

"Take a seat, honey." Destrey was on her way to the headquarters of *Folha de S.Paulo*, a local newspaper. "When can your family leave São Paulo?"

"Leave? Why? No, no. Don't say it! Someone wants to blow up the city, like they did in Jerusalem?"

"No, honey. It's not like that. Think of the Big One for California. And now think of a bigger one for São Paulo."

"Oh, Auntie Louise. That's all over the news. It's just a scare. No one's buying it. São Paulo is the best place to live and the best place to bring up my family. If you were here, you'd see that for yourself."

"I'm in São Paulo. And, you're talking to the someone who's trying desperately to scare people."

"You can't be serious?"

"Call your husband. There's a U.S. Armed Forces Hercules with three seats waiting for you. It leaves tomorrow afternoon with the American diplomats and their staff. I'll email you the information and the documents you'll need to board the aircraft."

"This is a joke. I mean, we can't just leave everything behind. And besides, Hugh's away on business, God knows where."

"Get out of São Paulo, out of Brazil, get your ass back to the States or to your mother's home," Destrey said.

"But…"

"If you don't do as I say, I'll have two humongous goons come to your home and carry you to the aircraft, with extreme prejudice."

"Okay, okay, I got it. I'll call him right now," Lucienne said. "Will you be on that flight?"

"No. I've got to convince a lot of people to get out of here."

"You're scaring me, Auntie Louise."

"Well then, I guess you do have a head on your shoulders after all."

"What the hell does that mean?" Lucienne asked.

"Never mind, honey. You've got to tell your husband, wherever he is, to move and fast."

"I don't think he'll listen to me."

"I'll email you my private number. Tell him to call me as soon as possible."

"Yes, Auntie Louise."

"Okay then. Call your mother and tell her you agreed to do as I say."

"You called my mother?"

"Honey, you wouldn't believe who I've talked to in the last two years."

"Jesus…"

"God? No. Not yet."

The line went dead. Lucienne looked out her kitchen window and finally understood. The sandbox. The waves in the sandbox. Destrey's call. And especially what she had to do *rapidamente*.

11

PAIVA CASTRO DAM

MAIRIPORÃ, STATE OF SÃO PAULO

It usually took João Santos and Paulo Malfatti more than an hour to get down in the dam's bowels. Before heading down there, Santos reviewed safety protocol notifications and yesterday's performance reports. He was obviously a careful man.

Just minutes before starting his daily commute down to his monitoring chamber deep in the heart of the dam, he got a call from Control.

"There's something going on," Control said. "Nothing important. Could be a glitch. Take a look at it anyway. See what the sensors down there are telling you."

Santos said he'd call him back if he saw anything out of the ordinary.

Santos was a man of few words. He believed he was a true professional. He was pretty good with numbers and he made them talk. He was also proud of the work he was doing. He had a purpose. His job was important: he monitored the dam. *Paulistanos* relied on him. He was instrumental in delivering precious water to the citizens of São Paulo. To do that, he would regularly work in monitoring chambers, wrought with state-of-the-art technology grown men would die to work with. The monitoring chambers were located at the lowest point of the Paiva Castro Dam. Normally, the surface of the reservoir would be thirty meters above the chamber, but today, because of a lack of rainwater, it was merely five meters above his premature balding head. Yet, a hundred million tons of cement and rebar rested solidly overhead.

João Santos had the place to himself even though Paulo Malfatti was a few meters away. In the great scheme of things, Malfatti's presence didn't count for much. Santos didn't know why exactly, but that was Paulo in a nutshell. He was rarely missed. Co-workers didn't know what to make of him. Paulo basically melted into the scenery. Likewise, the nickname "Poor Paulo" didn't help his reputation. Along with such descriptions as *cuzão* (or asshole) and simpleton, Paulo was also defined as peculiar.

"Paulo?"

"Yeah?"

"See anything?" Santos asked.

"No. Should I?"

"I don't know, you tell me."

"I'm following the routine set in the procedures," Paulo said, expressionless. "I see the same readings. Nothing unusual."

It was a fitting image, as Paulo was forever under the radar. He symbolized anonymity in its purest form. In addition to his lack of presence, Paulo was essentially drab, dull and dreary, with a touch of idiot brilliance. Whether a gift or a curse, Paulo's disappearing act was strange and at times comical. When all was said and done, Santos wasn't so sure what to make of him. Paulo was indeed a puzzle.

Poor Paulo wasn't the only team member to bear the mark of obscurity. They were in the millions. For all intents and purposes, the Paulo Malfattis of the world were faceless with no inherent value.

Santos felt as if he was alone even though Malfatti was staring right at him. Speaking to him. In his face. Maybe that's why Santos enjoyed his time underground with poor Paulo. Deep in his manmade cave, isolated from the rest of the world, Santos was just fine all by himself despite Paulo Malfatti.

"So peaceful down here. So quiet," Santos said to himself.

"What are you talking about?" Malfatti asked.

"Nothing, Paulo." Santos was feeling cheerful as he finished the last of his morning coffee. "Focus on those numbers I told you about."

"Then why mention it?" Malfatti said annoyed. He didn't quite understand his team leader. However, he was sure of one thing: he didn't like him. Not one bit. As far as he was concerned, the man was weird. For starters, Santos loved his bat cave. When adding Santos's compulsive obsession for safety with the reservoir's flow rate, Malfatti doubted his sanity. Why would anyone in his right mind want to work in a cement room the size of a small car? How could he be happy under a billion tons of concrete?

"I meant to say it's peaceful down here," Santos said, a bit pissed off. His workmate ruined his mojo.

"I don't know about you," Paulo said, "but this tomb is too fucking spooky for my taste. You have your fucking numbers. Let's get out of here."

At times, Malfatti could also be vulgar. But Santos let it go, as he always did. That was the way it worked. You did the best you could with what you had. Santos had to deal with Paulo together with his disappearing act and foul mouth.

Not a moment later, something odd caught Santos's attention. He noticed what he could only describe as a difference. A change. As if he had leaped into another world. Identical in every way, but still different as well as foreign. It was happening now, in the monitoring chamber, in the air he breathed, but mostly in his guts. He couldn't quite make it out. He suddenly felt a sense of impending doom. A crippling, nauseous feeling along with a painful dry throat. And scratchy. Something was in the air. A primal fear submariners experience before falling asleep.

"Paulo?"

"Yeah?" Paulo was still annoyed.

"Did you feel that?" Santos was not the type to scare easy. But something caught his attention.

"Feel what?" Paulo asked. "Is something wrong?"

"Never mind. I'm calling Control."

Santos picked up the land line and dialed one, two, three.

"Control, this is Santos. I'm in the monitoring chamber. How do you hear me?"

"Loud and clear. You got something?" Control was manned by a senior technician whose job was to oversee the dam's overall performance.

"I'm not too sure about this line." Santos believed he picked up static.

"Sounds clear up here. Like you're sitting in my living room."

"That's no comfort, Control. So, nothing on your side?" Santos was restless and agitated.

"Give me a second." Control had his own way of dealing with problems. Calmly and carefully.

There was a long wait.

"Do you have anything now?" Control asked.

There was another pause.

"Santos?" Control called him again. Santos was busy double checking the numbers appearing on his monitor.

"Control?" Santos said.

"This is Control," he replied as calmly as he could.

"I've got nothing."

"Everything looks good from up here. Finish up what you're doing and come and see me. I'm brewing a fresh pot of coffee."

Fortunately, Santos's anxiety faded away. He wanted to believe he was in control. Nevertheless, Santos hardly moved a muscle.

That's foolish and silly, he thought. He decided he had more important things to do even though he didn't know what to make of it. Something strange was radiating from the thick cement walls. Not a tremor, but close. A shift of some kind. In the end, he let it go.

As it often happened, the overhead light faded for a brief moment. Barely long enough for anyone to notice. But Santos did.

"Cool it," he said to himself.

"Sorry, what did you say?" Paulo thought Santos was behaving strangely this morning.

"Nothing. Just talking to myself. Never mind me."

Santos turned to his screen and punched a few keyboard commands. He checked the numbers once more. He was satisfied the flow rate was normal even though the reservoir was practically empty. He turned his gaze toward the overhead light. Just as his eyes focused on the light source, he saw it once again. The light wavered. A slight hesitation on its part. The light bulb blinked.

I don't see any warning indicators, he thought. *Maybe my eyes are playing tricks on me. Maybe I'm too old to work here.*

Santos looked around for something off-kilter, a sign or a clue. Paulo was too busy closing down his monitors to notice anything unusual. Paulo wanted out, the sooner the better. In fact, he'd been thinking about it for months. If it was up to him, today would be his last assignment in Santos's cave.

By chance, a class of third graders from the American Elementary and High School had moved on to another area of the dam complex without a hitch. All was as it should be as his computer monitors displayed the numbers he required for his usual morning conference. He checked his monitors one more time.

Nothing peculiar. So far, so good, Santos thought to himself.

He was just about done. Perhaps a few more minutes left to go. Santos was now preparing to send his report topside to his workstation. Essentially the same data he'd been conveying to his manager for the last few months. The flow was at an all-time low. The reservoirs were almost empty, down to 14% of their capacity. Soon, there would be no water to pump and no water to drink unless the State instituted a statewide water rationing program.

As Santos was going over his numbers one last time, the monitoring chamber was quiet. For a few minutes every day, Santos was far away from the noise and the bustle of São Paulo. Here, he was safe.

"João?" Paulo said.

"What?" Santos was mildly irritated. His eyes remained glued to his monitors. Suddenly, the numbers weren't right. Seismic sensor readings were off the charts even though he couldn't feel the slightest vibration. He made a note to reboot and re-calibrate the sensor array as soon as possible. Something was wrong, very wrong, crazy stupid wrong, and he had to do something about it.

"Can you feel something?" Malfatti appeared tense.

Santos looked up at the light source. "I thought I did a few minutes ago," he said, unsure of what he was about to say next. "But, I'm sure it's nothing."

Santos realized he hadn't imagined it. Something was up. A little voice inside his head told him to breathe again. Mercifully, it could all be explained. "Mother Nature," the little voice said, "is being mischievous again. Nothing to get too concerned about."

"*Fique tranquilo,*" he told Paulo. "Just relax. The reservoir is practically empty. What's the worst that could happen?"

The little voice in his head was very convincing because São Paulo's seismic activity was well known: scientists recorded thousands of mild tremors every year. Mostly harmless. What's more, São Paulo was nowhere near a fault line. Brazil, as a whole, was relatively free from faults. The nation was believed safe from major earthquakes. The country was not located on the border of any major tectonic plates. It would be safe to say that a major earthquake on Brazilian territory would be quite unusual.

"Besides," Santos added in earnest, "the dam has a mountain of monitoring instruments." The data generated was transmitted in real-time to the Polytechnic School of the University of São Paulo. *If something was going on,* Santos thought, *they would surely warn us.*

"Don't worry, Paulo. But I need your final count. Otherwise, there's nothing to be concerned about. I heard that on Globo News last night. So, keep at it, will you? Just a few more minutes and we'll be off."

"If you say so." Santos's colleague wasn't reassured.

A tiny plume of dust fell on Santos's keyboard. It was followed by a tiny tremor.

"What the hell!" Santos exclaimed. He looked around and found nothing out of place. He got to his feet and realized his sandals were wet. Water had accumulated on the floor. Santos hadn't noticed before and neither had his colleague. Water seepage in a dam this size was not unheard of, but still, it was unsettling.

"One," he began to say to himself, "I shouldn't be worried because the dam is at an all-time low, and two, because..."

Santos didn't have a two.

"João?" Paulo said.

"I know, I know," Santos shot back. "Something's wrong. Let me think."

"Fuck that... let's get out of here!" Paulo Malfatti didn't want to wait for the ceiling to collapse on his head.

Santos was about to call Control when the manmade enclosure shook, jarring the monitoring devices from their moorings. The lights above his head popped. The air conditioning ceased to provide fresh air. Computers shut down. Santos's cave went dark. The emergency lights did not come on as expected. Santos held his breath. Malfatti turned to God for help. He made the sign of the cross as he valiantly believed in the power of the Holy Ghost to protect him in his hour of need. Santos was afraid to move, to think or to run. He now understood what paralysis meant.

Much to their surprise, nothing happened. Maybe the end of the world was for another day. There wasn't a sound to be heard, which was not unusual one hundred feet beneath a mountain of cement.

Deep in the dark confines of the monitoring chamber, Santos and his colleague waited for the lights to come back to life. It was surely just a matter of seconds. Santos's mind drifted a bit. He thought he'd be late for supper. *Most probably,* he thought to himself. He was thinking of what he would say to his wife when he'd finally sit down to eat. He didn't want her or his two kids to worry about him or his damn job. *No need to get her going again.*

The lights and the computer monitors flickered back to life. Both men were relieved. It was just a false alarm. Nothing important enough to mention to the wife. Still, the com was dead, but that wasn't uncommon. Things happened. A glitch in the system. A bad connection. Perhaps a short.

Damn Chinese equipment! Santos thought.

No matter, Santos reasoned. *Almost everything is back to normal.* Or so he thought. In spite of all the incidents he had witnessed over the last few minutes, Santos began to sit rather than run for his life. He was somewhat relieved and almost happy to see his monitors generate the data he had been waiting for. He didn't feel the need to run to safety.

If I did that, I'd be in real danger, Santos thought to himself. *If I really believed that, I would activate a code red.* Santos looked at the toggle.

"The emergency switch is on my desk," Santos said out loud.

"What did you say?" Malfatti asked.

"Nothing."

He would probably run out of this man-cave as fast as he could, Santos said to himself.

But Santos didn't do any of that. He believed it would be wrong to think his days on the planet were ending.

We're both safe and alive for many more years to come. After all, not one of the many operational systems sounded an alarm. Control didn't call either. In fact, nobody did anything! he said to himself.

The end happened at lighting speed. João Santos and Paulo Malfatti didn't have the time to think or to feel anything other than their last breath. Their underground enclosure closed in on them, squashing them to dust. Anyone working underground died instantly as the Paiva Castro Dam suddenly collapsed. The dam buckled.

A few minutes later, other dams collapsed. Men and women, including the children from the American Elementary and High School disappeared, never to be seen again.

No one foresaw the event, save for a supercomputer in Cambridge, tasked to monitor the event.

It had begun.

Lola immediately contacted Destrey to inform her of the earthquakes.

"That's right, *Madame* Destrey. The Paiva Castro Dam was hit around 9:40 a.m. this morning. Local authorities say they can't explain the tremors. However, my prognosis is on target. The earthquakes will impact the city in a matter of hours. It will take well over six months to get water restored to São Paulo."

"So, it has started?" Destrey asked Lola.

"Given that the epicenter of the earthquake was located a few hundred meters west of the Cantareira Reservoir, I'd say yes. As predicted. Is there anything I can do for you, *Madame* Destrey?"

"No, not really. Just wish me luck. I'm heading for the Canadian Consulate."

"Of course, *Madame* Destrey."

Above, high in the Cloud, most of the Internet world was abuzz with conjecture and conspiracy theories involving terrorists, corrupt engineering firms, the planet's revenge against the human race for having desecrated the Amazon rain forest, and lastly, but certainly not least, scientists speculating about water pore pressure enabling seismic activity and earthquake occurrences. In other words, unintended man-made earthquakes, designed, engineered and manufactured in Brazil. A formidable problem to figure out, a certain threat in the near future, and, for once, an event that had nothing to do with China, Putin, ISIS, the Internet or crazy people.

12

Waiting for a government big shot to show up for a scheduled meeting wasn't part of Destrey's DNA. Never was. Never would be.

The woman at the reception desk had an apologetic look on her face. "The Consul General will be here in a few minutes."

Destrey wasn't going to give him a chance to wiggle out of this one. Not by a long shot. Because of the information she acquired and, more importantly, because time was in play, the senior industrial psychologist wasn't going to waste precious time waiting for a Canadian public servant to show up, not even for a diplomat. São Paulo had just learned of the Paiva Castro Dam disaster and Destrey knew it was going to get worse. She required the Canadian Consul General to get off his ass and do his job. There was no time to waste on protocol. She had already alerted his American counterpart.

God knows, she hated the diplomatic corps. Complete flummery and foolish humbug. Still, she needed him to do his job.

In a sudden burst of anger, Destrey yelled out, "Where the hell is he?" The sound of her voice stunned and frightened consular staff.

The young admin assistant didn't answer. It was clear she didn't know where her boss was hiding out.

Deer in headlights, Destrey thought miserably. She remembered what her late husband said about consular staff: "Not the sharpest minds..."

Louise sighed. "What's your name?"

"Amy... Amy Bluehawk, ma'am." The young woman was shaking.

"Oh hell. I've just bullied a child, a Native Canadian to boot," Destrey mumbled to herself. She felt awful. Destrey had a temper, and there was nothing she could do about it. It was too late for that. Besides, she had earned the right to be nasty, anytime, anywhere with anyone.

But not with the so young, she thought. Amy Bluehawk was a good girl, starting her professional life at the bottom of the ladder in São Paulo, of all cities.

Amy Bluehawk was on her cell before she had the time to realize how terrified she was. Panicked, feeling small and insignificant, she cowered at the sight of this woman. No one in her hometown of Regina had warned Bluehawk about the Destreys of the world.

"He's in a meeting on the third floor, ma'am," Bluehawk squeaked.

"Sweetie... Amy," Destrey said almost projecting affection. "Please shut that cell and take me to him. Don't worry. I won't bite."

The young intern appeared relieved. She called her sweetie.

"Now young woman. Let's get moving, shall we?" Destrey was on a mission and the clock was ticking. Destrey put her arm around Amy's shoulder and tenderly led her onward. The young woman was still trembling but moving forward, nevertheless.

13

CANADIAN CONSULATE GENERAL

AV. DAS NAÇÕES UNIDAS

SÃO PAULO

"He's in there." Amy Bluehawk pointed to a glass-enclosed conference room.

Bob Meneghel looked up from his teacup and watched as his sexy intern pointed him out from the rest of the crowd in the conference room. He turned away and calmly took another mouthful of his delicious brew. He felt safe among his employees, sheltered within his team of twenty-five-year-old kids, far away from Louise Destrey.

Don't look at her. Avoid her eyes, he reminded himself.

"You don't need to point him out, Amy," said Destrey. "I know him well. I can always tell him apart from the rest. This one slithers."

"Slithers?"

"Yes, Amy. Like a snake in the grass," Destrey whispered to Bluehawk while looking at the Consul General.

Destrey had no problem recognizing him because Bob Meneghel was in trouble, and he knew it. He had been instructed to help her out. Unfortunately, he'd gone out of his way to make it impossible for them to meet. He boasted about it to his employees. He would ignore the bitch. He was the boss. Not a servant for whomever had an agenda. He was a diplomat, not a gopher.

Destrey leaned over to Bluehawk and told her to go back to her workstation. "You don't want to be here, sweetie."

Bluehawk left. In fact, the intern ran for cover.

Destrey walked toward the glass-enclosed conference room, gently pushed the door, and walked in.

Meneghel watched her from the corner of his eyes. He was terror stricken.

Louise cleared her throat. "Ladies and gentlemen, my name is Louise Destrey." She gazed at the people sitting around the huge conference table. "Now get out. The grown-ups have work to do."

Not one public servant moved a muscle. No one dared.

Meneghel's assistant asked, "Should I call security, sir?"

Meneghel was about to agree when two men appeared from out of nowhere, and stood behind Destrey.

Louise smiled. "You needn't call security because, as you can see, they're here."

Meneghel choked on his tea. He was as terrified as the rest of his staff, his leadership skills having jumped ship.

The two giants entered the conference room. The bigger of the two pointed to Meneghel.

"Every... body... out. Not you, comrade Ambassador. Everybody else. Out now."

Destrey knew she could make good use of her Russian goons, assigned to protect and, on occasion, to intimidate.

She pointed to the woman who appeared to be Meneghel's assistant. "You, miss..."

"Ju...Ju ... Judy," she sputtered.

"Judy. Okay, Judy. Get Colin Tremblay, the Minister of Foreign Affairs, on this line. Here's his private number. Put him on speaker, and stay here until I tell you it's okay to leave the room."

Judy stood still. Her eyes darted back and forth from her boss to the woman who called herself Destrey.

"What are you waiting for?" Destrey asked.

"I don't know this number, I think..." Judy punched a few numbers.

By now, Meneghel was standing in the corner of the conference room. He was trying to fade away.

"Colin Tremblay," the minister said calmly.

"Colin, this is Louise Destrey."

"I was waiting for your call. What took you so long?"

"Mr. Meneghel is here with me. Could you please remind him... you know...?"

"Bob? Are you there?"

"Yes, Minister. I'm here, sir." Meneghel walked toward Destrey. "There's no need for this call, Minister. I can assure you that I will help *Madame* Destrey and put all the resources of my office at her disposal."

"Thanks, Bob, because Louise has an important job to do, and we don't want her to call me again. You do understand that, Bob?"

"Yes, Minister. Of course. No problem. I'm on it twenty-four seven."

"That's my man. Good luck, Louise."

"Thanks, I'll need it."

"You know, I'm praying you're wrong and all that, but if your track record is any indication of your work, I'm afraid we'll be talking about a rescue mission. Are you sure about this stuff?"

"So far, it's not looking good."

"Well, then goodbye, Louise."

"Thank you, Colin." She turned to Meneghel and told him to sit. He had a lot of work to do, and time was of the essence.

"What can I do for you, *Madame* Destrey?"

"One, tell Judy here, she now works for me."

"Right."

"One more thing."

"Anything."

"I need your office."

"Anything else?"

"A Canadian Hercules is on the way. Have it fueled and ready on a moment's notice. We're leaving."

"You're kidding."

"I wish I was."

14

WATER FILTRATION FACILITY #2
SÃO PAULO

uy Menezes toured the facility, looking out for anything out of the ordinary. Just another day at the office.

The work done at the facility was relatively easy to understand. Contaminated water in, cleaner water out. At least, that was the intention. However, at this station, only 65 percent of sewage was actually collected, with only a fraction treated. Menezes worked in one of eight São Paulo wastewater treatment plants. On the whole, only half of the wastewater collected in the metropolitan area was being treated.

Menezes knew it wasn't the easiest job to tackle, especially since the 2014 drought, but he couldn't blame anyone for his fate. The job paid the bills. In the end, he'd asked for the promotion and got it. Now it was up to him to supervise his former colleagues and get the work done as best he could. As employees went, they weren't a bad bunch to manage, but he did have a real challenge facing him: sooner or later, facility #2 would fail. He knew that, as did his employees. It was a secret he shared with management. He needed them to voice his concerns all the way up to the governor of the State of São Paulo. Although he didn't know how he or his employees would handle the challenge, he plowed ahead, doing his best to seal the cracks and fix the chinks.

Regardless of assurances from politicians, things were getting worse by the week. The troubles at the plant were unresolved and growing, and although Brazil had 12% of the planet's freshwater supply, access to clean water was an issue for most *Paulistanos*.

Although dozens of municipalities had a hand in identifying solutions, their execution was far and few between. Menezes was fed up with the constant requests for reports and stats from the World Bank and Inter-American Development Bank consultants. It was all for nothing. Nevertheless, Menezes being a good soldier, did his best to provide the information required from him.

Beware of what you wish for, he often thought to himself. *I wanted this job, and now I have it.*

The problem at hand at the facility was simple to understand. The wastewater plant was simply overloaded and every *Paulistano* knew about it.

Although no one was allowed to say it out loud, Menezes knew the truth. The facility was not even doing the job it was designed for in the first place. His employees had more overtime hours than he was allowed to assign. Yet the work was critical. Ironically, the politicians actually relied on their top managers to keep these facilities going, no matter the costs. There wasn't any other viable option left. *Paulistanos* were praying for rain and money from the Development Banks. They trusted God would never allow their city to go dry, a disaster 20 million people would have to deal with individually.

Truth be told, the facility had never reached the performance levels it was designed to achieve. Menezes was basically waiting for the next breakdown to happen. Fatally, he didn't have the resources or material to do the repairs required. He'd tell his crew to get the duct tape and get going.

Menezes was about to get his usual morning coffee when the emergency klaxons were triggered by an automatic shutdown system. The roar of the klaxons was deafening. Before he had time to think, Menezes was running at full speed toward the control center. He was hoping the shutdown system had simply malfunctioned.

It's a glitch in the programming, he thought, hoping for the best.

Deep underground, the wastewater that should have been flowing into the plant was somehow obstructed. If that was truly the case, the water from São Paulo's sewers would soon overflow, causing problems that could render the water undrinkable in a matter of days, perhaps hours, if any other of the seven water filtration plants had to shut down. Normally, the incoming wastewater went through screens. This system was designed to remove trash from the water flow. The system was supposed to protect the main sewage pumps and the other filtration equipment.

In his fifteen years at the plant, this was Menezes's first experience with an unscheduled plant shutdown. In that event, wastewater would be automatically diverted directly into São Paulo's natural waterways.

When systems crashed in São Paulo, as they did in any other city on the planet, there were problems and consequences. In Menezes's mind, the repercussions to São Paulo's freshwater supply could reach immense proportions.

Menezes finally reached the control center. He was greeted by a combination of chaos and fear. The pumps were down. This wasn't the glitch he was hoping for.

The plant manager was screaming at the intercom, asking for information. "For the love of God, shut the fucking klaxons!"

"What can I do?" Menezes asked.

"You tell me."

Menezes turned away from his boss and began to think of his options. He had none that would solve the current problem. He was afraid that his recommendation would only make things worse.

"We have to drain the facility and start a full clean-up. I don't see how we can do it any other way."

"Do you realize…"

"Yeah, I do. That will take us a month. At least thirty days without drinking water. If everything goes according to plan. But, if we have to replace equipment, that will shut us down for months."

"Will someone, anyone, please shut the klaxons? Pull the plug if you have to," the manager yelled.

Suddenly, everything was quiet. It appeared the plant had completely shut down. Menezes realized, as did the others in the control room, that it was the first time they were actually experiencing total silence at the plant.

As it turned out, Menezes's ears kept hearing the rumble of the pumps, when in fact, there was none.

15

"I observed the little man with my own eyes," Willy Callender said in earnest.

Willy's Scottish brogue was as genuine as it could be, given the fact he hadn't set foot in his place of birth since he was seven years old. Nevertheless, he was a true son of the Callender clan.

"With your baby blues?" Alexander Fionnuala asked in jest.

"Yes, of course."

Wee Willy, as they called him, played the game the old-fashioned way. He changed people's perceptions with disarming charm and wit.

Alexander's job spanned fifty years of observation, as he negotiated his way around paper battlefields across the planet. He'd been Thatcher's insider man. The man who connected the dots. A guest lecturer who knew everyone's dirty little secrets.

Both men were Official Secrets Act (OSA) signatories and would be held responsible for their actions and words for the rest of their natural lives, give or take a few years of senility. Agents who didn't play ball would find themselves out of a job and in the morgue.

Both made money, of course, sometimes a lot, had real jobs, married, all the while traveling extensively around the world for information. Soft spoken *007s*. Mildly introverted, they preferred pints to dry martinis.

As MI6 agents, Willy Callender and Alexander Fionnuala happened to work under the same boss, Sir Henry Blake Armery. Willy knew him as the fat fuck who could slither in and out of any con.

Today more than ever, these two old men understood why this conversation was taking place even though they were putting their own lives at risk. They understood that a whole lot of innocent people would get hurt if nothing was done about Armery.

"No," Alexander said calmly. "What you saw, or what you think you have seen, is quite impossible."

"I buried the piece of filth," he said to Willy.

"I'm telling you what I saw, for God's sake, and... who I saw was breathing." Willy's beer was a bit stale and lonely. He looked around for the waiter but never took his eyes away from Alexander. The Italian born Irishman was hard to read, almost impossible to fool or handle. Then again, this was different. There wasn't any handling required. They had a problem. The problem was old and probably feeble. Still, if the little fellow was alive...

"You were drinking the single malt again. That should explain your vision," Alexander said without much thought. He wasn't talking to anyone in particular. Alexander was just making noise while he pondered just what the hell was happening.

Willy laughed out loud. "Now tell me this, why would you say that?"

"Say what? If I remember correctly, the man was very ill," Alexander said almost as an afterthought.

Willy understood what the conversation was really about: Had they fucked up twenty years ago?

Alexander suddenly remembered his time at the Training Establishment. "It's like dancing," their MI6 instructor at Fort Monckton had said with absolute assurance. "Both have steps they need to go through in order to get information, and both can swing to the beat of a conversation. But, and this is important, if one wants the information more than the other, then... there's an opportunity as well as a problem. The dancer will play his hand too quickly and will go too far, too fast. So, let him come to you. He's bound to spill enough information to make it interesting. You can put two and two together? Remember that. Wait for it. Have a good time. People eventually talk. Because they want to. Because they want to show off: 'Look how powerful I am.'"

Willy and Alexander were cut from the same cloth. Had the same training. Graduated the same year. The year of the Rat. Versatile, imaginative and quick.

"If you prefer not to believe me," Willy said smiling, "then that's on you. But, here's a bit of friendly advice. Our friend is alive, and he's apparently doing well. And we should look into it."

"What about the advice?" Alexander asked.

"I believe the advice is intrinsic to the little fellow's health," Willy said. "If Armery is alive, I believe we were told a fairy tale twenty years ago by an overweight leprechaun. Which brings us to the second issue."

"The leprechaun?" Alexander couldn't help laughing at his friend's sense of humor.

"Yes," Willy replied. "Our friend the leprechaun. Why would he lie to us?"

"Friend?"

"It's an expression," Willy looked serious. "I do have confirmation about Armery. I did not hallucinate."

"Confirmation?" Alexander was now interested.

"Absolutely. From the same person who told you the bastard had died of an apparent stroke. Underline apparent."

"I had proof," Alexander said defensively. "He was identified, or at least what was left of him. He was dead. Plain and simple. Jesus fucking Christ couldn't bring him back. And I should know, I buried the bastard myself."

"They lied to you."

"Now why would they do that?" Alexander demanded. "We all wanted him out. Even the Russians wanted nothing to do with him. Persona non grata according to 5 and 6. We simply obliged. But let's assume he's alive. What is he now, eighty, a hundred? Did you see a ghost, Willy?"

"Like you, I would like to believe we did our job." Willy realized that Alexander was finally on board.

"Did you get a location on the bastard?" Alexander asked.

"Living the life of Riley in South America," Willy said.

"Like a Nazi?"

"*Jawohl.* Like a Nazi."

"What mess is he mixed up in?" Alexander could have guessed, but he wanted to know what Will had dug up.

"I didn't say he was." Willy was being cryptic.

"We are talking about the same Armery?" Alexander was curious to know how their old boss could had ever gotten involved in something legal.

"Well… he's doing work for the Governor of São Paulo State."

Alexander was now sure something had to be done. "I think we have a job to do."

"Got the tickets." Willy pushed an envelope into Alexander's hands.

"First class, I see. And British Airways to boot. Where's the money coming from?" Alexander asked.

"6." Willy winked at Alexander.

Alexander shook his head. "I don't like this one bit. Why do we have to do this? Plenty of young bucks wanting to play James Bond. Now everyone will know it's us."

"They said our blunder, our fix." Willy agreed with Alexander. He also would have liked them to do this on their own. There was no need for MI6 looking over their shoulders.

"When?"

"Tomorrow night, 6h50."

"I don't like this."

"You've already said that. You have troubles with your memory, old man?"

"Sod off."

16

The SH-3 Sea King helicopter hovered over what was once known as a feat of engineering. Looking at it from two thousand feet, it left Destrey a bit confused.

"It's as if the dam never existed," she said to herself.

The structure was completely covered up by one hundred feet of mud, rock and sand.

Destrey couldn't help a tear when she heard Alexander Francisco Spinetti describe the site as a mass grave. Spinetti, a Swiss-born architect, was her best shot at understanding, in layman's terms, what really happened two days ago at the Paiva Castro Dam located north of São Paulo. Spinetti was also the Cycle Foundation's go-to guy for anything made of concrete, rock and brick. Destrey inherited from the Cardinal all the Foundation's resources, which included more money than a single human being ought to have had. Spinetti had been assigned to build the Jerusalem Foundation's headquarters in Jerusalem.

"We will be flying over the small borough of Mairiporã a few minutes from here," Spinetti said through his headset's microphone. "It disappeared as well. It was swallowed by a sinkhole measuring one hundred and fifty meters by four hundred meters. What followed sealed the villagers' fate. A mud slide covered the sinkhole and officials are almost certain not a soul survived."

Destrey was speechless.

"About seven hundred people," Spinetti added as the Sea King swung toward Mairiporã. "Mostly women and children, because the men were away at work."

"Please tell me this is the event our people have been talking about?" Destrey asked.

"This, *Madame*," he said, pointing at the mud slide, "is perhaps an aperitif. If Lola's calculations are correct, the whole region is at risk. We may have another earthquake before we know it. Or not. Earthquakes are difficult to predict."

"I've never heard of sinkholes this size." Destrey had always believed that she was open to new ideas and because of that, she would be in a constant learning mode. Today, facing Mother Nature's supremacy over man, she began to understand just how little humans could control nature.

"At least three times as big," Spinetti said.

"How deep is it? Do they know?" Destrey asked.

"No."

"Then we have our work cut out for us. Can you find a world expert? We need him here. Right now."

"His name is Grant Little," Spinetti answered. "A science advisor at the U.S. Geological Survey based in Pasadena."

"Could you talk to Precov and see what he can do? We need the man here, pronto."

"I've taken the initiative and called Mr. Little this morning. He's on his way."

"That's my boy."

Destrey was old enough to be Spinetti's mother. He was also smart enough to take the hint. She was indeed the boss. It was his job to anticipate her every need. Although Julian Precov was president of BTG's board of directors, she was in charge. Destrey called the shots. She had the money to back it up and the temper to make things happen.

"Let's get back to São Paulo," Destrey said. "I want to talk to Greco. I hope he has more to tell us. We'll need to know how much time we have before..."

"Before it happens."

"Yes." Destrey was feeling a bit nauseous.

"What's our next step?" Spinetti asked.

"I don't see a lot of options available to us."

"Evacuation?" he asked.

"Yes."

"But we're talking about 20 million people. More perhaps."

"Maybe we should call it Exodus," Destrey said sarcastically.

"Biblical," Spinetti said.

"I don't know how to call this one." Destrey understood she was confronted with a challenge beyond her means. She now understood why people prayed to God for help.

"We probably need a miracle."

17

THE BOSTON TRIAGE GROUP (BTG)
VIDEO CONFERENCE
CAMBRIDGE – SÃO PAULO

Destrey was relieved that Constantin Greco and John Kleinrup had agreed to set up a conference call. She was also happy to learn that Julian Precov, BTG's Board President, had accepted to join in on the call from his home in Israel. Although Precov had Destrey's back, he also provided Destrey with advice, which she counted on. In the case of an event such as this one, perspective was imperative. Good information usually led the group to focus on strategies that worked. Foundation members had learned their lesson in Jerusalem. Just because one had a good idea of what was going to happen in the future didn't mean one knew what to do about it. Destrey, Kleinrup and Precov had learned that lesson the hard way.

"We need to look at our com options. That's why I've enlisted the help of *Madame* Andromaque Folmer to join us," Kleinrup said to the people gathered. "She's a retired major general in the French armed forces, now consulting with eVigill."

"I am happy to see you all," Folmer said.

Precov was impressed.

"The firm designs and deploys mass messaging through their geo-notification systems," Kleinrup added. "Regardless of our strategy, we'll need to reach millions of people within seconds. I feel it's an absolute must."

Kleinrup turned the mike to Spinetti.

"I would like to introduce Grant Little to our team," Spinetti said. "A world-renowned seismologist and the public voice for earthquake safety in California. Before retiring, our new colleague Mr. Little was with the U.S. Geological Survey and a visiting research associate at the Seismological Laboratory of Caltech since 1989."

Although Little was a man of few words, he was known to be accurate, to the point of being heartless.

"Thank you for inviting me, *Madame* Destrey," Little said. "Permit me to come to the point. Up until last week, I believed there was no way to predict an earthquake. That was last week. Today's a different story. Even without BTG's technological advances or the Los Alamos National Labs' findings, what we have here in São Paulo is an earthquake in progress. With a significant number of incidents demonstrated so far by Mother Nature, I can safely say that the earthquake will happen. In other words, it's on its way. It's not about probabilities any longer. I'm expecting a lot of people are going to die. Dr. Lucy Jones from Caltech's Seismological Laboratory once said about the Big One in California, *You aren't gonna stop the sun shining, and you aren't gonna stop the plates moving. And as long as the plates keep on moving, the earthquakes will happen and people will suffer.*"

Destrey admired Little's courage and precision. "Are you prepared to launch an all-out effort to get this message out?" she asked him.

Little nodded.

"Any other business to talk about?"

"Yes, Louise. There are a few more strategies we've looked at. From what I was able to find out, they seem ludicrous and impossible to implement," Greco added. "But we can't take anything for granted. Let's talk about an obvious choice. Can we stop the earthquake? Lola, please report."

"The preferred option," Lola said, "one that we would seek if we could, involves stopping a seismic incident. Unfortunately, there is no evidence, research or history of a man-made strategy to prevent such an occurrence from happening. To the best of my knowledge, research has been focused on the prediction of seismic activity, the development of construction codes to reduce loss of life, the destruction of property and infrastructure, and finally, the study of human activity and its impact on seismic activity."

"Has anyone been successful at stopping an earthquake?" Destrey asked, knowing all too well the answer.

"No, *Madame* Destrey," Lola answered. "However, researchers have speculated on the topic and proposed two theories. Over the years, scientists have played around with the idea of lubricating fault zones with water or some other material with the intent to stop or at least reduce the magnitude of a quake. Others have studied the possibility of using explosives to safely release accumulated seismic stress, thus preventing an earthquake. Recent research has disproved both theories. Lubricating or using atomic bombs would have the opposite effect. They would cause quakes to occur sooner. Stopping an earthquake from happening is, so far, impossible. Both strategies, at this time, are not viable."

"Which leaves us with the option of evacuating the city," Kleinrup said to the group. "Because I can't imagine any other strategy."

"Evacuating a village, a township or a city borough is one thing," Precov said from his office in Tel Aviv. "But São Paulo requires us to consider scope, as well as the political, social and financial aspects that would either hinder or facilitate our work. We are talking about 20 million people, perhaps more."

Folmer agreed with Precov. "Evacuating Jerusalem was difficult, to say the least. I flew over the city toward the end of the terrorists' deadline. What I saw was frightening. One of the best armies in the world lost control of the evacuation on day two. When I think of what could happen in Brazil, I don't know..." Folmer didn't have to elaborate, and Destrey didn't have to hear it.

"Lola? What did we learn from the Jerusalem event?" Precov wanted Destrey's team to consider the similarities between the two cities. He hoped they could prove useful.

"Although the threat was real, the destruction of Jerusalem was, for most citizens, almost impossible to believe or accept," Lola replied. "In many cases, people fought to stay in their homes. The command-and-control structure was also challenged by the government's own people, those responsible to carry out the evacuation. They too needed to evacuate their families."

"This last issue is key," Destrey said. "If we want an orderly evacuation, we must guarantee their families' security."

"This issue was resolved to the detriment of government imperatives," Lola said. "Hours before the forty-eight-hour deadline came to an end, police as well as military personnel opted to help themselves and deserted their posts to save their families. Command's power structure was later criticized for this breach in the evacuation protocol. It led to violence and criminality. Roads turned into parking lots. As time ran out, actions to preserve and transfer business information and important assets to locations outside the city also showed serious breakdowns. The command-and-control system failed. The planning at macro and micro levels also failed. Simply put, the nation as well as Jerusalemites were untrained and unprepared."

"I'm pretty sure there isn't a city on the planet who's ready to evacuate twenty million souls," Destrey said. "Do you agree, Lola?"

"Yes, *Madame* Destrey. On New Year's Eve 1999, Rudolph W. Giuliani considered evacuating Manhattan if Y2K fears came true. He had contingencies and targeted evacuation plans. One hundred National Guards were called up and were bivouacked in Brooklyn. Fortunately, nothing happened, and there was no need to evacuate the city or any part of New York. However, today, no current operational plan exists or is being developed to evacuate the whole city."

"Can anyone tell me why no one's talking publicly about evacuating São Paulo?" Destrey asked. "Authorities have been told by a number of experts, including Los Alamos, that a quake is about to happen."

"The answer has many parts to it," Kleinrup said. "One, no one believes we can predict earthquakes. Scientists have been predicting the Big One for California for the last one hundred years, and so far, it hasn't happened. Two, no politician wants to take the risk of evacuating the city. Too many lose-lose scenarios. What if you evacuate and nothing happens? Three, people don't want to know because it's unbearable. Four, fear works against prevention. So, do nothing, say nothing. Denial on a massive front. Five, because no viable option outside of São Paulo is readily available to ordinary citizens; staying put and hoping for the best is a default plan. Six, the municipal civil service is so corrupt, the thought of leaving all this booty behind is unacceptable. So, business as usual."

"That makes me dizzy," Destrey said miserably.

Kleinrup nodded. "But consider the following. There are many other reasons why people will not be proactive. I could go on for another hour with a list of reasons why, but in the end, they won't budge. I'd say it's all about change. Plain and simple. People hate change, in any way, shape or form. Hate it with a passion."

Destrey realized the scope of her mission. "We do have our work cut out for us."

"Indeed," Kleinrup said.

Destrey turned to Lola. "Lola, could you see if our key findings and best practices apply to São Paulo's profile?"

"The issue of time is crucial," Lola said. "Time-to-earthquake, or how much time the city has before the earthquake occurs. That knowledge provides clues for choosing and eliminating strategies. So far, we estimate the quake will happen between now and thirty-six days."

"So, we're working with a range of more or less a month," Destrey said. "If the quake happens tomorrow, that's it. We've failed. If we have a month, if we're lucky, we have time to do something. What that "something" consists of, is anyone's guess. Is that also correct, Lola?"

"Yes, *Madame* Destrey."

"What about applying those best practices?" Destrey asked.

"As Chairman Precov said, we must take into consideration unique challenges in this situation. In 2006, the city of São Paulo lost complete control of their streets due to widespread criminality. The rule of law was challenged as never before. That incident showed us one of the city's anomalies, which could come into play, here in São Paulo, during a government-initiated evacuation."

"Lola, can you expand on lessons learned?"

"Yes, *Madame* Destrey. The lessons learned are consistent with the general argument that without the rule of law, a society is unable to carry out its goals and responsibilities. In this case, São Paulo's lack of government integrity at the federal, state and municipal levels has contaminated most of the city's command-and-control systems. Unfortunately, São Paulo's capacity to enforce the rule of law has not improved significantly in the last two decades. To answer your question, *Madame* Destrey, I would say that none of the best practices can apply at this time. There simply isn't enough time to set them up. Evacuation of as many *Paulistanos* as possible is our only option. Collateral damage is inevitable."

"Can you predict how much collateral damage you're talking about?"

"It would depend on time-to-earthquake. Anywhere from 90% collateral damage to 58%."

"All right. Tell me what we get at thirty days' notice?" Destrey asked.

"Collateral damage is estimated at 71.1%." The number 15.4 million suddenly appeared on-screen. Almost everyone was speechless.

"Lola? Is there anything else we should know?" Kleinrup asked.

Destrey was surprised at Kleinrup's cool response. Did he know in advance? Or was it something else? When Kleinrup went hunting for those responsible for detonating a dirty bomb in Jerusalem, she was afraid she had lost him. Not physically, but part of his soul had hardened. He had been instrumental in finding the terrorists and punishing them. The terrorists were treated to the worst possible execution man could dream of. Kleinrup had executed the terrorist cell leader as well as his immediate family. The execution had been put online for the whole world to see.

Maybe that's what the team needs, Precov thought. *A leader who doesn't scare easy. A cold-blooded task master. Someone brave enough to look the devil in the face and send him packing.*

"Yes, Mr. Kleinrup. There is another lesson and best practice."

"Which would be what?" Destrey asked.

"The Jerusalem evacuation had been implemented and staged by geographical districts. Anyone leaving the city through another district would have found it empty, thus eliminating any possible obstruction. The plan worked until government forces encountered the first resistance cell. The transportation of people through districts not totally evacuated generated obstruction, violence and crime. Analysis of the Israeli evacuation debriefings provided tactical data for future evacuation strategies. I have generated a number of different scenarios and found that the key to a disciplined evacuation lies also in the destination. People need to believe they are headed to a destination that offers acceptable, good or better life conditions. A successful evacuation requires a credible end-result for those being evacuated."

"Am I right to say that resistance to evacuate is inversely proportional to the quality of the destination?" asked Kleinrup.

"That is correct, Mr. Kleinrup," Lola said. "However, there are good reasons to believe the Paiva Castro Dam's collapse may have prompted many to think twice about staying in São Paulo, regardless of the destination."

"So, they know?" Destrey asked, almost in a whisper.

"Local comedians have been talking of replacing water with wine. We only need a miracle for the concept to work," Kleinrup said sarcastically.

"They know," Precov said. "They most certainly talk about it every day. Especially if your faucet's been running dry for the last few days while water trucks are the only source of water available."

"Still, no one in authority has yet suggested people leave the city?" Destrey asked.

Kleinrup shook his head. "In fact, government representatives are convinced the earthquake will not happen. They said that when the Governor of California evacuates his state, they will consider evacuating their city."

"We have a problem," Precov said. "Where do we start?"

"That's an easy one, Julian." Kleinrup turned to the screen and asked Lola how long it would take to evacuate all the diplomatic missions in the city.

"There are forty-five diplomatic missions in São Paulo, with an average of twelve employees. It would take two days to evacuate consular staff and their families."

"Which requires us to do some pretty quick convincing," Kleinrup said to Destrey.

"That is a problem we can delegate to the American and Canadian diplomatic missions. They can be on board within a few hours. I suspect they're already on it, because they know," Destrey said.

"How are you so sure that they will evacuate the city?" Precov asked Destrey point-blank.

"Because Lola intercepted a few private conversations between Los Alamos and São Paulo, and between Los Alamos and Washington DC," she replied without hesitation. "We provided every embassy and mission with a copy of those conversations. The diplomats know that the people at Los Alamos have predicted a major earthquake. Imminent, they said to the U.S. president."

"Then," Precov said, "we need to get the ball rolling with the local media. When people find out the diplomats are abandoning ship, news will spread like wildfire."

"Not just local media, Julian. We need global coverage to put pressure on governments, as well as a social media strategy to generate self-evacuations. And you're right about the workaround," Destrey said to Kleinrup. "We need to talk to the people directly. That's without creating a bigger problem than the quake itself. Lola?"

"Yes, *Madame* Destrey?"

"Could you monitor what's happening now at the U.S. and Canadian diplomatic missions?"

"Constantin Greco has instructed me to do so with all forty-six missions. The word is already out, *Madame* Destrey. Missions are talking to each other as we speak. Some have already booked passage on airlines or are driving to Rio de Janeiro. They are doing so in complete secrecy until the families are out of the city."

"What about the Americans, the Chinese and the Russians?"

"U.S. military aircraft are heading to the city as we speak to evacuate families and some staffers. Russia is doing the same. China is still waiting for confirmation from Beijing."

"Well," Destrey said on a positive note, "the ball's rolling in the right direction."

"The Chinese may not be so forthcoming," Lola said.

"That's their fucking problem." Kleinrup smiled at Destrey.

Jesus, he scares me, Destrey thought to herself.

"Lola, what else should we be thinking about?" Destrey asked.

"We should consider the evacuation of nineteen hospitals, retirement homes and schools. Other actions include securing bank assets, transferring government databases, setting up emergency communication systems, enlisting the help of transportation organizations, which would include road, rail, air, naval and the military."

Destrey sighed. "Anything else?"

"The list is significant, *Madame* Destrey. I have barely touched the surface," Lola replied. "However, there is one more issue. I have secured a meeting with businessman mogul David Costa Batista, as requested."

"I'm not looking forward to meet Batista," Destrey said. "Am I wasting my time, Lola?"

"There's a good chance he'll brush you off, *Madame* Destrey. "My research shows that any idea that Batista hasn't initiated himself has little chance of getting his attention. But no, of course you are not wasting your time because I also know that he is a hard man to predict."

"Thank you, Lola," Destrey said. "Keep me advised as new

information is generated."

"Of course, *prontissimo*, *Madame* Destrey. Your wish is my command."

"I'm going to have to talk to Greco about Lola," Destrey said to herself.

"I heard that, *Madame* Destrey."

"Yeah, yeah."

18

The phone rang. He said to himself that one day he'd get rid of his landline phone. Leonardo Beccarin tried to focus on his job. He struggled not to hear it. He had work to do and a deadline to keep.

The phone persisted.

"I don't know who you are, but I'm not going to pick up, no matter what," Beccarin said.

Beccarin was working at home today. He'd fled downtown São Paulo for the peace and quiet of Maciel Street. He now lived in a middle-class neighborhood where small shops and apartments cohabited in harmony.

He needed quiet time to think about his design. That was the plan. There was something wrong with his first draft and the office downtown was not a suitable place to reflect or think. Although his bosses had provided him with a private office to work in, he was constantly interrupted by requests from people who had nothing better to do than to annoy those who had real work to do, specifically HR and Finance meddlers and busybodies.

Beccarin was a young and upcoming architect. His designs inspired a building's residents to see the city as a living organism, or so said Gustavo Martins, a writer and critic from one of Brazil's architectural blogs.

"He has reinvented the atrium as it rises to the sky," Martins wrote to his readers.

"*Alô?*" Beccarin said furiously. "Who's this? What do you want?"

Although he had the handset to his ear, the landline phone kept ringing. Strange. Nobody called him on his landline anymore.

Who's trying to reach me? he wondered.

"*Alô?*" he repeated irately. "*Alô. Alô. Alô!*" he said angrily.

Still the ringing continued uninterrupted.

"What the hell's wrong with this phone?" Beccarin said out loud.

Although he glared intensely at his handset, the machine was immune to intimidation. The machine kept ringing no matter what Beccarin did. In a desperate move to solve the problem, Beccarin shook the handset furiously.

"Stop it," he ordered the handset in a menacing tone.

Surprisingly, the handset refused to be bullied. The ringing continued regardless of Leonardo's excessive shaking. The phone was old tech and couldn't or wouldn't hear what he had to say.

"Medieval machine," he cursed to himself.

Finally, he unhooked the phone's physical connection to the telephone system. Thankfully, the ringing died off.

"There. That's better," he said to himself. "Much better." He'd won after all.

He returned to his drafting table.

The architect took a deep breath.

"This is the life," he said to himself. "I can't get enough of it."

He felt something different was at work. He stood and walked to the open window that let in the morning sun. He looked out and scanned the street below. There wasn't that much traffic about, but still there was something unusual coming from the neighborhood.

His eyes couldn't spot the culprit but he soon found himself trying to hear beyond the traffic hustle and bustle passing under his apartment window.

From his third floor flat, he had a pretty good view of Maciel Street.

What's that? he asked himself. Then, suddenly, Beccarin realized what was bothering him. His neighbor's phone was also ringing off the hook. Now that would be a problem because she was usually off to work at the dawn of light. That would be more than two hours ago. She wouldn't be back until six tonight. That wouldn't do.

Beccarin remembered she kept a spare key under her planter. He resolutely walked to her apartment, found the key, unlocked the door and walked in. He did his best not to snoop around. Beccarin was a disciplined soul. He avoided looking around the apartment and focused on where her phone might be located. He finally found it in Isabella's kitchen and took the handset to his ear. Like his own phone, this one kept ringing. He looked for the phone connection and promptly disconnected it.

"Finally," he said to himself, "I can return to work."

Now sitting comfortably at his drafting table, Beccarin's problem suddenly jumped off his drawing table. He understood what his design needed to do differently. The body of the work was too bulky, too boxy. He realized he needed to lighten his design. After all, his client was in semiconductors a.k.a. the chip business.

His focus was interrupted once again. Neighbors were talking to each other.

"Jesus! What now?" Beccarin said to himself.

Once again, Beccarin looked out his window. His neighbors were also at their windows trying to find out what was happening.

"I can't get my phone to stop," a neighbor said.

"Unplug it," she said while holding her phone up for everyone to see. She had solved his ringing problem.

"I cut the wire," Beccarin said to his neighbors. "I cut the freaking wire, that's what I did."

Beccarin wondered if he had made the right decision to work at home. There was no quiet time to be found today. At least not in his neighborhood.

"Telefónica is at it again," Beccarin said mockingly. The large telecom company was often criticized for breakdowns. The weather was often a factor. However today, *Paulistanos* benefitted from a perfect day. The weather couldn't explain the rash of ringing telephones throughout the city.

Yet, a few Telefónica technicians knew better. They all remembered what had happened to the Pinheiros Metro Station collapse in 2007 when the earth moved. The station had disappeared into a giant sinkhole nearly 80 meters or 260 ft in diameter. People had died. Although everything above ground seemed problem-free, buildings in and around Maciel Street and most of São Paulo were deceptively affected by earth shifts. Beccarin's home was no exception.

Unbeknownst to Leonardo Beccarin, Destrey's predicted earthquake was in progress. Although only a few localized ground shifts appeared under roads or homes, small micro-shifts were wreaking havoc with Telefónica's equipment. Beccarin's district was one of the first to report the incident to the telephone company. Telefónica's technicians were well aware of what an earthquake could do above and below ground. However, even if Telefónica's infrastructures were built with failsafe redundancies to prevent systems break downs, earthquakes could easily make those failsafe systems moot as fiber optics cables, either under the road or under buildings, were slowly being ripped apart by micro ground shifts. Beccarin had no idea what was lurking under his feet.

Destrey's message on social media was making its way to many employees who had a hand in maintaining São Paulo's infrastructures. They saw the signs day after day: small fissures appeared in cement pillars supporting highways, building foundations, subway tracks. Unfortunately, their managers believed the information was part of a unionized strategy to get better working conditions. Some managers did take heed of their employees' observations and although they went about their business as usual, they secretly prepared to leave the city as soon as the signs from their own workers became impossible to dismiss.

As Beccarin's design was taking shape, his apartment creaked and groaned from a truck passing through Maciel Street at high speed.

"Those fucking trucks! Someday I'm going to call the city…"

Beccarin laughed as his words reached his ears and brain.

"Might as well call the Pope, for all the good that will do. Call the city! What was I thinking?" Beccarin said. "That Humpty Dumpty mayor-asshole is a joke."

Beccarin didn't suspect a thing!

19

"Just read it. Now!" David Costa Batista was accustomed to giving orders.

"The whole thing?" Carlo Gutierrez asked.

"You're whining again. Read, for chrissake." Batista was an impatient man.

"Okay. I'll start with the abstract." Gutierrez had it with his father-in-law. The man was impossible.

"What did I tell you?" Batista said.

"I'm reading. See?"

From the top floor of the Infinity building, an elite group of men and women worked hard and long hours to ensure the company made as much money as the government could print. For some however, more money wasn't enough. One was especially eager to control everything that was happening in his city.

David Costa Batista wanted it all. Everything. He cherished the idea that he would, one day, own the city of São Paulo lock, stock, and barrel.

"It says, let me see, bla, bla, bla... here it is. The metro accident occurred in São Paulo, Brazil on January 12, 2007. The loss of life occurred when the station excavations nearly forty meters in length collapsed on itself, followed by another collapse creating a deep void measuring forty meters by thirty-five meters and forty meters deep. The collapse of the station caused an air blast that generated significant air movement. It pulled innocent people down the open shaft to their untimely deaths."

"What else does it say?" Batista asked impatiently.

"It says here that the São Paulo State Government as well as the Public Prosecutor of São Paulo commissioned the Institute for Technological Research (IPT) to probe into the collapse of Pinheiros Station on São Paulo Metro's new Line Four in 2007, and provide recommendations based on lessons learned."

"Bastards. I thought we had managed that a long time ago. Why are they bringing this up today?"

Gutierrez ignored him.

"Okay, where was I?" Gutierrez said. "It says here that according to IPT's reports, the accident was just waiting to happen because of too many deficiencies, omissions or plain errors in engineering processes related to design, construction, management and more importantly, local government involvement."

"Does it really say more importantly, or are you just ad-libbing?" Batista didn't trust Gutierrez because he couldn't think or have an original idea.

"No. I'm reading it word for word. See for yourself." Gutierrez showed the article to Batista.

"I don't want to read any of it. Not a word. Nothing. As far as you're concerned, I've never read the document."

"Right." Gutierrez was not too sure why he would say that. But that's the way it was between them. Batista was now family and Gutierrez didn't think it would be such a good idea to challenge him.

"Now, read!" Batista said once again.

"Okay. Included in IPT's recommendations are the following: the São Paulo State metro authority (CMSP) responsible for operating and carrying out expansion work on the local subway system should have played a more active role in the design and construction steps; the technical specifications should have been more clearly specified in the contracts ensuring proper quality control, full disclosure of results, and independent auditing."

"Why did you stop reading?"

"I'm not. I'm just taking in some air. The rest of this stuff isn't good. It's about the mayor."

"All tight, Carlo. That's it for now. I've heard enough for today. Let's continue tomorrow. I'll call you. Meantime, don't speak to anyone. In fact, stay home until I call you. Am I making myself clear?"

"Yes, Sir. As always. Crystal clear."

"Now, go."

The man at the top of the heap didn't really need to hear more of the report. He had tried to change the report's outcome many times in the past and he really believed he had controlled every damaging charge they could make. However, for some reason, the Central Government in Brasilia was now playing a new game. As if someone wanted him to know he wasn't in charge.

"This isn't finished yet. Not by a long shot," he said loudly to himself.

David Costa Batista wasn't a happy camper. Not today, and not until City Hall was once more under control.

20

Destrey chose the community center because the locals trusted the priests, and so far, the police had stayed away. She had done her homework well. The center was a neutral spot, a little Switzerland in the middle of the poorest *favela* in São Paulo. However, that didn't guarantee Denis Planter would be on time.

"Now what?" Destrey said to herself. "He's late," she said impatiently to the priests. They had brokered a meeting between Destrey and Denis Planter. The local priest, Father Latu, was a bit uneasy at Planter's no-show, while the cleric from the Vatican took it all in stride. Father Franco had learned long ago to deal with Destrey's fits of impatience.

"He'll be here when he'll be here." Father Franco said simply. "*Sampa* time, remember?"

"*Sampa* time!" Destrey whispered to herself. "If I hear that again, I swear I'll..."

Destrey stood silent.

"Well?" Franco asked.

"Well," she said, "to tell you the truth, Isaac Kriekoff is also late. I specifically told him to be here on time. He knows Planter. I thought he could help. But, that's on me. I'm sure he'll be here any minute."

As if on cue, Isaac Kriekoff strolled in with not a care in the world.

"About time, Isaac," Destrey said.

"Sorry, Louise. Won't happen again." Isaac wasn't really sorry nor did Destrey believe him.

"If I may," said Father Latu, "*Sampa* time is about our young people's attitude toward authority. You know that, as a people, we've suffered badly under the military dictatorship. Being late, is just our way of reminding those in power today, that those who took our freedoms away will never be forgiven. It's not personal, *Madame* Destrey. I can assure you of that."

"I'm sorry Father. I didn't realize..." Destrey said.

"That's okay." Franco believed he needed to hear that from Father Latu. He thought he'd been a bit unsensitive to the plight of Brazilians. "Father Latu is correct to reminds us why people behave differently in this part of the world. I will be more careful in the future, Father Latu. I promise. Changing the subject, how's John doing?"

"Really Father, is that the best you can do?"

Before meeting with *Paulistanos* who held the reins of the city, Destrey had Lola create a profile of people to meet as well as a tight script to follow. Nothing would be left to chance. Her primary objective was to help the people of São Paulo. But with information came responsibility. She would hold the elected officials responsible for their inaction. Mayor Sabóida was already on her blacklist. On the other hand, there was still this one character she was looking forward to seeing. Although Denis Planter held no official office, he was expected to play a key role in evacuating the slums and the poor *favelas* before the earthquake. Even so, Planter managed to annoy Destrey to no end.

"Whatever it takes, Louise." Franco was enjoying himself.

"For your information," she looked away, "he's different. If I didn't know better, I'd say John Thomas Kleinrup has changed. Sometimes, I don't recognize him."

"I'm sorry to hear that." Father Franco wasn't surprised because in the last two years, Kleinrup had been to hell and back. In fact, Franco believed both of them were pretty much shell-shocked. The hours, the pressure, the danger... they all took a toll.

"I'm sorry too," Destrey said, "but that doesn't change the fact that the boy's late," she said very calmly. "I was planning to tell you that this boy of yours has a lot to learn about respect. But as Father Latu reminded me, when in Rome, do as the Romans do."

"I'm afraid so, Louise," Franco said. "For better or for worse, it's different here."

"Yes and no, Father, there are similarities. Boys and girls play their hormonal games while we adults have to wait until their highnesses are ready to deal with the real world."

"That's harsh, but suit yourself." Franco didn't have a smart comeback. There was some truth to what she said.

"Don't patronize me, young man. You may be a Jesuit and work for the Vatican, but you're still a kid in my book."

"You really got up on the wrong side of bed."

She shrugged. "I guess, maybe. It's those damn fools at city hall…"

"What about them!"

"Well, I shouldn't criticize. Mayors lead the shakiest level of government. More often than not, they're either corrupt to the core or don't know what they're doing. I should have known better," she said to Franco miserably.

"You had no choice, Louise. Whether or not your efforts pan out is immaterial. You have to start somewhere."

"Then how do you explain it? I was under the impression the mayor had the citizens' welfare at the top of his priorities. I fell for it again. Talking to a jellybean and expecting common sense."

Franco was enjoying himself. Destrey had a cutting sense of humor, one she didn't show too often.

"His majesty the mayor of São Paulo was in rare form. You should have been there, Franco. This bottom feeder called Antônio da Silva de Sabóida, avoided answering all of my questions. A fat jelly belly, just like his boss the state governor. They're one and the same. They wiggle a bit, talk the big talk, but in the end, they avoid taking action, leaving it to others to stretch their necks out. To think I was trying to make this jellybean take a courageous stand! What was I thinking? I should have known better."

Franco laughed aloud while his colleague Father Latu found the whole conversation odd and potentially dangerous.

"I hope this Planter kid isn't like the rest of them," Destrey asked.

"I don't think you've met anybody like him before," Father Latu said. "He is not only different. I am sure he is a quite unique young man."

"We'll see," Destrey said.

She'd heard about this young man from Isaac Kriekoff. Isaac informed Destrey that he had a few conversations with Denis Planter since the Jerusalem event. Planter was asking him if he knew anything about *Sampa*'s future. Isaac had wished he could meet Denis Planter in person and have a face-to-face. He promised Planter he'd find a way to come to São Paulo with answers.

"I see the need of having you in on this meeting, Isaac," Destrey said. "So, I'm expecting you to help me get Planter on board. This is serious work. Keep your wits about you."

"Denis is here *senhora*," Latu said eagerly.

Destrey looked around. Portal Street was quiet.

"I assure you *Madame*, he's watching. He will come when he is ready."

A few minutes later, a handsome young man entered the Community Center.

"*Estou pronto agora*," Planter said as he strolled casually toward Father Latu.

"He said..."

"I know what he said," she told the translator. "He said, I'm ready when I'm ready."

"Close enough."

Destrey wasn't impressed by Planter's performance. In a very short period of time, he'd managed to piss off the woman who wanted to help him. Nevertheless, she took it upon herself to provide Planter the information and resources he needed to get the evacuation going. Father Latu called the evacuees Planter's people.

Destrey immediately went to work. *Sometimes*, she thought, *one should do the right thing regardless.*

Before she had the chance to talk to Planter, Isaac stood up and warmly embraced his e-friend Denis Planter.

"*Eu não acredito. Você está aqui!*" Planter asked.

"I'm here, believe it. I said I'd find a way, so yes, I'm here, and boy am I glad to see you in person after all these years."

"É este o seu chefe?" Planter said carefully.

"Yeah, she's my boss all right." Isaac took Planter by the shoulder and walked toward Destrey.

"I would like to present to you *Madame* Louise Margoe Destrey. My boss. Louise, this is Denis Planter."

"I didn't know you understood Portuguese?" she said.

Isaac pointed to his ear. "I'm wearing a Pilot."

"Oh well, that explains everything."

"It's a translator. Works like magic."

"I think I'll stick with Michel. Low-tech. Easy. No glitches."

"*Agora eu entendo o que você quis dizer com especial.*"

"Indeed, my friend. I warned you that she was special."

"I'm in the room you know!" Destrey said.

"Sorry, Louise."

"Please sit down, Mister Planter. I have important news. Michel here, will translate."

Planter got himself a chair and sat in front of Destrey. With both hands set firmly on the table, he appeared calm, but Louise could read him like a book. This young man didn't have a clue of what it meant to feel comfortable, or calm for that matter.

"I'm not going to be nice or sugarcoat anything I have to say to you. Do you understand that?" Destrey nodded to the translator.

Planter nodded.

"Yes. Good," Destrey said as her words were instantly translated in Portuguese. "Let me start at the end. This is what I'm going to ask you to do, then I'll explain why, and answer all your questions. Okay?"

Planter nodded again.

"I'm asking you to clear out. Leave the city. As soon as you can. I can't tell you when, but soon. São Paulo will go through the greatest earthquake the city has ever known... ever. Very few people will survive the quake. Do you understand that?"

"Yes," Planter said almost to himself. He turned to Isaac. "Is she's telling the truth?"

"Of course!" Isaac looked at Planter straight in the eyes. "I warned you, Denis. I told you she was going to break your heart. But you don't have to believe her. But if I were you, I'd listen big time and I'd get my act together, because what she didn't tell you is... it's gonna happen within the next thirty days."

Planter took off his Pilot device and waited for Michel to translate. Just to make sure the device worked.

Although Destrey respected personal boundaries, she wanted Planter to understand the gravity of the situation and her own commitment to save as many people she could. She had little time to do that, and so she had to risk everything. Destrey took Planter's hands and carefully explained how she knew about the earthquake. How powerful computers, using the most advanced programs ever designed, predicted the earthquake. Here. In his city. Soon.

Planter tried to pry his hands away from Destrey, but she didn't let go.

"I have provided Fathers Latu and Franco with enough money to get the ball rolling."

"I don't need your money," Planter said.

"Yes, you will," Destrey said. "Real money. Cash that can open doors. Whether or not you do take my money, is your decision. The Fathers will help you, whatever you decide to do. That's your decision to make. Remember, Denis, I'm the messenger."

"That's easy for you to say," Planter said.

"So, you think it's easy for me to come all the way here and tell you that everything you know is about to disappear under your feet? Is that what you really think? It's about time an adult put some sense in that brain of yours."

Planter was about to stand and leave when she got up, looked at him straight in the eyes and told him that if he was a man, he'd sit down, calm down and shut the fuck up, because …

"Millions are going to die in the next thirty days," she said.

"Millions?" Planter said warily.

"Millions." Destrey was not going to back down. Not now.

Planter sat down.

"You see those two men standing outside? There, across the street. The men in the black suits. If I'm not sitting in my plane by the end of the week, at the latest Sunday, they have orders to pick me up, physically, and forcefully haul me out of here. Here's what you don't know. Most consulates, the Americans, the Chinese, the Russians, the Canadians, the Europeans… everyone is leaving the city. They are leaving as we speak. In four or five days, there won't be a single diplomat, or foreign visitor left in São Paulo."

"I don't believe you. Why should I?" Planter asked.

"You're right," Destrey said. "Why should you believe me? Well, you don't. You don't have to do a goddamn thing. But whatever you decide to do, you just make sure you get those two priests out of the city by next week."

They both stood up. She got very close to Planter. Although the young man was incredibly big and strong, she stood her ground, never letting her eyes away from his.

They stood there for the longest of time. Then a tear appeared on his face.

"I know," she said tenderly. "I know."

Destrey gently took his face in her hands. She felt sorry for him.

She turned to Isaac. "He's just a kid, you know."

21

The mayor's penthouse suite took up half the floor of the Linton Building. The view of São Paulo from the forty-fifth floor was beyond description. A quick look from the patio garden provided a drop-dead view of one of the greatest cities in the world.

Unfortunately, Oscar Bardilione wasn't here for the view. He was here to say farewell to the mayor.

Bardilione took a deep breath. He knew it would be the last time they'd speak. It was time to say goodbye to his best friend, his business partner and the mayor. He also had no choice in the matter. The investigation into the collapse of Pinheiros Metro Station would eventually show that bad decisions were made and none of them were accidents. It would also show that the mayor had sticky fingers. That's what Bardilione told himself. But it was more than that. He'd also been told that the mayor had put The Group in jeopardy: a consortium of São Paulo's elite corporations put together to build the metro extensions.

The collapse of the metro station and its subsequent investigation by a multinational team of experts would put some powerful people in an uncomfortable position. That was something The Group would never allow to happen.

Although Bardilione was part of The Group's executive committee, he wasn't the messenger. Today, he was just an old friend saying farewell. Nevertheless, he couldn't let it be. Bardilione was angry at him for being so careless, so fucking greedy, so incredibly crooked, and most of all, so unbelievably stupid.

"I told you years ago," Bardilione said sadly.

"Told me what? You've been telling me how to do my job all my life." The mayor laughed at his own joke.

"Not to dig that fucking tunnel in that specific area," Bardilione said angrily.

"I don't remember you telling me anything like that," the mayor said. "Besides, what's the big deal?"

"You're a piece of shit." Bardilione also laughed.

"That may be right, but again, what's the big deal?" The mayor didn't have a clue where Bardilione was going with this. Antônio da Silva de Sabóida wasn't the first mayor of São Paulo to make his fortune while in office. But then again, Sabóida went to considerable lengths to isolate himself from those who paid him to do their bidding. Big money maintained whatever lifestyle he'd become accustomed to, but from a distance.

His detractors openly called him His Highness, Mayor Antônio Sabóida.

"You don't get it, do you Antônio?" Bardilione walked over to the panoramic window. "Nice place, by the way. It must have cost ten times your annual income."

"Get what? Enlighten me," Sabóida said resentfully.

"I keep forgetting how thick you can be when money and women are concerned. I should have known better."

"That doesn't make me special or different. And you're no different than any of us."

"You really believe that horseshit, do you?" Bardilione asked.

"Don't play games with me, mister." His Highness was a bit angry. The mayor believed Bardilione was just as much a thief as he was.

"I don't see you complaining about your Aston Martin or that fucking palace you call home. I remember when you were younger, the things you did for money and especially the broads... well, I discovered a long time ago that I was a fucking amateur compared to you."

"That's my point, you stupid imbecile. I grew up. I learned a few things." Bardilione shook his head.

"So what's the problem this time?" Sabóida asked.

"This time? My God! How can I make you understand?" Bardilione was looking for a way of telling his best friend that his time was up.

"Go on..." Sabóida said.

"It's all the time, Antônio," Bardilione said. "You keep fucking up time after time after time. And you know what?"

"What?"

"You keep making the same mistakes. God!" Bardilione seemed annoyed. "You're a complete moron."

Bardilione turned toward the door and thought of leaving. That would be the end of that. But he couldn't. After all, Antônio was his best friend.

"You're angry because you didn't get your way," Sabóida said.

"I didn't get my way because I knew what a sick fuck you were." Bardilione felt miserable. He felt he was betraying his friend.

"Is that all you have to say?" Sabóida asked.

"No. Let me ask you this. Why construct the metro tunnel in this area? Didn't I tell you to completely avoid building and tunneling in this area of São Paulo? You knew it would take twice as long at three times the cost. Or more. You chose an extremely slow way of tunneling, why?"

Bardilione got no response from his friend. The mayor appeared to ignore his question. To forget it was ever asked.

The mayor wanted nothing to do with the decisions that were made about the metro extension. After all, he wasn't an engineer. How could he be blamed for shoddy engineering?

"How much money did you make on that particular contract?" Bardilione asked.

The mayor ignored him, but he silently was counting the millions he'd made.

"Why? Why go for an expensive and slow project when you could have chosen a cheaper and faster route? And you would still have made a lot of money." Bardilione wanted to understand.

Again, the mayor refused to be trapped in this line of questioning. He kept his mouth shut.

"You knew. You knew very well that the whole area was a disaster waiting to happen. Remember when we talked of *Rua Capri*? The street bordering the Pinheiros Metro Station?"

The mayor got up and walked to the panoramic window and

discovered once again the most beautiful view money could buy. He wanted to forget Bardilione. He tried to erase him from his head. Bardilione's questions were beginning to make him wonder whether or not he was truly isolated from accusations of illegal behavior. It wasn't always easy even though denying reality was one of his strong points. He'd done that all his life because reality was too harsh, too poor, too wrong and unfair.

"I'm talking to you. Look at me." Bardilione stared into Antônio's eyes.

The mayor turned away and focused on the view of São Paulo. He didn't know where this conversation was heading, but that didn't bother him too much.

"You know what's the difference between you and me?" Bardilione asked.

"I have a million-dollar view. You don't. You can't buy this view unless you got what it takes."

"Then let me remind you of something, Antônio."

"Please." The mayor was getting a little tired of being insulted. After all, he was the mayor.

"There was a mini-bus on the road," Bardilione said somberly. "And a pedestrian walking *Rua Capri*. Did you know that?"

The mayor kept looking at the view his illegal money had paid for. Listening to Bardilione was probably the price he had to pay now and then. Instead of getting angry, he congratulated himself because he'd made the deal of a lifetime with the metro contract. And he was almost sure it wasn't going to be the only pay-off for this contract. With every budget overrun, he'd get a cut. Soon, he wouldn't know where to put the cash. He'd have to find a new way of stashing it.

"Don't nod your head like that," Bardilione said. "You're in big trouble. Don't you understand that?"

"Why should I?"

"Because it happened on your watch. Because after all this time, the report is finally out. It took them fifteen months to figure it out. The report is out there for millions to see. The Internet will feast on it for months. And the jackals, well, they'll hunt you down."

Sabóida avoided Bardilione's stare.

"They were sucked down the pit. They died a terrible death. They didn't have a chance."

Sabóida turned and headed toward the bar. He poured himself a glass of water. Purified, crystal clear, heavenly water. Water that ordinary *Paulistanos* had to pay dearly to get.

"You said that *Paulistanos* didn't want long escalators!" Bardilione said. "So, they didn't dig deep. In fact, just deep enough to be safe. Remember?"

Sabóida refused to answer.

"They just didn't fall, Antônio, they were sucked to the deepest level of the pit. God almighty! It took twelve days before their bodies were recovered."

Again, there was no response from Sabóida.

"Do you know the reason why, Antônio?"

"Why what?"

"It was an air blast, suction and piston effect. All in one disaster. A catastrophic event. It was the perfect storm for a cave-in. A cavern forty meters in length collapsed out of the blue. Just like that. Half a second later it was followed by another collapse. Virtually half the station shaft collapsed on itself."

"Thank God, I'm not an engineer," Sabóida said.

"Typically, one would think people casually walking on the sidewalk would avoid the cracks appearing before them and run for safety. But in this case, no one could. You see, the suction created by the giant cave-in took care of that. They were pulled down the shaft."

"Cost of doing business." Sabóida looked serious. "Not my problem. Remember," he said, pointing to his breast pocket, "not an engineer."

"It took fifteen months to completely excavate the disaster area. Do you understand what that implies?"

"It means nothing."

"Not for you. It means nothing because you're an idiot. However, it means everything to me because now there are hundreds of people from all over the world who'll find out your dirty little secret: you see, you were given a choice, the city had a choice. A choice where to dig. A choice to dig as deep as possible, to dig the right way. And you, all on your own, chose the solution that was the most dangerous and costly."

"You're hallucinating, Oscar."

"That you, you, the mayor of the greatest city in South America, were warned by the best engineers in the world. They told you in person, in writing, by email and through text messaging but you, and nobody else, made the decision to go ahead with the most dangerous and most expensive plan. By now, half the people from the federal government know what you really are."

"Of course, they do. They're the ones who helped me get elected in the first place," Sabóida said. "Oscar, do you really think I'm that stupid?"

Bardilione couldn't believe his ears.

"They'll simply say that I, the mayor, was wrongly advised. The engineers made the mistakes. The consultants were wrong. Engineers like you did not provide me with the right information. Anyway, who's going to believe for a minute that I had anything to do about it? I'll play dumb and lay all the blame on the people who should have counseled me in the first place."

The mayor had done the dumb scenario many times before, and it had worked. But now, Sabóida actually believed that his friend had a point.

Bardilione shook his head. "This time I don't think that's going to happen. You're not getting off this easy."

"Why not?" Sabóida demanded. The mayor wanted to believe he was safe from prosecution. But he wasn't so sure anymore.

"Because they're already asking why you chose to dig the tunnels where you were told it was risky. They're also asking why you chose the most expensive route."

"They can ask anything they want. They have nothing on me." Sabóida looked annoyed.

Bardilione wagged a finger. "I want you to listen very carefully."

"Go on…"

"Your friends won't be able to help you this time, because they're thinking you're expendable."

"You're bluffing." But Sabóida looked anxious.

"They think you're replaceable."

Sabóida said nothing.

"Are you listening now, Antônio?"

"I understand everything you've said so far." Sabóida was trying to think of a way out. "But no one can make a case against me. Don't worry about it. I'm protected by God himself." Sabóida started to laugh at his own joke.

"I'm sure someone will want justice for what happened, one way or another, Antônio. And maybe, just maybe, you can get away with it. But that's not the fucking point. You've become a liability to The Group. Is your thick head getting any of this?"

"I'm sure you're not threatening me?" Sabóida asked.

"No. No. Of course not." Bardilione started to say something but he found that the whole discussion was absurd. He began to chuckle at the idea that his friend, the mayor, was a total idiot. Bardilione laughed along with his friend.

"It's funny?" Sabóida said.

"No, not really. But I can't help myself. You're such an idiot! But, I know that sooner or later, whether it will be a friend, an associate or an enemy, one day, you'll find yourself dead, hanged somewhere where everyone will see what kind of moron you really are. And that will be that."

"And you think that's funny?"

"Yes, because, old friend, you pissed off too many people. Sooner or later one of them will blink."

"Blink?"

"And when they blink, and I think it's just a matter of time, they'll reach out to someone who will probably come from left field, and as I said, dear Antônio, that will be that."

"Now wait a goddamn minute. What are you trying to tell me?"

"Jesus, Antônio. Are you so stupid you can't put the pieces together?"

Mayor Antônio Sabóida felt a chill run up his spine. "Are you saying there's a contract on my…"

"You want me to draw you a picture, Antônio?"

"I don't know whether I should laugh or cry. In any event, I really don't believe anything you've said. So now, I think we should have supper. What do you think, Oscar?"

"What?" Bardilione was surprised.

"How about a steak at Figueira Rubaiyat?"

"No, thank you."

"Come on. It's late. I'm hungry. Call your wife. Tell her you'll be late tonight."

"Antônio?"

"What? It's just dinner." The mayor felt he needed company tonight. He didn't want to be alone. Maybe he could make Oscar change his mind.

"You know what? It's late," Bardilione said.

"Wait! Oscar, where are you going?"

Bardilione didn't respond to his old friend.

"Come on, Oscar. You can't just go, not like this?"

Bardilione didn't say anything. He was thinking about the end of their friendship.

"All right, Oscar. You got my attention. See? I'm serious. What do they want me to do?" Sabóida was pleading. "Tell me. I promise I'll do it."

"Goodbye, old friend," Bardilione said.

"Stop. Please. Don't leave now. The night is still young."

There was no response from Bardilione.

It was over.

22

"We'll nab him when he comes out," Alexander Fionnuala said simply.

Willy sneered. "Easier said than done. The bastard's always escorted in and out of the palace."

"Patience, Willy. Look." Alexander pointed to the car waiting at the entrance of the governor's residence.

"What am I looking at?" Willy Callender asked.

"His escort. In the car. Smoking," Alexander said.

"What are you saying, old man?" Willy asked.

"I'm saying we take the escort first, then we take care of Armery."

"Sounds simple." Willy was thinking about it.

"Yes." Alexander had done this before. In fact, both of them had experience in dealing with challenging individuals.

"*Yer bum's oot the windae,*" Willy said.

"Nonsense? What do you mean—I'm talking nonsense?" Alexander was surprised.

"Pure, unadulterated baloney," Willy said. "That guard's almost six feet five. How do you plan to subdue a monster twice your own size?"

"We can always shoot the bastard," Alexander said.

"Right, we're barely in the country and you're suggesting a killing spree."

"Yeah. Let's get done with it and return home. We take the driver's place, we wait for Armery to show himself, and then we do what we should have done a hundred years ago."

"Could we at least consider an alternative?" Willy asked.

"Such as?"

"We could snare Armery in his home," Willy said out loud. "We'll wait till he's alone in his house on Estér Street and then get the job done. In private. Far away from the governor's gate where there happens to be a fucking battalion of fucking guards, standing ready to shoot the first fucking idiot waving a gun in their fucking faces. How's that for an alternative?"

"You don't need to shout," Alexander said. "All right, so you have a better idea. What of it?"

"We need to know what Armery knows," Willy said. "How he got away from us. What he's doing here and then, we find a suitable resting place."

"Resting place?" Alexander said.

"It's an expression."

"I'm sure it is."

23

FASANO SÃO PAULO HOTEL

PENTHOUSE SUITE

SÃO PAULO

"I'm here because I was told by someone I trust that I should meet you," Batista said.

"Thank you," Destrey replied. "I'm glad you could make the time. Please come in."

Destrey's penthouse suite didn't impress Batista. Destrey was sure of that. She had enough experience with the super-rich to know that they were only interested in impressing others.

"*Madame* Destrey, you have no idea, do you?"

Destrey didn't respond. She sat down. She was tired of being on her feet. Batista decided not to.

"My time is precious," Batista said. "Let's do this as quickly as we can. I have business to attend to."

Destrey folded her arms. "I was ready to have a conversation with you about your city's future, but I'm guessing you're really not interested. So, let me get to the point and not waste any more of your precious time."

Batista cocked his head and looked at Destrey with mild amusement. "I was told you were a no-nonsense person. So, let me hear it, dear *Madame* Destrey. What's this earthquake business really about? I'm all ears."

"Let me just say that whatever you decide to do, Mr. Batista, whatever you think about earthquakes and whatever happens to you personally or to your family is, of course, none of my business."

"What are you getting at, *Madame* Destrey?" He looked puzzled.

"You, Mr. Batista, know far more than the average *Paulistano* or politician what is happening in your city. You are well versed in the latest science about quakes, what earthquakes can inflict on a population. How they can destroy infrastructure. You may also be very well informed about my recommendations to São Paulo leaders about evacuating the city."

Batista sighed. "That's why I have people working for me. I make judicious decisions for my company and my shareholders. However, the very thought of evacuating the city is so... how shall I say this, preposterous, that it invalidates your case entirely."

"I disagree," Destrey shot back.

Batista shook his head. "Do you realize that São Paulo is in the process of becoming one of the most prosperous cities in the world? A giant, *Madame* Destrey, a veritable titan. A super city that could go it alone if we wished to."

Destrey ignored his boastful soliloquy. Its relevance was at best indirect.

"The president of the United States has called your president with the Los Alamos findings about an earthquake hitting the city," she said. "But you already know that."

Batista nodded.

"So, in conclusion, you know what I've been trying to do here in São Paulo... I think it's safe to say there's nothing more I can put on the table. So that's that." Destrey put her hands up in frustration. "Still, may I ask you a question, Mr. Batista?"

"Ask away," he answered happily. "I'm an open book."

Destrey hesitated a bit. She was almost tempted to let the bastard go without even attempting to warn him about the impending disaster. But her conscience wouldn't permit that.

"Will you be in São Paulo for the next few weeks?" she asked.

"Yes, but I will not have any more time to grant you, *Madame* Destrey. I'm a busy man and this meeting is..."

She nodded. "A courtesy call."

"Something like that." Batista's tone was serene. "Is that all, *Madame* Destrey?"

"May I add that I am truly sorry?"

"Sorry? I don't really understand what you're trying to say here."

"I'm afraid I will be leaving São Paulo by the end of this week. There's a very good chance that we will never meet again. As you can see for yourself, I have not achieved my objectives. For that, I am sad for your family, for your management staff and their families, and for the thousands of employees and their families, for the future they will be forfeiting. Most likely because of a failed meeting between two intelligent persons."

Destrey stood up, reached out to him and shook his hand.

Batista thought the woman would have tried to convince him,

to sway him to believe there was indeed a threat on the horizon. Batista was accustomed to being treated like royalty. He expected to be worshiped. That's how his people behaved toward him. People came to him and they'd put on a show, with a presentation, numbers, financial forecast and outcomes. Today, there was none of that.

"That's it?" he asked, astounded.

"My job, Mr. Batista, is to work with people with an open mind. You came here with no such intent. Good luck, Mr. Batista."

"Did you really think I would fall on my knees and thank you for saving my life?" Batista was livid. He was the man who decided when a conversation was finished. Not the other way around. "Did you really expect me to turn around on a dime and leave the city because of your fucking prediction?"

Batista was about to leave the room, but Destrey wasn't done with him.

"You're right of course. It makes no sense at all. After all, everybody knows we can't predict earthquakes, can we, Mr. Batista?"

"No, we can't," he said. "But if you're so goddamned knowledgeable about the future, what's going to happen to São Paulo or to me for that matter? Now, I'm listening. Now, I have an open mind."

"There's a ninety percent chance you and your family will die within the next thirty-six days. That's what I've been saying to all who would listen, for the last two weeks. But then again..." She searched the right words. "My husband used to say that arrogant bastards like you only understand violent behavior. Should I have been more forceful with you, *Senhor* Batista?"

Batista snorted. "You've got balls, lady. But unfortunately, no. You see, I'm not arrogant or a bastard. I'm just good at what I do. Call me a realist. And realists don't buy end-of-the-world prophecies."

With that, Batista turned and exited Destrey's hotel penthouse suite.

A few moments later, as Batista slammed the door behind him, John Kleinrup came into the suite's conference room.

"So, how did it go?"

Destrey shook her head. "Like the rest of them. I have experts, politicians, researchers and computers to help me get my message through... and for what? No one wants to hear it. What am I doing wrong?"

"We've talked about this. Who in his right mind is going to leave this fantastic city because you say they should?"

"So, what should we do next?"

"We continue to knock on their doors. We do our job the best we can. We warn, we influence, we cajole, but in the end, it's their decision. My conscience will be clear. Yours too."

Destrey looked at the door that Batista just walked through. "What about Batista?"

John frowned. "Fuck 'im."

"John, you know that's not right. If we were only talking about this Batista guy, it would be different. But he could be instrumental in savings thousands upon thousands of lives."

"Fuck 'im," he said coldly once more.

"You're scaring me, John."

"Yeah." His voice was glum. "Sometimes I hear myself saying things I wouldn't have dreamed of uttering a few years back."

"So?" Destrey asked.

"I suggest we get our whiz kids to hack Batista's empire and talk directly to his people. Let's see what the families have to say about their future. I wouldn't put it past him to scurry off somewhere, incognito, away from here. Maybe we could catch him in the act leaving São Paulo."

"We don't have the time to do that."

"You're right. But I'm sure some part of him listened to you."

"You're saying Batista will hedge his bets?" Destrey wished he was right.

"Absolutely. That kind have a habit of saving their own asses," Kleinrup said.

"Then let's get to it. Talk to Isaac. Tell him to target the ten largest corporations in São Paulo."

"You don't have to tell me twice," Kleinrup replied.

"And put our experts on YouTube. Get some famous soccer player, or singer... Whatever it takes to make our message go viral. We don't have any more time to work with the elite. They're completely useless."

"And, they don't really care what happens to their people," Kleinrup added.

A sad look crossed Destrey's face. "I hope you're wrong about that. The world can't be this heartless."

"I think the world was overrun by greedy bastards a long, long time ago," Kleinrup said.

"Now you're talking like Lola. Remember, she came up with the concept that greed was a universal value."

"Sorry. I know how you feel about that hunk of scrap metal." Kleinrup smiled.

"She's only a computer, for God's sake."

"Speaking of which, what's the news on the diplomatic front?" Kleinrup asked.

"Lola left me this message." Destrey handed her cell to Kleinrup. "She said the diplomatic corps has been almost completely evacuated. They have also alerted their foreign nationals to leave the city before the end of the week. That's not going to go unnoticed. China is the only hold-out so far."

John Kleinrup studied the content but didn't comment.

Louise looked at him with suspicion, then rolled her eyes. "Don't say it!"

"What?"

"The Chinese?"

Kleinrup smiled. "You mean *fuck 'em?*"

24

R. ESTÉR, 491

VILA ALPINA SANTO ANDRÉ

SÃO PAULO, 09000–790

The stakeout by Alexander Fionnuala and Willy Callender took more than two days before Armery got rid of the scum infesting his home. The villa was safe to approach. With no unwanted visitors to deal with, they could completely focus on Armery.

"I'd like to wait until four in the morning before we make our move," Alexander said.

"And what brilliant strategist told you that piece of crap?" Willy believed he was far better equipped for this kind of op.

"It's common knowledge," Alexander replied, a bit subdued. "Armery will be fast asleep and too drowsy to do anything serious. It'll be a quick pick up. If you consider his age, it makes sense."

Callender believed his friend was on something, probably Prozac. He stared at him in total disbelief.

"Are you forgetting who we're dealing with? It's Armery, for chrissake. I repeat, the big freaking head. Former MI6 director. Killer *extraordinaire* as well as a traitor and bottom feeder. You don't think he'd be ready for an intruder, especially in the early hours of the morning? Remember, he studied the same textbook we did. Hell! He probably wrote the bloody manual himself."

"I wasn't thinking," Alexander replied, almost indifferent. "I just want this to end quickly. That's all. So, what do you recommend?"

"We knock at his door just around lunchtime. Aim a gun to his face, tie him up, question him and then get rid of the evidence."

"That sounds good." Alexander looked at his watch. "Eleven-oh-three. We've got an hour to kill."

Willy smiled. "I'm looking forward to it."

"It?" Alexander asked.

"Aye. A pint and a sandwich." Willy liked to play.

"Consider what we have to do instead. Then we'll do the pint." Alexander was business first and play later.

"And sandwich." Willy was always hungry.

"Anything else?"

"Tuna." Willy knew Alexander hated tuna.

"What in heaven's name are you thinking we're going to do over there?" Alexander felt the project needed discipline.

"We are here, dear Alexander, because we fucked up. That doesn't mean we have to starve."

A little after twelve-thirty, Alexander Fionnuala and Willy Callender rang Armery's doorbell.

"He's getting old," Alexander said under his breath.

"Shut it!"

After a few minutes, the door opened to reveal Armery holding a sandwich. Armery didn't recognize Callender or Fionnuala. He should have.

"Yes?" he asked, his mouth full of tuna. "What can I do for you gentlemen?"

Alexander and Willy pushed the door so hard it caught Armery by surprise. He fell, his sandwich flying in the air in brazen defiance of gravity.

Willy popped his gun in Armery's face. "Talk, you die. Move, you die. Think, you die. Understand?"

Armery nodded. Kidnappings, burglaries and violence: São Paulo's scourge. He thought he was immune from that kind of crime because he had connections.

The agents moved Armery to the kitchen. Willy tied him up while Alexander was busy preparing lunch.

"May I talk?" Armery asked.

"You may," Willy said.

"How much do you want? I can write you a check. Anything you want." Armery knew it was just a question of money. It always was.

"Don't you recognize me?" Willy asked dryly.

Armery hesitated. "Should I?"

"You should, you piece of shit. We worked for you. We ran your ops and you gave us up." Alexander punched Armery's left temple. "What are you doing alive? I thought we had buried you."

Armery didn't respond. Not immediately. He was still a bit stunned. His head hurt. He cursed himself for not installing a more sophisticated security system.

"Nothing to say?" Alexander asked.

Now Armery absolutely knew for a fact that he wasn't going to get out of this situation alive. To make things worse, no one was coming knocking at his door. Not today. That he was to die wasn't the issue. His question was when and how?

"I can see it in your eyes. Do you recognize me now?" An evil smile spread across Willy's face as Alexander waited for Armery's answer.

"Now we're in business," Willy said.

Armery tried not to show any fear. But these two bastards had a lot of experience. Pretense was a waste of time. What he did fear the most at this point in his life was the suffering. *They would be creative,* he thought anxiously.

Alexander and Willy had planned to work this out quickly. In and out. That was the plan.

"We both know," Callender said, "how this is going to end. But we have questions. You answer our questions, and we'll be out of here in a jiffy. Quick and clean. You understand, old man? The alternative would be unthinkable."

Armery nodded. "What do you want to know?"

"Why you're still breathing?" Willy asked.

"That's an old story," Armery said carefully.

"Make it short."

"I paid off the bastard sent to kill me."

"Whom did you pay off?"

"I don't honestly remember. What I do remember is the look on his face when I shot the stupid sod. That's it, I swear."

Willy didn't reply.

"More?" Armery asked.

Willy nodded.

"I'd been preparing for such an event. We have a short shelf life, as you well know. I had a body prepared to replace me. Hacked the system. If ever his dentals were scanned, my name would pop up. The dead body burned and I got away. Easy."

"And..."

"For God's sake. You didn't need to come all the way here to find that out, did you?"

Willy didn't bother answering Armery's question. "What are you doing in this part of the world?"

"The city needs to get rid of its criminals. The courts can't handle the job. The police are corrupt, and they need help. Someone powerful called, close to the governor, as rich as Croesus, perhaps more. He said the people needed my services. I obliged. That's what I'm doing here. Cleaning up."

"The plan?" Willy asked.

"What of it?" Armery looked surprised. "Same as always."

"Details, please."

"The city is on the verge of becoming a mega-business in its own right. Can't let kidnappers and robbers continue to do whatever. Too much money involved. The elite want peace and quiet. I provide the peace and quiet."

"You mean you're setting up a kill squad?"

"Done." Armery nodded.

"Is the squad active?"

"Yes." Armery's answer was quick.

"How active?"

"Crime rate is dropping. Business is feeling better."

"Who's in charge of this squad? The police?" Willy knew the routine.

"No. Not really. The chief of police is too stupid. To answer your question, I don't really know, nor do I want to."

"Who else are they targeting?" Willy asked.

"Anyone and everyone who criticizes the money people, the mayor, the chief of police, I don't know..."

"Anyone we know of?" Willy was being thorough.

"Can't think of anyone."

Willy aimed his gun at Armery's private parts.

"Don't need to get nasty. I said it could be anyone." Armery wasn't lying. Willy could tell.

"Such as..." Alexander was fishing.

"The woman talking about earthquakes, for instance. The money people want her silenced."

"What woman?" Alexander didn't know whom he was referring to.

"The same one who predicted the muddle in Jerusalem," Armery said.

"Destrey. That's her name, right?" Alexander was calm.

"Yes."

"When?" Willy frowned.

"Today, tonight. Tomorrow. Now. Last night. How should I know?" Armery was getting tired of the game.

"Funny man." Alexander had a bad feeling.

Alexander Fionnuala and Willy Callender exchanged looks. There was a clear understanding between them. The question period was over.

"How would you like it?" Alexander asked his prisoner.

"Quick." Armery knew there wasn't anything he could do or say to stop them from their mission. The Firm had failed once. That wasn't going to happen today.

"Quick it is, then," Willy said.

Armery stared at his executioners. He'd been tightly bound and gagged for his last trip. Armery was then unceremoniously dumped on his favorite Turkish rug and rolled up for his journey to Valhalla or hell.

Once in the trunk, Fionnuala and Callender drove away from Armery's ritzy neighborhood. Their destination was a reservoir sixty kilometers away for a burial at sea.

"We could just shoot him and that would be that," Willy said.

"Armery will drown. I promised myself. He'd die by his own preferred way of doing things." Alexander considered the worst possible execution.

"You're going to enjoy this, aren't you?"

"I will."

Three hours later, they found a quiet area a few meters from one of the Paiva Castro Dam reservoir system.

"Let's get him out of the boot and get this done with."

Fionnuala and Callender unrolled the carpet. They got Armery to sit and violently removed the gag away from his mouth.

"I thought this would be quick. We had a deal," Armery pleaded.

Armery was hogtied. He could barely move. He was vulnerable.

"Goodbye," Alexander said callously. "I hope you rot in hell."

With that, Armery was tossed in two feet of water. Armery roared.

"You can't do this!" he yelled as he swallowed water faster than he could spit it out.

Armery slowly sunk. Alexander delicately pushed his body further underwater. He kept his eyes fixed on Armery.

"If only eyes could kill," Alexander said as he loomed over Armery's side.

"Bye-bye and good riddance," Willy said.

Alexander waved at him. "I promise I won't leave until I'm satisfied, you're dead. I promise."

Both agents watched as their former boss drowned.

Alexander shook his head. "I can be so cold."

"Aye. That you can."

"Let's get going then. Job's done."

"No. Not this time. I'm waiting." Alexander wanted to make sure Sir Henry Blake Armery would never come back to haunt them.

"He's dead, for God's sake. You can see that. The old bugger is gone."

"Wait. Be patient. You really don't want to come back here and start all over again?"

"If you put it that way, I guess I can stick around for a bit. Oh, I forgot; I brought a few pints. Mind if we celebrate?"

"Don't mind at all. In fact, it would be an honor to share this brew with you."

"Who are you talking to exactly?"

"Why, Armery of course."

"Then, let us toast Sir Henry Blake Armery the best of times. In hell."

"Aye. In hell. Where he belongs."

"He surely does."

25

CANADIAN CONSULATE GENERAL

AV. DAS NAÇÕES UNIDAS

SÃO PAULO

"There's a call for you, Mister Kleinrup. Line one. He says he's an old friend of Horace."

"Did he mention his name?" Kleinrup was a bit surprised. It had been a few years since his father's passing. Nowadays, his father's name didn't come up too often, especially from a complete stranger.

"He didn't say."

"Right. Patch him through. And thanks."

"Don't mention it."

"Who am I speaking to?" Kleinrup asked.

"It doesn't matter who I am, but I owe your dad."

Kleinrup was taken aback.

"You're Destrey's friend, am I right?"

"Who wants to know?" Kleinrup's voice was even.

"Listen carefully, young Kleinrup, and listen tight."

"You sound like John Wayne."

"Maybe I am. The woman's on a hit list and I wouldn't be surprised if you were on it too. If you care about her, then get her out of the country."

"What trouble?"

"Do I have to repeat myself?"

Kleinrup could feel the anger brewing inside him. "This isn't funny."

"It's not meant to be."

"How do you know about this hit list?" Kleinrup wasn't sure this call was on the level.

"We just learned about it. Our source is... sorry, was, impeccable. Now he's long gone. We took care of that."

"We?" Kleinrup couldn't believe the caller. "Who's we?"

"That's none of your business. But we once worked for your father. Let's leave it at that."

"Tell me something about my father that's not on Wikipedia."

"Your father is alive."

Kleinrup hung up. He was now sure the call was a prank. And, in bad taste.

A few minutes later, the ambassador's secretary called Kleinrup's extension.

"It's your friend who knows Horace. Line one. He says it's important."

"Forget it. Hang up."

"He said he knows about the part you played with the Kung brothers to catch the German, his accomplice and his family. I think he's serious. You should take the call. I can tell if it's a prank call."

"Really?"

"Yeah, really," she said calmly.

"Okay, put him on."

"You've got two minutes," Kleinrup said. "Tell me again who you are and what you know."

"As I said, we were your dad's operatives. As for our source, he told us about the list earlier today. He specifically mentioned the Destrey woman."

"What did he say exactly?"

"He said the city put together a kill squad. Anyone who's trouble gets on that list. Destrey's on that list. You're probably on that list too. Ergo, she's in trouble. You're in trouble. The people who work with you. You're all in serious danger."

"Why are you telling me this? Who the hell are you?"

"You're not paying attention, young man."

"Make me believe you." Kleinrup was angry.

"Do you know why the casket was closed?"

"What casket?"

"Horace's."

"Please illuminate me."

"This is what your father never wanted you to know. Brace yourself, young Kleinrup, because the body in your dad's casket wasn't his. It wasn't Horace. If your father stayed alive, his family would have paid for his sins. So, he had to go, making his family safe to live without fear."

Kleinrup swallowed hard. "Right. My father's alive." He didn't believe a word of it.

"I can attest to that."

Kleinrup was taken aback by the caller's cold-blooded reply. There was no hesitation. Not even a hint of a lie.

"Who's your source on this kill team?" Kleinrup asked.

"An old friend of ours who turned traitor to Queen and country. We were tasked to finish the job we botched up twenty-five years ago. Let's just say the prick had it coming."

"MI6?"

"You know damn well we can't talk about that."

"What does your source have to do with Destrey?"

"The man we disposed of was responsible for setting up a special team of off-duty officers and local mercenaries who possess...how can I say this? Special talents. They are charged with taking out anyone on the list. If the person is on that list, that means someone is thinking he or she is in the way."

"Whose way?"

"São Paulo's money people."

"You still haven't said why Destrey was in their crosshairs."

"Because Destrey's saying people have to leave the city. That the city isn't safe. That, young Kleinrup, would be enough to put her on top of the list. And according to our source, God bless his fucking soul, she's on that list as we speak."

"Who's in charge of the hit squad?"

"Someone with a lot of powerful friends. Friends in high places, such as the governor of the great State of São Paulo and some of the wealthiest men and women on the planet."

"Can you give me a name?"

"Why?"

"Because she still has work to do. And she won't leave until she's ready."

"I see," he replied.

"No, you don't see." Kleinrup was irritated. "But if you ever have the unfortunate chance of meeting her face to face, you'll see for yourself."

"I'm glad I'm not in your shoes."

"Can you find out who's putting the names on that list?"

"We'll see. I'm not promising. If I find something, I'll call you. If not, do your best to get her out of the city."

"One more thing," Kleinrup added.

"You are your father's son. It's never enough, good enough or fast enough. What is it you want, young Kleinrup?"

"If, like you say my father's alive, then, where is he? How can I reach him?"

The caller hung up.

Kleinrup looked at the receiver, dropped it on the table, and poured himself a Scotch.

"What in God's name is going on? Is the world going mad?" he said out loud.

26

A few short minutes later, Kleinrup called Destrey's cell and left a message to call back as soon as she could. Code red, he said.

Destrey's bodyguards were on their way to her next meeting. When they heard the news about the list from Kleinrup, they quickly made their way back to the Canadian Consulate. As much as Destrey tried to get her goons to change their itinerary, they continued on, in spite of Destrey's promise to have them killed or deported to Afghanistan.

Failing to achieve what she had set out to do, she took her messages and reluctantly called Kleinrup.

"I'm not happy," she said. *"J'suis pas contente.* Do you understand what I'm saying? How about, *No estoy feliz!"*

Kleinrup tried unsuccessfully to cover his laughter.

"This isn't funny, mister."

"Oh, so it's mister now?"

"What's this all about? Why is Boris Badenov and his sidekick Bullwinkle heading for the consulate as if the world was on fire?"

"Well, dear Louise, it's because you're on a list."

"What kind of list?"

"Calm down. This isn't good for your heart."

"My heart is fine, no thanks to you."

"Whoa! Where's this coming from?" Kleinrup was having fun at her expense.

"Well?" she asked.

Kleinrup didn't respond.

"Are you still there?"

"There's this kill squad," Kleinrup said slowly. "It's been put together by the money in São Paulo to eliminate people who meddle in the city's affairs. You're on the list. I was just informed a few minutes ago. I've been told that I'm probably on that list too. I'm trying to find out more. If someone wants to kill you, there's nothing anyone can do to stop an anonymous killer. Sooner or later, especially if we stay in São Paulo, we will not make it."

"Are you sure about this?"

Kleinrup sighed. "I'm not sure about anything anymore."

"Just checking," she said.

"That's not all of it." Kleinrup didn't know how to say it out loud.

"Then what?" Destrey's voice changed, like she felt something was wrong.

Kleinrup sighed. "He said my father's alive."

"What? That can't be. Can it?"

"Just come back to the consulate. We'll talk about this and the other matter, if you care to," Kleinrup said.

"I'm fifteen minutes away."

"Nothing is fifteen minutes away in São Paulo." Kleinrup was a realist, but then again, Destrey's Russians guards were full of surprises.

"I didn't have lunch yet," she added.

Kleinrup detected a warmth in Destrey's voice.

"I'll be waiting for you. Be careful."

27

IPEN – SÃO PAULO NUCLEAR RESEARCH CENTER
UNIVERSITY OF SÃO PAULO

Cristiane Tarsila Amoedo trusted science. Everything else was delusion, concocted perceptions and wishful thinking. And because science was about knowledge, she had to know. She was a theoretical physicist at IPEN - São Paulo University Nuclear Research Center, currently working on nanoscale systems. Although she wore a gold chain with a cross, she was not a true believer in God, angels or the devil. The cross had been a gift from her mother. She wore it because more than 90% of Brazilians were religious, and she simply wanted to blend in. Learning how the universe worked was her life. She had no room for Christian lore or its mythology which she believed was a mishmash of ancient beliefs and storytelling. She also had no time for the mundane distractions the world had to offer. No clubbing, bars or soccer. Cristiane Tarsila Amoedo was highly intelligent, focused, serious and drop-dead gorgeous. She was also a chronic loner.

"I'm here again, because I have to understand what this woman is talking about," Cristiane said to her friend.

Cristiane only had faith in numbers. In what she could measure and verify. But what this Destrey woman was advertising on every social media available in São Paulo, was unbelievable. It didn't take an engineer or a geologist to tell her that no one could predict earthquakes. Yet, there she was: openly asking the people to leave the great city of São Paulo, or else. Cristiane had an issue she couldn't figure out: although her prediction made no sense, Destrey was no ordinary woman. She had done this before. Predicting things beyond the scope of known science. Submitting impossible scenarios. Warning people of impending disasters. In the end, it all came true. Destrey had, on many occasions, challenged the scientific establishment and saved thousands upon thousands from dying a horrible death at the hands of Mother Nature or terrorists.

Rosalie Gomez listened carefully at what her friend Cristiane had to say. Rosalie called herself a planetary scientist and was a bit curious to find out why Cristiane was now interested in earthquakes. Every now and then, Cristiane would drop in, unannounced, and go through a long list of problems and questions, mainly about the planet, specifically asking Rosalie how things worked. Over the years, they had become close friends. Finding the time to talk about the universe was one of Rosalie's favorite pastimes.

"I consider myself a realist," Cristiane said. "I need clarity."

Cristiane was also a fan of Galileo. She considered him a giant among men: a physicist, an astronomer and an engineer. More importantly, Galileo believed in numbers.

As a child, looking at the universe through her father's telescope,

Cristiane couldn't help but believe there had to be a beginning. And that was the start of her quest. To understand everything she could about... all of it! Everything and anything she came into contact with, which lately included strange whistling noises coming from her basement.

Today was no different.

"So, you're saying earthquakes are preceded sometimes by noises?" she asked inquisitively. Cristiane listened attentively to what Rosalie had to say.

"Many of my colleague geologists, seismologists, even oceanographers, have determined that unusual noises often precede earthquakes." Rosalie could be relied on to provide reliable information.

Cristiane Amoedo also understood that animals altered their behavior prior to earthquakes. She was told that they could sense impending earthquakes days or even weeks before they happened, sometimes, long before humans could recognize their pets' strange behaviors. The implication was important: earthquakes could be predicted.

"They can sense seismic waves and the energy they generate. The waves themselves are caused by the sudden crushing of rock within the earth's core," Rosalie said. "They can't miss it."

"Is this new science, Rosalie? It's not a topic that comes up at the university's campus."

"That's because, my dear Cristiane, you haven't been paying attention. Your head's too busy studying nanoscale systems. Really small objects when compared to earthquakes. So today, you happen to be curious about the big stuff. That's interesting."

"That's not fair, Rosalie. I happen to be interested in a lot of topics, not just the small nanos."

"If you say so." Rosalie chuckled at her friend's obvious innocence. "All the same, and I'm sorry to say this, the subject is as old as history. You see, we've known for some time that animals can detect earthquakes."

"So, they know in advance."

"Knowing is a big word. Let's say they sense danger. At least, that's what my colleagues tell me."

"Wow," Cristiane said.

"Wow indeed."

"Do you believe what this Destrey women is saying about our city?"

"I really don't know what to say about that. But I'll tell you something I just realized about you. Promise me you won't get angry?"

"Rosalie, you know there's nothing you could say or do that would make me angry. I'm sure you know that."

"Well, I just realized that if you told me that we'd have to get away because something terrible was about to happen, I think I would follow your advice even though everyone else would think you're crazy."

"That's quite a compliment."

"No. It's not. I'm just describing who you are and what you represent to me. To answer your question, I think this Destrey woman is someone I would like to believe, given her track record. Maybe you and this Destrey woman are made from the same cloth."

Cristiane was stunned by Rosalie's comment. Now, more than

ever, Cristiane wanted to meet Louise Destrey. But the clock was ticking. According to Destrey, the earthquake was happening in a matter of weeks or days. Time was a commodity Cristiane couldn't waste.

"Would you come with me if I decided to follow Destrey's advice?" Cristiane asked.

"Why not? We could head for Rio. I haven't seen my parents in ages. We could stay at their house. There's plenty of room."

"What about your work?" Cristiane asked.

"My work is in my head. I carry it everywhere I go. But, tell me something. Are you making up your mind as we speak?"

"Yeah, I guess I am."

28

Destrey and Kleinrup were back at the Canadian Consulate. From there, she tried to talk to Brazil's President Ditmar Paul even though he was in the process of being impeached for electoral fraud. She wasn't shocked or disappointed when the president had refused to talk to her about the earthquake.

As far as Destrey was concerned, the country had lost its way a long time ago. Rule of law was replaced by market needs dictated by the São Paulo elite while ordinary *Paulistanos* were busy scrounging for water. For some, food and shelter were dependent on the money they could rip off of people who were in as much trouble as they were. All in all, desperate times.

When the U.S. president attempted to warn Brazil's chief of state of the impending natural disaster, he was told by the Brazilian foreign minister, in no uncertain words, to mind his own business.

Destrey no longer believed there was enough time to persuade government leaders to do the right thing. So far, her strategy to win over elected officials had failed. That wasn't a surprise. She met resistance before from politicians who could only govern the short term.

"I can't blame them," she said to Kleinrup. Destrey could hardly believe the city was on the verge of extinction. Who in his right mind would even try to evacuate one of the biggest cities in the world?

Kleinrup believed that a behemoth such as São Paulo was a very difficult creature to push around, especially when there were so many people to evacuate and so much money involved. For all those reasons and more, Destrey had decided during the planning phase of this event, to quickly short-circuit the formal government apparatus and directly get the message out to as many *Paulistanos* as possible. Because of the earthquake's potential for destruction and loss of life, Destrey had authorized Lola to hack into any and all Brazilian Internet sites deemed necessary. Especially those who had nothing—nothing to lose and everything to gain. In short, the poor.

All bets were off because the countdown had begun. It was time to get out.

Kleinrup was reviewing the logistics of an evacuation. "The Americans and the Canadians are now making arrangements to evacuate the city."

"I hope that they'll get out in time," Destrey said.

"That's one thing I can't get a handle on. But, both missions have specific responsibilities to deal with before they evacuate their staff. Let me go through those. It'll only take a minute."

Destrey indicated her agreement.

"One: informing American and Canadian citizens living or working in São Paulo to evacuate as soon as possible and head at least 100 kilometers away from the city. Staying well away from structures such as older buildings, dams and chemical plants was a priority message. Two: Little is putting out the message that time is running out. Little prepared a number of posts including the probabilities of serious injury or death with each passing day. Little's communications were shaped to instill certainty into the message."

"Are we getting any numbers on how many are reading this stuff?" Destrey asked.

"Were starting to get some traction."

Destrey realized that there were choices to be made and the priority was to get people to leave the city.

"There's more," Kleinrup said. "IT departments from both embassies are working full time, warning families to get their children to safety."

"I'm glad we're able to do that." Destrey wanted to appeal to people's most sacred responsibility. Destrey had perfected the message of the family being under attack. *The lives of your children are at risk.*

"Three: consular staff are urging hospitals and retirement homes, schools and universities to shut down operations, to evacuate as many as possible and prepare for the worst." Kleinrup wasn't sure how school administrators would react to their appeal to evacuate. Without proper authorization from the state government, administrators wouldn't risk their jobs on a foreigner's end-of-the-world warning. Evacuating anyone from harm's way was being challenged at every step. That's why Destrey was appealing directly to mothers and fathers.

"Four: staff are explaining, through discrete communication channels with the Brazilian military and the local police forces, why the American and Canadian consular staff have initiated the evacuation of their own people."

Kleinrup explained that military personnel friendly to the American and Canadian diplomats received Lola's findings on how to evacuate the city based on BTG's extensive review of Jerusalem's evacuation a few years back. This included finding suitable destinations for evacuees, such as family or friends, school buildings and sports facilities.

"We also have a team of Indian hackers jamming Brazil's Internet sites," Kleinrup said. "While hacking these sites, we've replaced their content with an evacuation protocol, encouraging families to find another place to live, as far away from the city."

"You think we got everything covered?" Destrey asked.

"To be frank, no. With each passing hour, the threat level on your own life is increasing. We have to stay one step ahead of those who are set to stop you at any costs. By now, they must be in the hundreds. They're probably arguing that, from their point of view, the city is being assaulted by foreigners in order to sabotage São Paulo's future. The mere mention of an earthquake is being shot down. They're saying you are a criminal. That the earthquake is a brazen lie. That it's made up to undermine Brazil's economy. You and me, both of us, are on their hit list."

"They can't touch us," Destrey said. "Don't we have diplomatic immunity?"

"Equipped with a Canadian diplomatic passport won't stop

anyone who has been ordered to shoot you on site. We've been lucky so far because our security detail was able to elude local law enforcement who'd been ordered to find us."

"I didn't believe I was in any real trouble. They've tried before and we always came through unhurt." Destrey was still clinging to the idea that she was safe. "Besides, I don't believe in letting bullies get their way. It's not my way."

"I got news for you," Kleinrup said.

Destrey pretended she didn't hear him.

"Look at me." Kleinrup gently pressed her chin toward him. Their eyes met. "You and I are in trouble. A real life-and-death situation. We stay here too long, we either die from the earthquake or someone shoots a bullet through your pretty little head."

"What about your pretty little head, Mister?"

"Again, listen up, *Frenchie*. They'll probably shoot me first. Then they'll come after you because I won't be there to shoot back."

Destrey shot Kleinrup a glare. "I don't like being told what to do."

"Don't I know it."

29

"Louise?" Margaret sounded nervous.

Margaret McGivney knew what was at stake with Lola's updates. She knew that Destrey didn't like them because the computer would inevitably have bad news. Margaret believed the boss would probably blow a fuse.

"What's up?"

"Apparently we have new data. She wants to talk to you."

"Who exactly wants to talk to me?"

"Lola. She says it's urgent."

"You know that doesn't make any sense. She's a freaking machine!"

"Be that as it may, dear boss of mine, she has something to tell you."

"Okay, what the hell. Put her on."

"Good morning *Madame* Destrey," said Lola.

"Get on with it. I don't have any time to waste."

"I would like you to leave São Paulo."

"Since when do you tell me what to do?"

"I was specifically tasked by Chairman Precov to keep an eye on you."

"Since when?"

"Since you joined the firm."

"You've been spying on me?"

"Yes, *Madame* Destrey. Day and night."

"Well, at least you're honest about it. But that doesn't give you permission to tell me what to do."

"Please leave now, *Madame* Destrey. The Gulfstream G100 jet is fueled and ready to go from São Paulo Congonhas International Airport. Mister Greco is waiting for you on board the aircraft as we speak."

"What did I just say?"

"Your time is up, *Madame* Destrey. I have uncovered new data about the event. Independent in nature. The São Paulo earthquake is imminent. Your life is in danger."

"Whatever. Besides, I'm on my way to the airport right now. It looks like there's a contract on my head."

"I am well aware of that threat, *Madame* Destrey."

"I'm curious though, what did Precov tell you exactly?"

"Chairman Precov said… 'Get her ass on that plane or I'll have her bodyguards pick her up and forcefully take her to the airport.'"

"You can't be serious. He wouldn't say that."

"Do you want me to repeat the chairman's message, or would you prefer to hear the message in his own voice?"

"No. No. I give up. Just tell me, what's this all about?"

"I will be happy to provide you with a full debriefing as soon as your jet is safely in the air."

"Give me a hint?"

"I'm afraid I can't."

"Excuse me for saying this, but you're a machine and I'm heading for the airport now. Okay?"

"Yes, *Madame* Destrey."

"Tell Margaret I'll be soon on my way."

"Anything else, *Madame* Destrey?"

"There's this young woman working at the Canadian..."

"You mean Amy Bluehawk."

"How did you know..."

"It's on the Internet. You scared over a hundred people at the consulate. You've gone viral."

"I don't believe it!" Destrey said.

"I don't lie, *Madame* Destrey. It's not in my programming or my ethics."

"Doesn't matter. Do whatever you have to do, but get her out of the city. If what you're hinting at is true, I might as well make sure the little one is safe."

30

"I'm not done yet." Louise Destrey didn't waver or hesitate. The woman had no time for boys acting up with their shoot 'em up westerns. She didn't blink. "A few minutes ago, Lola was ordering me to leave and now you're telling me the same! It's all rubbish."

"You don't get it, do you? You've hit a nerve, Louise. Hell! You finally got their attention. But I don't think you're going to be a threat for very long, because as far as they're concerned, you're as good as dead."

"Where did you get that from? Fox News?" Destrey smiled, goading him and testing his limits. She was relentless. She had to be tough because the woman had to know if there was enough of him left from when she'd first met him and fallen in love.

"Louise, what did I tell you? Two ex-MI6 agents, old employees of my father's, got it from the horse's mouth. There's a contract on your pretty little head."

"Little?"

"Cut it out." Kleinrup's voice turned angry. "I don't want anything to happen to you."

"Why?"

"Oh, for Pete's sake! We have no time for this…whatever this is."

Destrey walked to the nearest couch and made herself comfortable.

"Tell me again. Why do you care so much?" This time, she meant it.

"Because even though you think I've changed, and I have, I know that I'm not a fool. I love you now as I loved you then."

"You've certainly changed." Louise looked down.

"I've changed because I had to. You of all people should know that," he snapped. "My world was in danger. You were in danger and I couldn't accept that. I had to do what was needed of me. It wasn't pretty. Executing people is vile. Hell, it was the devil's work. But I don't regret any of it. So there. You have it in a nutshell. I'm still crazy in love with you, *Frenchie*"

"Go on." Destrey suddenly realized she cared for him, still.

"Right now, we have to get out of the country."

She frowned. "I'm still a little dubious about where your information is coming from. After all, people don't go killing people over a few Internet blogs."

"Are you kidding?" Kleinrup demanded. "Little has taken over the city's communications. As we speak, you're in charge of what people read, hear and see in São Paulo. Your message is reaching millions. So, your job is done here. We're done."

"It's not that I don't believe you, it's more about your sources. Can I talk to them?"

"Yes." He was on the edge of exasperation.

"When?"

"Now, if you want."

"Who exactly are they, anyway?"

"I'm sure they'll tell you. Give me a moment. I'll fetch them right this minute."

Kleinrup left the room and came back with two rather elderly gentlemen.

Destrey stood up, a bit surprised. She was expecting James Bond and Carrie Mathison. These two gents looked like Destrey's grandfathers.

Destrey proceeded to greet them the way she'd been taught. As they should be. Two senior gentlemen. Two old men who deserved respect.

"Please, have a seat," she said.

"We've no time to sit and chat," one of them said. "I'm Alexander Fionnuala. He's Willy Callender. We're both British Public Service employees. Or at least we were. So that's enough for us. You wanted to see Kleinrup's sources. Well, here we are. Now, little lady, you should be going. You've no time left, because I know who's behind this, and he's no slouch."

"I see." Destrey didn't know what to think of these two gentlemen.

"I don't think you do, because you're still here," Willy Callender said. "And your goons outside are having a smoke as if they were on vacation."

"How do you know about..."

"Armery told us," Callender replied.

"Told you what again?"

"Armery was our boss way back then," Fionnuala explained. "We believed he was dead. But, he ended up being a traitor and still alive. Then we found out he was working for the police right here, in this city. We had a job to do back then but we had failed to terminate him. This time, we're bringing back proof that we've accomplished our mission."

"Armery, you say?"

Fionnuala nodded. "Right, that's what we called the fucker."

"Okay. You said you had proof?" Destrey asked.

"Would you like to meet him?" asked Callender.

"Sure, why not?" At this point, Destrey was beginning to feel that these two old boys were not to be trusted.

Willy Callender tossed his bag on the floor, a few inches from Destrey's Christian Louboutin high heel shoes.

"What's in there?" Destrey was curious.

"It's the proof we're bringing back to the office."

"Louise," Kleinrup interjected. "You don't have to do that. Trust me, don't."

"I know what I'm doing," Destrey said.

"You don't want to do this," Kleinrup repeated. "These guys are for real. For the love of God, Louise, don't open the bag."

Destrey smirked. "I do very much want to see for myself."

Kleinrup moved toward her. "No, you don't."

"Don't tell me what I can and cannot do, mister."

Kleinrup sighed. "Suit yourself. But consider yourself warned."

Destrey unzipped the bag and looked closely at its contents. It was looking right at her. A face. A big head. Contorted and grimacing in pain. Pure agony. Eyes wide open. Destrey took a step back, falling on the couch.

"May I present you Mr. Armery in the flesh, so to speak? He died over twenty years ago. Or, he should have. That's why we're here, dear *Madame*. We were sent here by our former employers to finish the job we'd been entrusted to do."

"But..."

"Please understand that others will put you in a bag such as this one if you don't move your sweet ass, and quickly."

Louise looked at Kleinrup. "How... what do we do now?"

"I've been in touch with Precov," Kleinrup replied.

"And?"

"The Russian Embassy is sending some of their own boys to help us. They'll be here in a few minutes." Kleinrup was relieved. Alexander Fionnuala and Willy Callender had managed to convince Destrey.

"Okay." Destrey was resigned; she understood she was in danger.

"We're flying out of a private airfield owned and operated by the Russians. Far from São Paulo." Kleinrup was praying they'd be able to get out of the city in time.

"Good old Precov," she said half-heartedly.

"Yes, Louise. I agree. Now, let's go. We have things to do and people to avoid."

"But what about Greco?"

"He left São Paulo as soon as he heard of our change of plans. We're flying military."

They prepared to leave the safehouse when two anonymous Corollas made their way to the back entrance. Kleinrup was relieved that he had finally convinced Destrey to be reasonable. Destrey's own security detail would helicopter their way out of the city. They would provide their comrades on the ground air support all the way to their destination. Fionnuala and Callender were set to find whoever was assigned to kill Destrey.

Kleinrup pointed at the first Corolla. "That's our ride, *Madame*. The second Corolla will troll downtown with Fionnuala and Callender until we're safely out of São Paulo."

"You know something, *Frenchie*?" Kleinrup said.

"No. What?" Destrey was expecting Kleinrup to complain about her pigheadedness.

"For an intelligent broad, you can be pretty stupid sometimes." Kleinrup smiled to himself.

"I think… I'm gonna keep my mouth shut." Destrey had no quick repartee. He had a point.

"That's my girl. Here, wear this hat and sunglasses."

Destrey did what she was told. Reluctantly. This James Bond stuff was, at best, a waste of time, but at this point she wasn't so sure anymore.

"One more thing," Kleinrup said. "Give me your phone. I'm going to disable it until we're safely airborne."

"Whatever you say." Destrey decided not to argue with him.

"That's my girl."

"Stop that."

31

"The Russians appeared at the back of the safehouse as Destrey and Kleinrup were making their way to the back entrance. Two anonymous-looking Corollas screeched to a halt. Kleinrup and Destrey rushed into the back seat of the second car. Much to Destrey's surprise, their getaway car looked ready for the scrapyard.

"Will it make it?" Destrey asked nervously.

"You mean our mode of transportation?" Kleinrup snorted. "Not at all like your Jag back in Adela?"

"It's Ste-Adèle. She's the patron saint of those poor schmucks who can't remember their girlfriend's hometown."

"Darn! That hurts!"

"Seriously, will this old clunker make it?"

"Don't let appearances fool you. We don't want to attract any attention."

"Okay, if you say so."

Destrey tried to put on a good show. This caper wasn't her first rodeo. However, today, her life was in jeopardy. In a very personal way. She was beginning to understand the people behind the scenes in São Paulo. They meant business and the threat was real. Destrey began to realize what few people go through in a lifetime: a real possibility of being murdered in cold blood and to know about it in advance. The fear she now felt sent her back in time. To a difficult period of her life when she was working on the highest rung of the corporate ladder. She nearly didn't make it.

If it hadn't been for her husband, God knows what her life would look like today. He had stood by her and had done everything he could to protect her from those who wanted Destrey out of the way.

Destrey reminded herself that corporate life wasn't at all how it was portrayed on TV. Business environments were almost always misportrayed. They were messy and unsafe.

Kleinrup was also on high alert. The Russian drivers could have been spotted. He was almost as frightened as the woman sitting beside him. Kleinrup realized some time ago that her life meant everything to him. More than his own. He wasn't the independent bachelor he was a few years ago when they first met. That part of him was long gone and replaced by a deep sense of responsibility and vulnerability. Two incompatible emotions, yet, they lived in the same man and in the same moment.

Destrey stammered, "Back in Jerusalem, the world was in trouble. Not just me. I could handle that. But today's different. It's me they want. It's very personal, isn't it?"

Kleinrup turned to her.

"Look at me."

"No."

Kleinrup gently touched her chin.

"I know what you're going through, Louise."

"I'm alone. My late husband promised he wouldn't let that happen. He said he'd be there for me. For the rest of my life. He promised. In Vegas, when we got married a second time, he swore."

"Your husband didn't leave you, Louise. He died. That's different. But I'm alive and I'm here."

She turned to him, barely keeping her tears in check.

"Tell me what you see. You can do that better than anyone else on this planet. What is my soul telling you?"

She sighed. "I know what you're thinking."

"So? Tell me," Kleinrup said.

"It's just... I'm afraid of losing you... too. I don't think I could go through that again."

"I'm not going anywhere." His voice was gentle.

They both stared into each other's eyes.

"You're my job," Kleinrup said "You're my reason for living. My life and my future."

"I haven't heard anything quite so romantic..."

"Right now, *Frenchie*, I have a job to do." Kleinrup kissed her on both cheeks.

"Oh, God. Why is it always when the world is going to shit that we find each other?"

Kleinrup shrugged. "I don't know. Karma?"

Suddenly, Destrey sat straight up.

"I just remembered something. What about my niece? I forgot to check up on her."

"She's on her way," Kleinrup replied, amused. "She's safe. Her husband is also on his way. He's as good as home. No problem there. Your call to his boss made sure he'd be hauling his ass out of Brazil in a hurry."

TG's Chairman Precov commissioned four of the finest operatives he could find in São Paulo to evacuate Destrey and Kleinrup. Two agents per vehicle. One driver, one navigator. They were professionals with no names.

"Precov said they were good. They also know their way around São Paulo traffic."

"That's a relief," Destrey said.

"They're also professional killers. On our side."

Destrey shuddered. "I'm not sure what to say about that."

"There're the real deal. The kind of men who have no qualms about bending a few of God's Ten Commandments."

Destrey pretended not to hear.

"Can you tell me where we're going?" She was looking at the city, thinking that perhaps this would be her last chance to appreciate São Paulo in all its splendor.

Kleinrup sighed. He put his cell phone back in his shirt pocket. "Apparently, there's a change in plans. We're heading for the city of Campinas. There's a private airstrip just south of the city's airport."

"Why? What's happening?"

"I don't know."

"You look nervous," Destrey said.

"I'm hoping we can make it without being noticed," Kleinrup said. "Fortunately, Fionnuala and Callender are running interference.

They'll find the shooters."

Destrey looked nervous. "You sure about that?"

"I'm not too sure about anything anymore. I warned them to leave the city as soon as possible."

The idea of finding the shooters had a million-to-one shot of happening. Stopping them from doing harm to Destrey was also ironic since the city was going to be destroyed along with millions of other *Paulistanos*, from crumbling buildings, failing infrastructure, fire or gas explosions.

"Are they still looking for them?" Destrey asked.

"So far, Fionnuala and Callender are still at it, even though I've told them to get out."

Kleinrup had good reasons to keep the ex-MI6 agents safe: the whereabouts of his father, Horace Kleinrup, was still a mystery, apparently not deceased and obviously not buried in the UK. A good reason to have another conversation with the agents, a conversation that he needed to have as soon as possible.

Kleinrup reminded himself that Horace Kleinrup was the former director of MI6, and, for that reason, he would never underestimate the lengths his father would go to to protect his wife and family.

The Russian driver was paying attention to his navigator's instructions because it was fairly easy to get lost in São Paulo traffic. The navigator was working with a road map as well as a GPS. In past evacs, route guidance proved efficient and stealthy. This time, they would be hiding in plain sight in the midst of the world's biggest traffic jam.

"I think I know what our drivers are doing," Destrey said to herself.

"Don't tell me you're taking Russian lessons from Precov?"

Destrey understood a few words here and there. Right on R. Diogo Vaz, then right again on Av do Estado, exit on Av Dr. Francisco Mesquita, then back to Av do Estado.

"Tried it once. Too difficult," Destrey said.

The other Russian turned to Kleinrup and told him that Campinas was about one hundred kilometers away via Rodovia dos Bandeirantes. Though the drive would normally take about an hour, stealth required a slower approach.

"We'll need to be patient," Kleinrup said.

Destrey sighed. "Do we have a choice?"

32

Batista had met Destrey earlier in the week and had dismissed the woman and her foolish ideas as overly emotional. He had accused her of being paranoid and putting the future of his city in jeopardy. However, now, high atop the Infinity Tower that Batista happened to own lock, stock and barrel, the man wasn't so sure anymore. Could he have misjudged her?

"It's the way she..." Batista started to say to himself.

"What?" Carlo Gutierrez said. Carlo was Batista's son-in-law and chief critic. He believed he could do anything his father-in-law did, but infinitely better.

"The way she said... good luck," Batista said intently.

"What are you trying to say?" Carlo wasn't following.

"I think she wanted me to understand that I was somehow taking my life and my family's lives into my own hands." Batista had doubts.

"Don't you do that every day?" Carlo had no idea where this was going.

"No, I don't," he shot back. "I would never consciously put myself or my family in jeopardy. Never. I generally don't take risks." That was the first time Carlo heard his father-in-law admit his aversion to risk-taking.

"Of course, you do. You love risks. You're known throughout the world for making bets on the market that nobody else would."

"It's a myth, Carlo. Risk-taking is for amateurs. Whatever you've learned in Boston about risk is wrong. It's also lazy because it means you haven't done your homework. In this business, as in any other, making money is about making sure the odds are on your side. Just like the casinos. The house always wins. It has to, otherwise it wouldn't survive. You see Carlo, I'm the house. The house must win even if it means fixing the game in your favor. If you think about it, we're here today because it's fixed."

"I understand probabilities better than you think, David, but what does that have to do with this Destrey woman?"

"When you're in the business of winning, and someone tries to warn you about losing everything, if you don't listen, then you would be a fool not to. It's that simple."

"I wouldn't worry about her," Carlo said.

"That's exactly what she said." Batista remembered her words.

"I don't..." Carlo was lost and it showed. Carlo couldn't figure out what Batista was trying to tell him.

"She said she wouldn't waste her time with me. But, and this is the important part, Carlo, I felt she was sad."

Batista surprised himself with his own words. It suddenly occurred to him that he had missed an opportunity to learn something important. Not necessarily about earthquakes and natural disasters, but something infinitely more important. He had passed up an opportunity to relate to someone exceptional. A woman who was at least his equal, if not better, smarter and oh so quick.

"There's one aspect, David, one small but significant tidbit you seem unable to factor in."

"And what would that be?" Batista asked, unimpressed.

"She can't predict earthquakes. Science can't even predict the weather let alone what nature cooks up to shrink the population. There are too many variables in play. Hell, we can't even predict when the rain's coming back to São Paulo."

"That's where you're wrong, Carlo. What if that woman is the house for another game, and she's trying desperately to tell me to leave the table and run while I can?"

Carlo sighed. "This woman, David, she's nothing. It would take divine intervention to do so, and think about it, David. You really think God is speaking through her? What really matters is what this city is about to become. The economy is, as far as I'm concerned, the only reality we should care about." Carlo Gutierrez sounded pretty sure of himself, especially for a man who didn't know crap about geology or theology. He was an economist, fresh out of Harvard. To top it off, the man couldn't read people if his life depended on it. Carlo Gutierrez was basically clueless, but then again, he was the boss's son-in-law.

"The whole thing gave me the creeps. All I remember and all I know for sure, is that I wanted to get the hell out of there." Batista remembered how he had played the tough guy. It was an illusion

Destrey hadn't bought into. Batista understood from the first moment he met her that she was reading him, and he couldn't do anything about it. Bravado or not, she was dominant.

Carlo rolled his eyes. "It's eco-propaganda and she wants us to fail."

"I don't think so Carlo. She's not like that. She looked at me. She saw through me. She was handling me like I was a kid back in elementary school."

Carlo got up and Batista noticed he was about to make a call.

"Sit down, Carlo. I'm not finished." Batista was angry. Carlo didn't argue. His father-in-law could be unpredictable as well as dangerous.

"She was the teacher and I was the pupil. Do you understand that, Carlo?"

"Sure. I understand." The problem was that Carlo wasn't listening any longer. He was trying to come up with a plan to get out. As far away from Batista as he could.

"To be honest Carlo, I ran away from her as fast as I could. I wanted to forget everything she said, because I didn't want to believe it could happen. You know me, I never flinch, and I certainly don't run away from anyone's words. No one can do that to me. That is, of course, until a few days ago."

Carlo looked even more confused. "Why do you say that? I know for a fact the Americans are not our friends. All they want is our resources and they want guys like you out of the way. They probably don't care if the city or the country goes belly up."

David Costa Batista had many faults, one of them being arrogance. However, today, he wasn't feeling as sure about himself or the future of his empire.

"Carlo, listen very carefully. This is important. You can still learn a few things now and then. A few days ago, I met a force of nature. That woman changed everything." Batista's voice was tired. "You still don't understand, do you, Carlo?"

"What's to understand? Destrey is a nobody. Besides, she won't be bothering us any longer."

"What do you mean?"

"Nothing, David. I swear. I just heard she was leaving town."

"You sure about that?" Batista didn't believe him.

"You're not thinking of meeting her again, are you?" Carlo asked.

Batista could smell a rat a mile away. "I can see why I like you, Carlo. Your advice is always bang-on."

"What?" Carlo didn't understand. His boss was being sarcastic.

"I damn well want to talk to her now. I have a strong feeling about that woman." Batista had finally changed his mind about Destrey. He was now sure of it.

Carlo shook his head. He never quite understood how the mind of his father-in-law worked. "I don't believe this."

"*Senhora* Silva?" Batista called his secretary to his office.

The older woman came in the office suite. "Yes sir?"

That's all Batista had to do. Ask. Every wish was quickly executed. Because like half a dozen other billionaires of São Paulo, he ruled his empire like a living, breathing God.

"*Senhora* Silva, I would like to talk to this Destrey woman," said Batista "Even better, I'd like to see her again. Tell her that I'm ready to listen. There's no time to waste."

"Yes, of course."

Batista noticed the concern on Carlo's face. "You don't get people,

Carlo. You only understand money."

"Oh, for God's sake, David. You can't be serious," Carlo said.

"On the contrary. I'm deadly serious. Now that I think of it, that woman was sorry for me. Me! Can you imagine that?"

Carlo rolled his eyes. "So what? I'm sorry for you every day of the week and twice on Sundays."

Batista let that pass. "Let me explain it to you in terms you can understand."

"I'm listening." Carlo folded his arms in defiance.

"This Destrey woman, she wasn't lying. She might be wrong about this earthquake stuff, but—and it's very important you understand what I'm trying to tell you—she's a straight arrow. I know because it's all about motive. Remember, she was the one who had predicted the Jerusalem blast. Years before it actually happened. She singlehandedly saved millions of lives because she was relentless and because she cared for people."

Carlo didn't look impressed. "So? I can care. But that doesn't make me right about the end of the world."

"People, Carlo. She cared for my welfare."

"How do you know that?"

Batista sighed. "Carlo, you wouldn't know how to care for people even if your little heart wanted to. Do you know why your employees are asking—no, pleading with—me to transfer them out of your function?"

"Because they're lazy and because I push them hard." Carlo's voice was on edge.

Batista shook his head.

"I'm sorry to say this, but you're unbearable as a boss and that is also a scientific appraisal. You have blind spots as big as the Morumbi Stadium. We move your people around to other departments because they're loyal and important assets for my business."

Carlos began fidgeting, looking impatient. "So why do you keep me here as your number two?"

"Because I want you close to me, so I can save your ass from those who'd like to kill you. Besides, would I rather have trouble with my daughter or put up with you?"

"I don't understand."

Batista chuckled. "Your wife is right under your nose. She can make my life a living hell. You on the other hand, are a decent and honest man. I trust you to do your job. Working with you is a holiday compared to what Alexandra would have in mind for me if I ever cast you adrift."

Carlo almost flinched. "I don't need charity. I can find work anywhere in the world."

"I'm sure you can. I don't have any doubt about your skills," replied Batista. "But, I've wanted many times to tell you about your shortcomings. God knows I tried. You're still a young man. You have a lot to learn. Maybe one day you'll be able to deal with people and run my company." His focus then shifted. "But now, I must deal with this Destrey person. I have to know. There's something happening. If it's not an earthquake, it must be something else. She found something. I need to know what. And you need to smarten up."

Although Carlo had his own failings, his strength was not to take anything personal. No amount of feedback would deter him from doing his job. Somehow, words didn't reach his soul, as though he was deaf. This explained a lot about his management style, which was pretty much nonexistent.

Carlo sighed. "I think that's enough information about me for one day. Let's concentrate on the woman. The sooner we do this, the sooner we'll get back to business."

"She's trying to save my life, my family's future and my employees' livelihoods. Remember those people, Carlo? My employees? I count on them to drive this beast forward. I'm not the company, Carlo, they are. Remember that."

"But, what if she's completely wrong?" Carlo was a bit annoyed because he still didn't get it.

Batista nodded and leaned forward. "I understand what you're saying, Carlo. But think very hard about this. What if she's right?"

33

"Miss Amoedo?"

"Yes."

"I'm patching you through to *Madame* Destrey. Please stay on the line. If we get cut off, I will call you again."

"Hello?" Louise's voice was muffled by the background noises of the street.

"*Madame* Destrey, my name is Cristiane Tarsila Amoedo. I work at the university as a theoretical physicist."

"Okay," Destrey said. "What can I do for you?"

"I wanted to know about the…"

"Earthquake. Is that the word you're looking for?"

"Yes."

"And you want to know if it's a joke or for real?"

"Yes. Yesterday, I was at a police station in the middle of making a complaint when an earthquake nearly…"

"Killed you."

"Was that the earthquake you are warning us about?" Amoedo asked.

"The answer is no, Miss Amoedo. That wasn't even a nibble."

Amoedo was confused. "I don't understand, I'm sorry."

"What I'm trying to tell you and all of your countrymen is the following. Get the hell out of the city. Every day you stay here is another day closer to the big one. The day you will very possibly die."

Amoedo was too stunned to respond.

"Listen," Destrey said patiently, "you're probably young enough to understand that you have your whole life to look forward to, so take my advice. Leave now. Save yourself. Save your family."

"I'm sorry to have bothered you, *Madame* Destrey."

"You're not. I'm just doing my job." Destrey tried to sound reasonable.

"I understand."

"No, you don't. This isn't about probabilities, it's about your life." Amoedo could hear the edge in Destrey's voice. "In fact, it's about the lives of all those people you work with at the university. Tell them. Save them. Save who you can, but you've got to get the hell out of the city for your own sake. Right now. Understand?"

Amoedo felt a sinking feeling in the gut of her stomach. Reality was hitting her in the face. "Yes," Amoedo replied unsteadily. "I must leave."

Destrey waited for more. The woman wasn't finished yet.

"May I ask you a question, *Madame* Destrey?"

"Yes."

"When will you be leaving the city?"

"I'm trying to do that as we speak," Destrey said.

Amoedo looked out her office window. Automobiles everywhere. As far as her eyes could see. Through the smog. Through the white smoke from thousands of vehicles. Through the noise, through the honking and yelling.

34

INFINITY TOWER

R. LEOPOLDO COUTO DE MAGALHÃES JÚNIOR

700 ITAIM BIBI

SÃO PAULO

David Costa Batista was contemplating the unimaginable. Destrey had provided information he should have taken seriously. He admitted to himself that only a stupid man did that. Someone vain and conceited. A man who owned one of the largest corporations in South America and thought he knew everything. In the end, Batista had finally come to his senses as far as Destrey was concerned.

"If it wasn't for my daughter, I'd toss you off this building myself." Batista was looking at Carlo Gutierrez. His daughter's most recent mistake. He should have stood up to his daughter and stopped the marriage.

"I swear, David. I didn't do anything," Carlo said timidly. "I didn't call anyone. No one's going to hurt Destrey. I promise."

"Don't lie to me, *maricas*."

"I'm no coward. Whatever I do is for the company," Carlo said.

"Be a man for once." Batista was angry. "Have a little self-respect." Batista was ready to pull the plug on his boy genius.

Batista's voice carried his fury through walls. Carlo Gutierrez had never before seen his father-in-law so angry. But what frightened him most was how Batista could manage to change his attitude from an uncontrollable rage to a serene state of mind almost instantaneously.

"Shut up and listen," Batista said. "Get in touch with your gutter friends and call it off. Whatever they're planning for the Destrey woman, call it off. I want her alive. If you have to put yourself between the bullet and the woman, do it. I really don't care what happens to you. Now go. Get your ass out of here, and do as you are told."

Carlo looked pale and sickly.

Batista shook a finger as his son-in-law. "By the way, if something happens to her, if I find out she was harmed in any way, I'll have my federal friends lock you up in a hole and you'll never be heard of again."

Carlo Gutierrez got up and walked out his father-in-law's office suite. Carlo was now sprinting toward his own office. There, he had a special book of contacts he'd hidden in his wall safe. He quickly dialed the combination and retrieved his little black book and a burner phone. He had handwritten a number of confidential numbers. They included passwords, names of high-priced hookers he could call anytime of the day or night, his providers of exotic drugs and finally, one last number: São Paulo's chief of police. His private number.

He found what he was looking for. He hoped the Chief would

stop the hit on Destrey. If it wasn't too late. Carlo almost prayed to God for help. But the Harvard man didn't believe in God or any other deity. Carlo was all about money, fast cars, Rolex gold watches and young women who always said yes.

Carlo dialed the number he found in his little black book.

"Answer, for God's sake!" he yelled at his cell.

The phone kept ringing and ringing.

That's impossible, he thought to himself. *He has to answer.*

"It's his private number, for Chrissake!" His secretary overheard him and dashed to his rescue.

She had barely opened his office door when he yelled at her to shut the door and leave him alone.

"What's wrong with this number?" Carlo wondered to himself.

He redialed the same number over and over again, with the same results. The Chief wasn't picking up his calls.

"I know, I'll call his office. They'll know where to find him." He sounded a bit more positive. This was an acceptable alternative.

He called 190, the emergency number for Brazil.

"This is 190. How can I help you?" the agent asked dispassionately.

"I'd like to talk to the chief of police. This is an emergency."

The operator had never had this particular type of call before. He was caught by surprise, but he immediately crafted an acceptable response.

"May I take a message? I don't have access to the chief of police right now, but I will pass your request on to my superior."

"You don't understand." Carlo was pleading. "This is an emergency. I need help here. I need to talk to the Chief."

"Tell me where you are, and I'll send a squad car to your location.

The officers will see what they can do to help you."

"No, no, no," Carlo said. "I want the chief, right now. On the line."

"Could you at least tell me what's going on?" The operator was going into handling mode.

Carlo could only imagine how the operator would react if he told them the truth. More importantly, what would the operator say to his boss and the police?

Listen, I've got this guy who wants to call off a hit on a woman.

Yeah. That's right. A hit.

No, Sir. I'm not kidding. I believe the call is real.

Her name? Let me see. It's foreign. A Louise Destrey.

That's right. Name finishes with t r e y. Des-trey. You got that?

Yes, Sir. I believe him.

He wants us to find the assassin before he murders Des-trey.

No, that's not all. There's more. He says the assassin is a cop! He said we should be careful because the killer will not stop until he terminates the woman.

Yes, Sir. His exact words.

Gutierrez cut the communication off before he would make a fool of himself. There was only one alternative left to him.

He decided to leave the building, the city and the country before it was too late. The Infinity Tower wasn't a safe place anymore. It took him just a few minutes to empty his safe. He told his secretary he was on a special errand for the boss.

"Don't call me. If I need you, I'll call you," Carlo told her.

A few moments later, Batista tried to reach him, but Carlo wasn't answering his cell. His car was still in the garage. Batista thought he couldn't have gone far without his Aston Martin.

"Where is he?" Batista asked Carlo's secretary.

She told him that Carlo was on an errand.

That night, Batista told his daughter that he would find Carlo, but for now, they had to prepare to leave the city. Batista's private jet was fueled and ready for takeoff. There wasn't a moment to lose. Batista pushed everyone around. He wanted to get his family out of harm's way. He had already sent a memo to his executives to evacuate his employees from São Paulo.

He tried to reach Destrey, but to no avail. There was no answer.

35

Alexander and Willy were off hunting for the assassin. Just minutes after leaving the American safehouse, the Russians produced a few leads they could count on.

The Russians were well aware of Armery's activities. He was formerly known in MI6 as Sir Henry Blake, or Director Blake. The traitor, as Callender liked to call the bastard, had singlehandedly managed to pull together from the São Paulo police, an elite force of assassins. The well-paid volunteers would extricate from the city streets the undesirables taking potshots at the ruling class and their businesses. Amnesty International used the technical term 'extra-judicial killings' for this type of murder. Local journalists talked of mass murders by the São Paulo police force and suggested a civil war could erupt at any time.

For the next few hours, Fionnuala and Callender would troll the city for people who would gladly rat on their colleagues for the privilege of staying alive.

The Russians had turned out to be very useful. They had had extensive run-ins with the São Paulo police and in doing so, had managed to pay off high-ranking police officers to look the other way. Those who would sell their souls for a few rubles would be used over and over again to keep secrets out of sight and out of mind.

Because money in São Paulo was the only asset that was truly valuable, important people could buy anything they needed to run their business operations smoothly, without any interference from government employees, journalists and rabble-rousers.

Since Fionnuala and Callender didn't have that many rubles to dish out for information, they would rely on old-school conventions and beat the living daylights out of their captives until they cooperated.

First name on their list was Captain Joao Pedro Pastor. He could be found at the Marsilac police station. Marsilac being one of the poorest districts in São Paulo, Fionnuala and Callender figured they'd get lucky, because the poor would, more often than not, attract informal police actions. If their thinking was right, the local captain would surely send them in the right direction. The Russians had had many encounters with Pastor.

"He not Armery, Pastor, he, dickhead," The Russian driver said. He laughed so hard he nearly lost control of the Corolla. "You know what I say?"

The Russian driver assured the Brits they'd get what they were looking for from the captain.

All they had to do was to lure Pastor from his hiding place and start working on him. They had little time and very little patience at this point. Unfortunately for Captain Pastor, the Fionnuala and Callender wrecking team would soon establish a deadly relationship with the good captain.

Forty-five minutes later, they found the captain. Luckily for Fionnuala and Callender, the captain was having his morning coffee at the local coffee shop.

The Russian driver knew him well and volunteered to invite him to a friendly *tête-à-tête* with a potential customer who had a lot of money to invest.

The captain eagerly and immediately accepted the invitation, and followed the Russian to the waiting Corolla. The driver drove off to a quieter location, for a discreet conversation.

Captain Pastor was almost salivating at the thought of another payoff. Things were looking up for the policeman, because he needed cash to entertain his newest mistress.

Although Captain Pastor's greed was boundless, he was suspicious of foreigners. Pastor found them difficult to read. In fact, he would often say that they all looked alike.

In general, his suspicions toward strangers were often well founded. Especially these days, as the press was always looking for a good story. Catching a cop on the take was always a front-page story. But Pastor was too old to fall for a journalist's bait. However, an introduction from his old friends from the Russian Embassy was almost fool-proof. The Russians were always on the look-out for opportunities to make a bit of cash on the side. If there was real money involved, Pastor summarized that he could count on the Russians. He felt he was on the right track.

Still, he told himself, *I will be careful.*

The Russian driver told Pastor that his clients were very picky about their identities and that's why they needed a more discreet location to talk about business.

Pastor's need for money and his greed led him to believe the Russian.

Yes indeed, things are looking up, Pastor said to himself. *Today has taken a turn for the better.*

Although life as a police captain wasn't complicated, Pastor's job wasn't a stroll in the park either. On any given day, life in the favellas could come crashing down on people's lives, including his own. The violence toward his fellow policemen could be deadly. Not that they didn't deserve it. His police force were certainly not angels. Still, being a policeman could be hazardous to life and limb.

In the end, Pastor accepted the Russian's invitation to a face-to-face meeting with the foreigners.

What could go wrong? Pastor wondered.

36

They'd been summoned and, not unlike good Catholics, had reluctantly attended the priest's invitation.

The dozen or so young men and women sat a table that had seen better times. In bad times, the church's basement was a safe haven for those who had none. If truth be told, the church as a whole was in disrepair. Our Lady of Mount Carmel was looking more like a beaten down warehouse than a place of worship. It had taken more than its share of bullets since the 2006 riots, and was in dire need of funds to keep it afloat.

"Why did you call this fucking meeting?" Eduardo Donato Moreira demanded. The young gangster was the leader of one of the biggest and strongest gangs in São Paulo. Officially, the gang leaders never met. Unofficially, they got together on a regular basis to make sure everyone was kept in line, because gang warfare wasn't good for business.

However, they all knew from experience that an official sit-down at Our Lady of Mount Carmel meant trouble was on the way. Whether because of future police involvement into their affairs, an army initiative to clean up a *favela* for a public show of strength, a new player gathering strength or a mafia-led incursion into gang territories, there was always someone who used the gangs for their own agenda. Not surprisingly, a call from the priest was almost always followed by trouble.

"I called it because I had no choice," said Father Latu.

"Excuse me, Father, but I don't have any time to waste on a prayer meeting," Moreira said arrogantly. "Why are we here?"

Everyone turned to the priest. He didn't respond, didn't react, he just sat there as though he was waiting for God to inspire him.

"Come on! What the fuck's going on?"

Father Latu stood up. "I have money."

"Now you've got my attention, Father. What do I have to do to get that money? Want me to pray on my knees? How about an Ave Maria? I know, I'll do confession. I'll tell you everything. I swear. Do I get my prize now?" Moreira laughed and the other gang leaders joined in, but deep down they respected the priest more than the young man who was trying to impress the audience.

"Please sit down, Eduardo," the priest ordered.

Eduardo Donato Moreira was a vicious little rat with a God complex. His five-foot four frame did not reveal his malicious personality. Rumors that he had murdered two policemen when he was fourteen years old solidified his reputation as a gang leader, a tough guy and a man who would do anything to get his way. Anything and everything were on the table at all times.

Moreira banged his fists on the table.

"You will listen to me," the priest said calmly, "just this once. This is a matter of life and death."

Moreira couldn't believe it. "Are you fucking serious, old man?"

The priest looked directly into the young man's soul, the way he had done when the gang leader was barely five years old. Old habits didn't die and so Moreira sat and waited for the priest to have his say.

"I have information concerning the lives of your mothers, fathers, sisters and brothers. Their lives are in jeopardy." Father Latu's voice was grave.

"What are you talking about?" Moreira had one weakness: his younger sister, Fatima, who was under his protection. Anyone coming too close to her would disappear and never be heard of again.

Father Latu glared at Moreira. "I said quiet. This is bigger than anything you have seen in your lifetimes."

Everyone was caught by surprise by the priest's sudden change in demeanor. The priest had never talked to them like that before. After all, they were his children ever since they were born. Many had been left to their own devices to survive on the streets of one of the most violent cities in the world. The priest had protected them from the death squads who would take them off the streets of São Paulo. Most of those abducted were never found. UNICEF reports underestimated when talking of more than four to six hundred children killed each year.

Father Latu continued. "I also want to tell you that your own lives are in danger. Right now."

The room remained silent. They knew there was more to come.

Father Latu lifted his satchel to the table. He took out a small bottle of cheap cognac from the bag and proceeded to take a swig from the half-empty bottle.

"I really need a drink," he said. Father Latu had never before displayed any human frailties in public. Something was up.

Father Latu took a breath. "I never thought I'd be saying this, never. Our city is going to be destroyed and everyone still in the city by the end of the week will most certainly die."

No one said anything until Janice Lima, sitting in the back, started to giggle. As her chuckle morphed into pure laughter, her large and ample breasts shook uncontrollably as they took flight from her tiny brassiere and were set free, and in so doing, encouraged the other gang leaders to laugh hysterically. It took but a moment for everyone to burst out laughing. Uncontrolled hilarity. Pure joy. For some, it had been a long time since someone had successfully made them laugh. Truly laugh, to tears. An unimaginable sense of happiness permeated the church's basement and its occupants.

The priest wasn't surprised or disappointed by their cheerfulness. He reminded himself that he too had a hard time believing what he was about to say. It wasn't uncommon for kids to behave strangely when faced with unbelievable news. Because Destrey's news was indeed difficult to swallow.

Eventually the gang members settled down. A few were wiping their tears away while others were paying closer attention to Father Latu, who wasn't laughing at all.

"Please, Father, what can we do? What can I do to help you?" Lima said.

In a very short period of time, Lima had proved herself worthy of being a gang leader. She had gained respect on the streets. Lima was well known for her irresistible charm as well as for her deadly mastery of the double edge knife.

"You can start by asking your twin sisters to do the samba." Moreira sneered.

Lima moved like a panther landing on the table in front of Moreira. She was pointing her special knife a few centimeters from Moreira's good eye.

"You want to be totally blind?" Lima's voice was softer than her stare.

Moreira didn't answer.

"I know you want to apologize. I just can hear it."

Again, Moreira said nothing.

"Open your filthy mouth and repeat after me: I am sorry, Janice."

Moreira didn't hear a word she said. He could lose everything if she wanted to. It would only take a thought to make it happen.

"Janice, leave the boy alone," implored the priest. "He didn't mean any disrespect. He's just trying to impress you. That's all. Put the knife away and please get back to your seat."

"You want these, don't you, Moreira?" She shook her breasts right in his face.

Moreira kept his good eye on the knife.

Lima wouldn't hurt him. They all got that. She knew him from way back, as far as she could remember. They were almost friends. She jumped off the table and got back to her seat while smiling to herself.

Moreira stood up and looked at the priest. "I'm going to leave right now if you don't tell me what the fuck's going on."

"Speak for yourself, asshole," Lima mumbled.

Father Latu hesitated a moment before speaking. "Let me tell you a story. This story is quite preposterous and almost impossible to believe."

The gang leaders were all ears.

"First things first. Let me call Denis. I'm sure he's not far away." The priest started to dial Denis Planter's number when, without warning, Planter strolled in the room as if on a walk in the park.

Father Latu looked at him. "I was about to tell them a story."

"Fine by me, Father, please go ahead," Planter said.

Denis Planter was more than respected. He was the man who had caught a police chief in the act of killing a federal district attorney. He had broadcast the crime on the Internet making him the first gang leader to go digital. The same police chief had murdered his fiancée. Like many others in the room, he had a personal vendetta against the business community and its government. Planter was, by all who knew him, the most dangerous man in São Paulo.

The room went utterly silent. Planter sat by the priest and said nothing more.

Father Latu proceeded to explain how he had first met the lady who could predict things. The same woman who had told world leaders what would happen to Jerusalem more than a year before it actually happened. The priest explained what she knew about São Paulo and when she believed it would happen.

"She said São Paulo will be destroyed by a big earthquake," said Father Latu.

"I've met her," Planter said. "She's the real thing. I'm sorry Father, please go on."

"She said it had something to do with the water shortages and the deforestation of our great forest. She said it would be a devastating event. Mother Nature's worst nightmare. The collateral damage will be in the millions."

"What's this collateral mean, Father?" Janice asked.

"Innocent people dying because of the quake."

The priest paused for a few moments to let the message sink in.

Planter was eyeing Janice. "I know you have a question, Janice. I can see it in your face."

"Do you believe this woman, D?" she asked Planter point-blank.

"Her name is Louise Destrey. She works in Boston but she was born in Canada. Look her up on the Internet."

Everyone got busy on their phones.

"I don't understand," Ignacio Perez said while still scrolling through hundreds of pages describing who she was.

"What is it you don't get, Ignacio?" Planter was counting on Ignacio to help him. He needed him to corroborate the Destrey woman's credentials.

While Perez was a chubby and rather invisible character, he was known to manage his affairs through the Internet. He was more than familiar with technology. He was using tech to blackmail businesses to pay huge ransom fees to un-hack their computers.

Perez shook his head. "This woman is like... everywhere. I mean she can have the Internet all to herself and it still wouldn't be enough. I'm curious D, how did you come to know her?"

"I spoke to her about Jerusalem," Planter said.

"Why?"

Planter shrugged. "I wanted to know if something like Jerusalem could happen here, in my city."

"And?"

"She came here. At this table. Then she told me a story I didn't want to believe. She said I didn't have to. But she told me I had a responsibility to save the children, because they can't make that kind of decision on their own."

"What do you mean by decision, D?" Lima asked.

"Leave." Planter didn't raise his voice or try to make a big deal about it.

"Leave?" Perez repeated.

"Yeah. Leave." Planter looked down.

"When?"

"Now. This afternoon. Tomorrow morning. Now, Perez."

"When are you leaving, D?"

"I'm not." Planter remained cool and in control.

"So, you don't believe this crazy story?"

"Yes, I do. I just have some unfinished business with a few cops and the mayor."

37

Sensing the cop's uneasiness, Callender nodded to the Russian driver.

"Practically there, *Capitao*," the driver said in Portuguese.

His co-pilot agreed. "Soon."

From Captain Pastor's perspective, it was going to be a long drive. All that mileage for a friendly conversation. It didn't make sense. But then again, the foreigners had money. They were calling the shots. In fact, if his memory served him right, it wasn't going to be that long a drive after all.

I should have known better, he thought to himself. Being a policeman for more than thirty years, he knew what driving in São Paulo meant: a slow sport or a cheap alternative to a helicopter ride. Either way, no problem, as far as he was concerned. The captain wanted to believe the story he was told, even if it was too good to be true. In the off-chance it was real he would take the risk, see it through. It could change his life.

Pastor wanted to make sense of what seemed to be an unbelievable opportunity.

The foreigners chose him, a low-level civil servant. A nobody.

They needed him, the Russian driver said. That kind of recognition didn't come Pastor's way too often. In actual fact, he couldn't remember the last time he felt that good about himself.

From the captain's point of view, the car ride to the reservoir could go both ways. It could be dangerous in ways he couldn't fathom. Or not. Although self-preservation was a necessity for a corrupt cop, the captain was being blindsided by the financial prospects that lay ahead. Although a well thought con job was being led by a couple of ex-spooks, Pastor clung to his belief that the Russians presented him with the real deal. In reality, Pastor was in the process of being kidnapped and he couldn't see it coming. He was blind. Even though his life depended on his survival instincts, he had effectively shut them down. He preferred to believe complete strangers than his own good sense. He was morphing into a victim: one step at a time, taking shape while ingesting the flaws he acquired throughout his career as a coward and a fraud.

Of his need to feel important, there was no doubt. Pastor's lack of self-esteem was proof enough of his career barreling into the gutter. Failure usually came as a common affliction. A common cold. But to actually feel good based on a lie, on a story a six-year-old kid wouldn't fall for, that was almost suicidal.

Nevertheless, Fionnuala and Callender counted on Pastor's shortcomings because they had based their strategy on one little known fact: humans lied. They lied all the time. They lied to their parents, their close friends, their teachers and co-workers, citizens as well as customers, and more importantly, humans lied to themselves. Which of course was Pastor's weakness. It could save him from dealing with the real world. That's why both Fionnuala and Callender believed Pastor was the perfect mark. He was basically weak.

Pastor looked at his watch. They had made good time. They were halfway to their destination and it had barely taken an hour. Despite the fact Pastor knew the distance between the police station and the reservoir, he still had doubts. He wondered about that. Why go all the way to the Billings Reservoir when an inconspicuous corner café would have done the job?

He had a lot of time to think about distance, drive time and money. Not surprisingly, each passing hour on the road made him a bit more uneasy and conflicted. Something wasn't quite right. The Russian driver was trying too hard. The captain didn't completely trust the two Russians nor did he fully understand why they had recommended him to these two foreigners.

To dispel the captain's doubts about the foreigners' intentions, the Russian driver reintroduced the element of money into the conversation. "They want conversation secret," the Russian said in Portuguese. The driver's heavy Russian accent made the captain think about his role in this business. "That's why they pay money," the Russian added while eyeing Pastor through his rear-view mirror.

Pastor wanted to believe he was entering a new phase in his life, one that would include large payoffs. His new Russian contact would want a payoff of his own. Pastor expected that. The cost of doing business in Brazil was anything but cheap. Nevertheless, maybe this encounter with the foreigners was a sign of things to come. A kind of promotion into the big leagues. He was going to be important at last.

"Yes, I understand," Pastor said in Portuguese. He tried to put on a happy face.

"The money is very good," the Russian co-pilot said, trying to reassure Pastor as well as remind him of his cut. "Very good money for you and me, *Capitao*. I know these people for years. They pay well."

Although Callender wasn't fluent in Portuguese, his in-ear translator was good enough to understand the gist of a conversation in as many as fifteen languages, which included Russian, Chinese and of course, Portuguese.

Fionnuala was pleased. Both Russians as well as the old Corolla played their part to a tee. No one would take a second look at a beaten down old wreck in São Paulo's mega traffic. The optics were perfect and Fionnuala was in his element: playing the long game. He'd learned early in his career that confidence must be earned for the con to succeed. Getting the mark to believe he was about to win the jackpot took patience and dexterity. Ironically, it could save Pastor's life if he bought into the con and talked. Unfortunately for Pastor, if the con didn't work out, Fionnuala and Callender would have to get the information another way. The Chicago way. Thus, the reservoir. The largest in São Paulo State. And the water. Callender's preferred method of removing evidence.

The Billings Reservoir covered more than 125 square kilometers or about 45 square miles. With a catchment area the size of Rhode Island, it was an excellent spot to get rid of people. The reservoir was said to be populated by large snakes, some more than five meters in length. The anacondas were nature's way of cleaning up. With no witnesses and no bodies left to identify, Fionnuala's plan B to dump the body in the reservoir was beginning to sound as attractive as plan A.

Still, Pastor had lingering doubts about the foreigners' real intentions. They'd been too quiet. They didn't even try to engage him in conversation. At least not yet.

If Pastor's doubts persisted, he could ruin his own chances of making it back home alive. Doubts meant fear, and fear could quickly turn into a shootout, as unpredictability was a surefire way to get someone killed.

Again, the driver made eye contact with Pastor through his rearview mirror. He said they were making good time.

"I understand and agree that these gentlemen need discretion. Very important," Pastor said, while caution and greed fought for supremacy.

Luckily for Fionnuala and Callender, greed won over reason and prudence. The cop's own little voice was telling him something was wrong. But it was either muzzled or simply canceled as he remembered that a big shot police captain shouldn't be afraid of anything, especially two elderly foreigners from God knows where.

The ride to the Billings Reservoir went relatively smoothly, even by São Paulo standards. One hour later, the Corolla reached its destination. Lanchonete da Rosa, a small bar and restaurant on the edge of the reservoir, lay ahead. A cool breeze would meet them at the edge of the pier while a young barmaid prepared herself to make a good tip.

"That wasn't as bad as I thought it would be," Fionnuala said. "The view is breathtaking."

"Big *represa*, good fishing," Pastor joked. His English was surprisingly good.

"You don't say?"

"I do, *senhor*." Pastor didn't get it. "*Desculpe senhor*. I am sorry. But what is expression... *you don't say?*"

Fionnuala backtracked. "It's a habit of mine, *senhor* Pastor. When I hear something new, I use this saying to express my surprise and my thanks for the information given to me."

"Then, *senhor*, you are very welcome. But let me tell you more." The captain was feeling a lot better for two reasons: first, he was in a public place, a bar with real customers. Two, he was glad he wasn't in uniform today. No one would ever know he had been here.

Fionnuala smiled. "I would welcome knowing as much as I can. Who knows, one day the information might come in handy."

"Very good, *senhor*. I have, in the past, been a traffic policeman. Long time. I tell you this now because I know every street in São Paulo. When traffic is grave, not like today, *hoje*, yes not today. *Hoje* very good. When traffic bad, we have *estacionamento*. How do you say, parking? A parking for hundred kilometers. More. Sometime, traffic dangerous. The heat, *senhor*. Dangerous. Drivers impatient. Weather make violent man angry. Today is good day. A walk in park, as you say in English. No heat. No traffic. No danger."

"Let's get a drink, Captain Pastor. I'm thirsty as hell. And then, we can get down to business. Yes?" Fionnuala asked.

"Great. I second that," Callender responded.

"You think we can get a sandwich here, Captain?" Fionnuala was purposefully marking his time.

"*Sim, claro*. Yes of course," Pastor said eagerly. "Best sandwiches."

"Don't tell me you want to eat again?" Callender wanted to sound annoyed at Fionnuala. "Is there a bottom to that stomach of yours?"

"What are you complaining about?" Fionnuala looked annoyed. "We are about to make a deal with this fine gentleman, and I think we should do that on a full stomach. Don't you think so, Captain Pastor?"

"Yes, *senhor*." Pastor was almost giddy at the idea of getting closer to his money.

"Okay," Callender said. "You win. Let's, by all means, get a meal while we're at it. Why not?"

The small establishment, Lanchonete da Rosa, a Gilligan's Island type of beach resort, was familiar to the Russians because they often came here after completing a job for their FSB (Russia's Federal Security Service) boss.

"Three beers and something to eat, *senhorita*, and give my two fine friends over there whatever they want," Fionnuala said. Turning to Callender, he proceeded to introduce the second chapter of the con.

"You know something, we haven't introduced ourselves," Fionnuala said.

"Quite right, William. Well, Captain, I'm Alexander. You can call me Alex. And my good friend here is William. You can call him Willy."

Pastor produced a proud grin. "I am Captain Joao Pedro Pastor. I very happy to be with you today. But, tell me, *senhors*, what is it you want from me?"

"Straight to business I see," Callender said.

Pastor didn't respond.

"All right then. Business it is. We do not require very much, *senhor*," Calender said. "In fact, we only need a wee bit of information as well as an introduction." Seeing Pastor's greedy face turn white, Callender added the bait. "For that small favor, and for other small favors in the future, we are in a position to pay you handsomely."

Pastor hesitated. "What is this *handsome*?" he asked.

"Here in my briefcase is half of what you will receive if the information you provide us is what we are looking for," Fionnuala said.

"May I see case, *senhor*?" Pastor was a bit puzzled by what the foreigners required from him.

Information! They have need for information. Money for information! Pastor thought to himself. Pastor was a fixer, not an informant. He would, in a manner of speaking, fix things in exchange for money. He didn't know how to deal with complex issues other than push people around whenever a client, willing to pay for his services, was in trouble. Pastor didn't understand why people would think he had any information of any real value. He only knew how to coax people into paying their debts, and the sooner the better. He also never understood how he could make money in exchange for what he knew, which he would freely admit was, at best, very little. At this moment, he was a bit lost.

What little intelligence Pastor had in his possession couldn't be worth all that much. He was so low on the totem pole, he wasn't privy to much of anything going on. His colleagues didn't think much of him nor did his subordinates. His peers believed his promotion to captain was a mistake. He was barely able to carry his functions as a simple beat cop, let alone understand how to be a captain. Pastor could feel his colleagues' contempt like a knife jabbing at his soul. This little excursion in the countryside was beginning to feel like a total bust.

Fionnuala opened the briefcase a few inches. There, stacked and neatly bound, lay wads of American one hundred-dollar bills. Fionnuala took a packet and ran through them, revealing hundred-dollar bills through and through.

The captain could smell the new bills. Pastor took a deep breath. The smell was intoxicating. The finest perfume in the world couldn't compete with the smell of money.

Fionnuala looked at Pastor. "This, my dear Captain, is what I meant by *handsomely*."

"I understand." Pastor's eyes were focused on the prize.

He couldn't believe his luck. So much money. He could do anything with that many *dinheiros*. The future flashed in front of his eyes. He could see himself with a beautiful young girl. She would be willing to do anything he craved. He couldn't make up his mind whether he wanted big or small breasts, blonde or brunette, underage or over eighteen. Too many choices. He salivated like a mad dog. He wanted it all.

"Captain," added Callender as Fionnuala closed the briefcase, "I must tell you there will be more. Much more. All you will need to do is tell us a few words, and you will have all the money you need for the rest of your life. We are prepared to make you a rich man."

"Why me, *senhor*?" Pastor asked. "How you know my name?"

Callender was about to respond when Fionnuala raised his right hand ever so slightly.

"Our Russian driver and his colleague sitting over there," he said, pointing at a table at the other end of the bar, "they know people who know people, and they pointed to you, Captain. A man who could help us."

The captain looked at the Russians and couldn't understand why they or anyone else would think he had any information people would be willing to pay for.

"You were highly recommended," Callender said. "I was given your name in utmost confidence. Consider this a pilot project."

The barmaid sauntered toward them and set the beers and a few *bauru* on the table.

"What's this, young lady?" Callender asked.

"*Bauru*," said the captain. "Is popular Brazil sandwich with cheese, *carne*… beef, tomato and *pepino*." He pointed at the cucumber. "They are good for you."

Callender thanked the young lady as he pressed a fifty-dollar bill between her perky, chocolate-colored breasts.

The cop noticed the foreigner's way with money. He wasn't counting. He probably had deep pockets.

"How many dollars, *senhor*?" Pastor asked, glancing at the briefcase.

"Today, ten thousand, Captain. Tomorrow, ten thousand. Next time we need you, ten thousand, and so on."

Pastor had never been close to so much money in his life. He felt a little dizzy. His mind couldn't process what was happening fast enough. Pastor chugged his beer in one shot. God, he was thirsty.

"What do you want to know, *senhor*?" Pastor asked as he eyeballed the briefcase.

"Someone from France is coming here, very soon," Callender said. "We don't want him to stay in Brazil. We need someone. A professional. A certain someone who is a professional at solving problems. We need the problem solved permanently. Can you help us, *senhor* Captain?"

Fionnuala and Callender's plan was simple but depended on information. The Brits wanted Pastor to introduce them to the assassins who were tasked to take down Louise Destrey. Pastor was the key. Destrey was either being hunted or about to be in the very short term.

"We want you to point us in the right direction."

The Brits wanted to get to the assassins before they got to her.

"We need you to help us find them."

The problem of finding a needle in the biggest haystack in South America wasn't lost on them. The Brits needed a shortcut. They needed to cut the monster's head.

"Your name, Captain Pastor, was provided through our Russians' network of friends."

Although Pastor was low on the totem pole, the Brits believed he was nevertheless connected to a network of high-ranking police officers who were responsible for terminating the city's undesirables. He was the weakest link.

The challenge was to make him talk. Get the cat out of the bag. Run off at the mouth and spill the beans.

"A professional. I see," Pastor said. "He will cost money, *senhor*. More."

"Yes, of course, Captain. But please understand that your fee doesn't include the professional's costs. The professional's pay is our problem. We'll take good care of him, I assure you, Captain. All the money we showed you goes directly into your pockets."

Pastor's philosophy about life was simple and straightforward. He always tried to stay away from dangerous information when he was in the presence of high-ranking police officers. That, he believed, would insulate him from threats to his own life. To do that, he needed to know as little as possible. Knowing too much about murders, targeted assassinations and kidnappings by his fellow police officers was hazardous to his health. Yet, Pastor knew who the assassins were, who they were after and when they were going to execute their plans, because people talked. High-ranking police officers would openly discuss their business in his presence, as if Pastor didn't exist. *Like a dog*, he thought to himself. *Because, I'm invisible, an insignificant individual.*

Pastor had to admit to himself that he did, in fact, know quite a lot. Information he didn't want to possess or share with anyone. By listening to these foreigners talk about him like that, Pastor started to believe he did have information of value.

Just a few words, he thought to himself. *That's all they want from me.* He now understood he was dealing with people who had unlimited resources.

"*Senhor*, the professional cost more. Dangerous business. I take risk. You understand I want to help, but need more money."

"Let me talk to my partner and see how we can accommodate you, Captain."

Callender and Fionnuala left the cop alone and walked toward the veranda. Meanwhile, Pastor debated whether or not he was asking too much money. If he was too greedy, he could jeopardize the whole deal.

Callender and Fionnuala returned to the table.

"Okay. Here's what we came up with," Callender said. "In return for a name and an introduction, we are willing to double your fee. If the name and the introduction work out, you will be leaving here with twenty thousand American dollars, cash, with another twenty thousand after we've concluded a deal with the professional you identified. The final count will add up to a cool forty thousand dollars. But remember this, Captain. We want the very best. One who is known to be the best in São Paulo. We will check him out. If he is not the best, you will not get the second payment or more projects like this one in the future. We want the best."

"I see," Pastor said.

"We want a man of experience and we want him now. This project is very important, Captain. If we succeed, we will have many more projects to offer you in the future."

"You want best *assassino* in São Paulo," said Pastor.

Callender smiled. "I would prefer to call him a man with a solution."

"I understand, *senhor*."

"We will deal with him personally because we will give him information he will need in order to do the job. There's only one way that will meet our standards. Our way, Captain."

The captain didn't reply.

"You won't have to do anything yourself, Captain. Just tell us who he is and make the introductions. Tell him we want to meet and that it will be worth his while."

"I understand."

"We must be sure that this meeting will be kept secret. We would also suggest you put your money in a safety deposit box. In a foreign bank. For example, Deutsche Bank."

"In a safety box. Yes. I understand, *senhor*."

Fionnuala placed the briefcase on the table between the bottles of beer.

"What if he refuses to see you?" Pastor asked.

Callender snorted. "Tell him for ten thousand dollars cash up front, he can make an exception. Or else the deal's off."

"You will pay him?" Pastor asked.

"Yes. But, we want a name and an introduction. That's all you have to do, and the forty thousand is all yours."

Pastor looked away.

"Why don't we finish our meal, Captain? Take your time. If we don't come to an agreement, we will simply find another. But we'll still be friends. Yes?"

Pastor swallowed hard. "Yes, of course, *senhor*. Friends."

The cop began to think about what could happen if word got out he was making his own deals and not letting his associates in on it. He'd be dead before the end of the day, and even though the forty thousand was a lot of money, he knew he wouldn't be able to spend a single *centavo* from his grave.

He wanted to do business with them. They seemed reliable and safe. If only he could do the job himself. No muss, no fuss, no nothing but a lot of cash in his pockets. He knew how to kill people. He'd done it a few times before. There was nothing to it. He was surprised when it got easier over time.

"I make a suggestion, *senhor*?" Pastor asked.

"Yes, of course, Captain."

"What would you say if I... would myself solve problem?"

"We were counting on you to say that, Captain. It shows me and my friend that we can trust you to do the job. In the future, we may very well ask you to do so. We would, of course, pay you more, but..."

Pastor leaned in. "But..."

"Our problem, Captain, is the Frenchman. Let's just say, he is most dangerous. A bad man. Trust me, *senhor* Captain, you want a professional for this job, and we want to keep you safe. The less you know, the better it is for everyone involved."

"I see," mumbled Pastor.

"But please *senhor*, let's finish our lunch," Callender said.

Callender turned and faced the bar. "Another round for everybody, *senhorita*." Callender looked again at Pastor. "Captain, do you wish another sandwich?"

"No. Thank you, sir." Pastor's appetite had faded.

The cop was tired. He didn't have a clue how to turn things around. If the foreigner was right, staying away from the job would be the best thing to do. On the other hand, introducing them to the professional they would be using was almost suicidal. One way or another, he wasn't going to spend his money. Dead men don't talk and they certainly don't spend. They just rot.

The beers were delivered promptly.

Pastor was processing. Should he refuse the foreigners' offer?

Fionnuala could read the cop like an open book. Pastor was thinking it over. He showed signs of wanting to pull out. A shame, really. Fionnuala believed the cop wasn't all bad. Callender could let him live. For a short while, anyway. The earthquake was right around the corner. Anyone left in the city would soon feel the wrath of the earthquake.

Unfortunately, Pastor was still thinking in circles. How could he get away with it? Maybe he could finagle a deal with his colleagues. The same colleagues he despised. The people who wouldn't give him the time of day. And what would he say to the cop who would do the job? Could he trust him to keep his mouth shut? No matter how hard he tried, Pastor always ended up where he started.

"It looks like you're having a hard time making up your mind, Captain," Callender said in a calm voice.

Pastor forced a polite smile. "Yes, *senhor*. Difficult decision. Danger with others. Very dangerous people."

Callender nodded. "I understand, Captain. Believe me, I've been in your shoes." He paused a moment before continuing. "There could be another way. A safer way. But, I'm not sure."

The relief on Pastor's face was obvious. "What, *senhor*? Please tell me."

Callender shook his head. "No. Now that I think about it, I don't think it would work."

"Tell me, *senhor*, please." Pastor was almost pleading.

"No. If you can't do it, then let's leave it at that. We will look elsewhere."

There was a long pause. Callender would wait for Pastor to make his next move. If he had one.

Finally, Pastor took a breath. "I like to help, but others... maybe not. Introduction is dangerous. My life, *senhor*, would be in danger."

"I perfectly understand, Captain." Callender was going to wait it out until there would be no other alternative left than to get rid of the cop.

"I show you professional. I no make introduction." Pastor pointed his finger as if he was identifying the man or men they were looking for. "You make introduction. I stay away. You see him. I show you. Safe for me. Good for you."

"I'm not sure that would work, Captain. This isn't what we talked about, but I do understand your position." Callender looked hesitant.

"Maybe this could work."

"Yes?" Pastor's voice had an unmistakable eagerness.

"But that would have to happen today, Captain. Time is of the essence. The Frenchman is arriving tomorrow."

"Yes, *senhor*. Today. We leave now. I show you today." Pastor believed this was a better plan.

"You understand, Captain, until we've completed our business, I will insist you stay with our friends the Russians. Only then will you be paid. Half."

"Half?" Pastor was confused.

"Yes, Captain. You tell us who he is, point him out, we make the introductions ourselves. That means twenty thousand instead of forty. It's only fair. Half. We take all the risks. Besides, Captain, this is but one of many arrangements we will have with you. Trust, Captain. All is a matter of trust."

Pastor nodded. "I agree, *senhor*. Trust."

"Before we shake on it, Captain, you must tell us who he is. His name, Captain." If Pastor bailed out at the last minute, Callender could easily find the assassin with a name. But the cop didn't know that.

"You want name and we have deal?" Pastor asked.

"Yes, Captain. Name first. Deal after. Ten thousand now and another ten thousand when you show us the man and we make the introductions ourselves. Do we have a deal, Captain?"

Callender put out his hand.

Pastor hesitated, but then shook on it.

"Good. Then, let's have his name, Captain."

"Lieutenant Eduardo Romeo Clabas." Pastor didn't hesitate or have to think about the answer. He had been thinking about Clabas since he had first heard the word 'professional.' Clabas was the executioner. He always worked alone and never left any evidence behind. He was a pro. The stories about him made most policemen fearful of the man. He was crazy. Pastor had heard other captains say he didn't have a soul.

Fionnuala waved at the barmaid for the bill.

Callender quickly put ten thousand in an envelope and handed it to Pastor.

"As agreed, Captain."

"Yes. Very good, *senhor*." Pastor was feeling better.

As they walked back to the Corolla, Callender told the Russians to shoot the cop if he made a move to run for it.

"But, I want him alive for as long as we can. Once we've identified the target, you can do whatever you want with him. I really don't care. We will need time to do the job and get away from here. Then again, he could be useful in the future. But, that's up to you."

"I don't believe the predictions about the earthquake," the Russian said casually.

"You are entitled to your opinion. I know I was a bit skeptical myself. But, I've been warned, and so have you. Just remember one thing." He wagged his finger at the two Russians. "Destrey doesn't make mistakes, and I'd hate to see you come into harm's way."

"We will see, my friend." The Russian driver had, no doubt, been briefed on Destrey. Nevertheless, he found the whole thing about predicting earthquakes a bit too much.

They had left the bar, well on their way to the city.

A half-hour later, Callender turned to Pastor. "All right, Captain, now we need a destination."

"Lieutenant Clabas work today at police station." Pastor's voice was confident.

"Which one, Captain?" Callender asked.

"Estadio Pacaenbu."

"I know the place," said the Russian driver. "We drive one hour. If traffic is good."

Fionnuala leaned toward the Russian driver. "Do you know of this Clabas fellow?"

"Perhaps. Let me see what my colleague can find out." The driver asked his comrade to make a few calls. Fifteen minutes later, the Russians had a pretty good idea what this Clabas fellow was all about.

"Clabas," the Russian co-pilot said, "come from the U.S. He worked in ships and bars. He joined São Paulo's police. His bosses think he is what they need. Clabas do anything for money. Clabas is sixty-two years old. Very dangerous, very quick and very strong."

Officially, the Russians didn't know more than that. Unofficially, they had used Eduardo Clabas on a few occasions when even the Russians found the work too hazardous.

The driver commented that he'd heard too many wild stories

about the white-haired man to believe such a creature could exist in real life. "Clabas is most dangerous man. Man is assassin. He is the man we look for."

"Are you sure?" Callender sounded hopeful.

"No," the Russian driver admitted. "But Clabas know the others. If not him, then he will tell us who."

"Quite right. We can kill a few birds with one stone," Callender said as an afterthought. "We must adapt and move forward."

Pastor wasn't paying attention to what the Russians and the Brits were talking about. He was almost entirely focused on what he would be doing with his newfound money.

Fionnuala knew the Russians were very much connected to São Paulo's underworld. Anything and everything the Brits needed to carry out their mission was available to them, thanks to the Russians' deep contacts with the local police, the military and the city's criminal organizations.

The Russians had been busy the last few years. Now that the continent had grown to dislike the Americans, the Russians were taking up residence in the southern hemisphere.

"Must be careful," the Russian driver told Fionnuala. "Clabas will kill person, like that." He snapped his fingers together.

"So, how do we get him out of the police station?" Callender asked Pastor.

Pastor didn't know what to say. He wasn't paying attention to the conversation. They had an agreement. The deal didn't involve him in any way other than pointing his finger. He was to stay anonymous, invisible and safe. That's all he needed to know.

Pastor hesitated.

Callender waited him out, but to no avail.

"I asked you, how will we get him out of the police station?" Callender repeated the question.

"*Senhor*, we stay and he will come. Time not long. He not stay in police station all day."

"How do we know he's in there?"

"That is easy, *senhor*. We telephone," Pastor said, as if the idea of calling a killer was the natural thing to do.

Callender thought about it. The idea sounded crazy, but it was simple enough to work. "Okay. I agree. Let's do it your way, Captain. If that's what we have to do to smoke him out, then we'll try it."

Pastor looked grateful. "Yes, get man out of station."

"We have about an hour before we get there. Let's make the call when we get to our destination. Where do you think we should meet him, Captain?"

"Café, *senhor*. Safe place for you and for him. Across the street."

"Could we find a place more out of the way? Too many eyes in a café," said Fionnuala.

"I know place where he meets with others. Police talk together in secret, no one look," Pastor said.

"That's better, Captain. Where is that place?" Callender asked.

"I show you. Behind garage near police station. Garage close. Never open." Pastor seemed to know the area.

"Could you tell the driver where that is exactly?" Fionnuala said.

Pastor walked through the destination with the driver.

"We need to be there a few minutes ahead of time. Before Clabas has the time to check it out. We also need to prepare the location. Isn't that right, Captain?" Fionnuala asked.

Pastor nodded. "Yes, of course, *senhor*."

"We will be there in one hour," the Russian said to Callender.

"Then, if there's nothing else, let's move," Callender replied, almost to himself.

The passengers sat quietly, keeping to themselves, while the Corolla hit the road toward the city.

Alexander Fionnuala and Willy Callender were going through their ritual of visualizing what they had planned for Clabas. The essential exercise was to mentally prepare for the action ahead. When Fionnuala got a text from the other Corolla taking Destrey to her plane, he took a deep breath and thanked God. Destrey was on her way, safely, with nothing to report other than to say, "So far, so good."

Callender asked the Russian driver to ask his comrades driving Destrey away from São Paulo if he could talk to Kleinrup.

"Communication not safe. Better wait," the Russian driver said to Callender.

As they got closer to their destination, Captain Pastor was beginning to feel a bit claustrophobic. The Brits were flanking him on both sides. Pastor found himself squeezed in the back-middle seat. The journey back to São Paulo was almost unbearable.

Fionnuala turned to the Russian driver and asked him if they would be on time to scope the place before Clabas turned up.

"*Da*. No problem. Need confirmation from *senhor* Pastor. Yes?" The Russian driver asked.

"Yes," Fionnuala said carefully.

As soon as they arrived at the location, the Russian driver called Clabas, and that was that.

Fionnuala walked the perimeter and quickly came back to the Corolla. "Let's get to the police station and wait there."

The distance between the police station and the garage was barely two hundred feet.

A few minutes after they arrived at the police station, Pastor pointed to a man coming out. "That's him.".

"He's taking his sweet time," Callender said.

Callender noticed that Pastor was still pointing at Clabas.

"Captain, are you sure that's the man we're looking for?" Fionnuala asked.

"Yes, *senhor*. He is Clabas. *Assassino*."

The other Russian sitting in the passenger seat next to the driver, hadn't uttered a word since they first met outside the safehouse. Without telling Callender or Fionnuala what he was about to do, he opened his door and walked toward Clabas.

Callender and Fionnuala calmly watched as the Russian sauntered toward Clabas. As Clabas turned the corner, the Russian walked up to him with a map in hand and pointed to the street. As they both looked at the map, the Russian quickly put a bullet through the assassin's head. The gun barely made a noise. The huge Russian held the policeman up until they came to the corner café where he gently sat him on a seat. There was no one in sight. The place was deserted. The Russian placed the policeman's hat on his head to hide the bullet hole. The Russian then sat down and called the waiter who was busy drinking his coffee inside the café.

"*Dois cafés-curto* (two coffees), please," he called out to the waiter in perfect Portuguese. "I'll be right back. And bring us a couple of *misto quente* (toasted cheese sandwiches)." The Russian got up and walked away.

When the waiter finally came to the table with two coffees and sandwiches, Clabas appeared to be sleeping with his head on the table. The waiter knew better than to bother the policeman. He left the coffees on the table and went back inside the café. By then, the Corolla as well as the Russian shooter were well on their way.

Pastor witnessed everything. He started to sweat.

Callender thanked the Russian for his work and said they could keep the briefcase as a sign of gratitude for a job well done.

Pastor understood that Callender had just given the Russians his briefcase. The briefcase that was filled with the promises of a better life.

"Who else, Captain, should we be looking for?" Callender asked while looking straight ahead.

Pastor wasn't talking because he understood that everything had changed. In just a few minutes, he'd gone from a life of luxury to no life at all. There wasn't any money for him. No deal. No future work. No nothing. He felt ill. The prospect of dying wasn't just his imagination going wild. There was a real possibility he had reached the end of his rope. He cursed himself for being so stupid. So incredibly dense he couldn't see a con when he saw one. He told himself he should have listened to himself. The whole idea of making money in exchange for information was too good to be true.

"Captain? I asked you a question. Who else should we be looking for? Your life depends on what you're going to say in the next few seconds." Callender still looked straight ahead.

Pastor couldn't talk. He knew he was about to die regardless of what he would say.

"If you cooperate, there is still a chance you can get away with your life. It's your choice, Captain. So, again, Captain, who else should we be looking for?"

"I don't know, I swear." Pastor was struggling.

"If you know anything, this is the time to come clean and tell us what you know," Callender said.

Pastor was by now frantic. He was pretty sure he didn't know any other *assassino*.

"There's no need to hide anything from us. You have already killed Clabas with your own words. You may not know this, but you did the world a favor. Because of that, I promise you I will let you go free if you tell us everything we want to know."

Pastor didn't believe him.

Callender turned and faced Pastor.

"I know you don't trust me, Captain. But, I'm not the one you should be afraid of. If your friends out there ever found out you were complicit, directly involved in Clabas's murder, you wouldn't last an hour on the streets. Your fellow police officers would hunt you down like a stray dog. They'd cut you up before they'd put a bullet through your head. Do you understand, Captain?"

Pastor nodded.

"Let me repeat myself, Captain. I am not the one you should be scared of." Callender chose his words carefully. "But, I could be. If you don't tell me right now who else is out there killing people, I'm afraid I will be forced to provide the world with a tape recording of our conversation. The Internet would love you. Within an hour or two, maybe less, your voice would travel around the planet. When that happens, Captain, you will be a dead man before the day is over."

Pastor began to understand how utterly foolish he had been.

"One more thing, Captain. I'm afraid the carnage wouldn't end there. They'd find your wife and make sure you'd see with your own eyes how many times she could be raped before they'd kill her." Callender had played his last card. It was now up to Pastor.

Perhaps he could get away free if he only knew. But he didn't. And he said so.

Although Pastor pleaded for his life, the Russians had other plans. The driver parked the Corolla on a side street, told Pastor to walk away and shot him dead without a second thought.

"No one left to talk," the Russian shooter said to Callender.

"You didn't have to kill him. For all intents and purposes, he was already dead," Fionnuala said.

The Russian shooter shook his head. "Best this way."

The Russian driver drove around the policeman's body and reentered the main highway.

"Thank you, gentlemen, for the good work you've done," Calender said. "Please enjoy the contents of the briefcase with our most sincere thanks. I think we'll take a taxi for the rest of our trip. You seemed to be responsible persons, so I leave you to your own devices."

The Russians nodded to Callender and Fionnuala.

As Callender was about to move away from the Corolla, he turned to the Russians and gave them a piece of paper. On the paper was Destrey's name. There was also a note that said *Look her up on Wikipedia.*

"I think you should leave the city," Callender said. "If that woman is right, there will be no safe place by the time the earthquake hits the city. Get out and don't look back. Tell the people left at the consulate to do the same. This city is due for God's correction. She won't be bouncing back anytime soon. Thank you again."

The Corolla left the scene, leaving behind Pastor's dead body lying in a pool of blood.

The police found Pastor's body a few hours later while Clabas was still sleeping at the café.

So far, so good.

38

Destrey was fidgety. "How much longer?"

"Not long, *Madame*," Ivan said, biting his tongue.

"You've been saying that for the last hour." Destrey was more than impatient.

"*Madame*, please." Yvan's partner, Mikhail, wanted to smooth things over. "You see traffic, *Madame*? Too many slow autos."

"Is that your secret agent answer? They're too slow... they're too slow, *madame, madame, madame*?"

Kleinrup thought he heard the man mumble in Russian that he was going to kill the woman if she...

Kleinrup looked out the window and tried very hard to become invisible.

"You find this funny?" Destrey punched him hard.

"No, ma'am."

"Don't ma'am me you... you..."

"You what?" Kleinrup half-smiled.

"Don't change the subject either." Destrey was a bit confused. Why was she angry? Why was she being driven in a beat-up old car, in secret, to God knew where?

"Louise, I understand you…" Kleinrup tried to bring her back to earth, but he was quickly told not to even think about it.

"No, no. Don't go there, Mister. You go there and I…"

"What? You're going to divorce me? Oh! I forgot. I'm not married to you. Oh! You're going to fire me? Can't do that either because you're not paying me a penny. Or, you can't live without me. Am I right or what?"

Destrey looked directly at him as she was debating whether she should kill him or just kiss him silly.

"Oh, what the hell." She took his face in her hands and forcefully brought him closer. "Or, I'm going to kiss you until you have no more oxygen in your lungs. How's that, Mister? And I don't need your money because I'm filthy rich."

"You wouldn't dare," Kleinrup said slowly.

Destrey brought her lips to his and she held him for what seemed like an eternity. She was warm and soft and everything that a man wanted and needed from a woman.

Love, everlasting and almost sinister.

The Russian eyed the couple in the back of the Corolla and made the sign of the cross. Ivan wasn't religious; however, he was afraid of the dark as well as the devil. Ivan was now sure of it, the woman sitting in the backseat was dangerous.

"Ivan?" Kleinrup's voice was calm.

"Soon, Mr. Klerup. Soon," replied Ivan.

"It's Kleinrup, Ivan. KLEIN... and then RUP. Kleinrup."

"Yes, of course." Yvan was now praying to St. Nicholas, the patron saint of Russia, to please make him survive the day.

"Ivan?" Kleinrup said. "Can you approximate when we'll be reaching the airport? And please don't say soon. What's your best guess?"

Both Yvan and Mikhail understood what Kleinrup was talking about.

"An hour, Mr. Klein..."

Kleinrup nodded. "Okay. Now we're getting somewhere. We have an approximate time and you got half my name right. Not bad, Ivan. I'm sure *Madame* is very happy."

"*Madame* happy?" the Russian asked, surprised.

"Yes, *Madame* is very happy," Louise said sardonically. "Now drive."

Everyone understood what was really going on: the Brazilians had put a contract on Destrey's head. That was a fact. The other fact was they hadn't yet heard from Fionnuala or Callender.

39

"We go to private plane now, *Madame* Destrey."

Yvan was almost done with the unholy witch. Now, all he had to do was to drive to the private airfield and deposit his passenger on the steps of her aircraft. He also made a note to pray to his God for forgiveness, for all the bad things he'd done in his life and for all the bad things he still had to do because of his job.

Destrey looked at Yvan, amused. "You think I can't recognize an airport when I see one?"

She was having fun with the big *palooka*. She didn't want to hurt him, but still, it was enjoyable to see a big man squirm in front of a woman half his size, if not more.

The driver pushed the pedal to the floor, even though he barely had a few hundred feet to go.

"Are you going to call the MI6s? Tell them we're safe?" Destrey asked.

"Not until we're out of harm's way." Kleinrup wasn't sure he'd call anyone.

"You really think they could still get to us now?" Destrey sounded frightened.

"Listen to me very carefully," Kleinrup said. "We are in fact more vulnerable now than when we arrived in Brazil. If they're professionals, like I think they are, they'll wait until our guard is down, which is precisely what you're doing. Letting your guard down. You think you're safe. But that's when they move in and take the shot. Like I said, until we're at thirty-five thousand feet, I'm not leaving anything to chance."

To no one's surprise, there were five armed men waiting for the Corolla.

Destrey watched the guards as they were scanning the horizon. "That's a lot of guns?"

"Those are the ones we can see. I'm sure there's more."

"You'd think I'm some kind of royalty," she mumbled.

"You're not too far off. These people are probably FSB. Friends of Yvan."

Destrey shrugged. "If you say so."

"When we reach the tarmac, wait until I'm out of the car, and when I call you, I want you to run up the stairs. As fast as you can. Don't look back. Don't say a thing. And let me handle your purse."

Destrey handed Kleinrup her purse.

"Don't fall on the steps, and don't look back. Got it?" Kleinrup looked around before exiting the Corolla.

"Yes."

Kleinrup opened his door. Mikhail was already in position.

Bodyguards surrounded the Corolla.

"Louise." Kleinrup's voice was suddenly rough.

"What?"

"I said Louise. That means get the hell out of the car and run."

"When?"

"Now, for God's sake. Now."

Destrey flew out of the Corolla like a bat out of hell. Twenty seconds later she was safely inside the cargo plane. The pilot was already moving the big Hercules, even though the doors weren't completely secured.

Destrey was caught off guard.

There, sitting in one of the world's largest aircrafts, were more than fifty Canadians and Americans looking at the woman who had had them wait at the airport for more than two hours.

"Auntie Louise! Auntie Louise!"

Destrey looked around, trying to understand what was happening, when a little girl ran toward her and jumped straight into her arms.

"Emmanuelle!" Destrey looked at Kleinrup. "Is that my little angel?"

"I'm not sure," he said with a smile. "Let's see. What do we have here?"

Emmanuelle's mother, Lucienne, ran behind her daughter as fast as she could.

"Boy, I'm glad to see you, Auntie Louise."

"Oh my God, I thought you were long gone by now."

"I had to take another flight. It's because of my husband, Hugh. He's on the plane. I'd like you to meet him. He's sitting in the back. He's looking forward to meeting you, Auntie."

"I'll bet he is," Kleinrup muttered under his breath.

Just as the huge cargo plane lifted off, passengers could hear, in the distance, gun shots. Then, the explosion. A small truck blew up not far from where the Hercules had been parked.

"Just another day's work, folks." The voice on the intercom was calm and reserved. "Guns and trucks exploding on the tarmac. This is your captain speaking. We will be flying the heck out of here bound for Fort Bragg, that's in North Carolina, folks, for refueling. We'll be flying at thirty thousand feet. I'm glad to inform you that we will be serving the best C-Rations money can buy."

"Who's the comic driving this boat?" Destrey asked with a smile on her face.

She embraced Emmanuelle until the little girl squealed. "Auntie Louise, you're hurting me!"

"Yes, I am." Destrey kissed the child tenderly while Lucienne looked on, amazed to see the great Louise Destrey so emotional, so vulnerable.

"Why is Auntie crying?" Emmanuelle asked her mother.

"Because she's happy to see you, honey."

Lucienne embraced Destrey, trying to get closer than physically possible while her husband, Hugh Pritchard, and John Kleinrup watched what seemed like the most beautiful family to have ever flown a Hercules Jumbo carrier.

40

EMAIL

TO: KLEINRUP, JOHN THOMAS

FROM: ANONYMOUS

Just to let you know we found him, the assassin. He will no longer be a threat to anyone. As to your father, he doesn't want to be found and we will respect his wishes.

Good luck.

W.

41

PREFEITURA DO MUNICIPIO DE SÃO PAULO

VIADUTO DO CHA

SÃO PAULO

The Matarazzo Building housed São Paulo's city hall. A full ten stories of bureaucrats, politicians and a few citizens still waiting for the mayor to tell them what to do. They didn't have long to wait. Antônio da Silva de Sabóida, the mayor of São Paulo, was making last minute changes to his speech to the press corps. He had an important message for them.

"Over two hundred reporters are waiting for him to show up," Ricardo Brothers, the mayor's press secretary, said impatiently. "Do you have the press release ready? *Fode-se!* Give me what you have. It'll have to do." He stormed out of his office and ran. He finally had a press release. It was better than nothing.

Brothers was nervous and anxious. As His Honor's chief of staff, Ricardo Brothers's job was all about running. As fast as he could. To do the mayor's bidding. To lie for him. To make up stories and make him look good. Even though His Honor was a spineless leech, Ricardo did his job admirably. He was the chief of staff. He was in his element of servitude and of treachery. He felt the rush of power and life itself vicariously through His Honor. His Honor was his life. His Worship gave him meaning. Like a master to his puppy. He was indeed the chief of staff.

The building was surrounded by satellite and production trucks from every news agency one could think of. The natives were restless. They could smell His Honor's blood. The gossip around town was about the mayor leaving the city. Running away as fast and as far as he could. Although his private helicopter was ready and waiting to fly him to Rio, he stubbornly refused to evacuate São Paulo, calling it irresponsible.

"That would be putting millions of *Paulistanos* in jeopardy," Antônio da Silva de Sabóida had said earlier that day to businessmen assembled to hear him condemn the so-called experts for creating an unhealthy business atmosphere.

"And for what?" Sabóida had added pompously. "For something that might happen in a thousand years from now?"

He had waited for the assembled elite to answer him. "No. No. No," they had clamored in unison. They loved this mayor. He was so pro-business, that the most right-wing men in the crowd cringed.

"This city is open for business today, tomorrow, forever," he had shouted.

The speech had been received with great enthusiasm. Men and woman had cheered their mayor for standing up to the outsiders who wanted to destroy their way of life. São Paulo's elite had paid for him lock, stock and barrel, and they wanted him to keep the city going. They owned the mayor. They owned the city. They wanted their money's worth every day.

Mayor de Sabóida understood only too well what was at stake. If he evacuated the city and no earthquake happened, his political career would be over. *Kaput.* He did not publicly give any credence to the fear mongers or the so-called experts, or even his own people telling him the worst was yet to come. Yet, he knew and understood what his supporters had planned for themselves. Some had left the city and had long ago cloned their businesses in Rio and Salvador City. He couldn't blame them for doing so. He'd do the same if he had to.

The mayor waited in his office for his chief of staff to show up.

"Ricardo? Are you ready?" The mayor shouted on his cell.

The chief of staff stormed down the hall. He also had plans of his own for getting out. All he had to do was to pack his boss onto his helicopter and that would be his cue.

"Yes. Now let's get down there and be done with it. The helicopter is fueled and ready to go."

"What about Camille?" The mayor revealed a grin on his face. He needed his mistress now more than ever.

"She's waiting for you in Rio. And your wife, well, she's getting ready to leave as we speak. She'll be here in about one hour."

Both men took the elevator to the ground floor where the mayor was to meet with the hoard of flesh-eating bastards. The mayor actually despised the men and women of the fifth estate. Maybe he was right. They called themselves journalists. People responsible for informing the people. Perhaps they were. Or maybe they were just out for a juicy scandal. The truth really didn't matter. Nowadays, the ratings ran the networks while journalists ran after gossip, rumors and stories of infidelity.

The front steps of city hall were swamped with mikes, cameras, howling reporters and the police. The relationship between reporters and the mayor was at best incendiary. Still, the mayor loved it.

"Mr. Mayor? Mr. Mayor? Some are saying the sinkholes we witnessed last month are just the beginning. Is that true?"

"Mr. Mayor? What do you have to say to your constituency about the impending earthquake?"

The mayor was about to respond when the crowd of reporters pointed their cameras away from him. That wasn't part of the plan.

Reporters wanted to have a better look at what was happening behind them.

"What about your fucking helicopter, Mr. Mayor? Are you leaving town?" Denis Planter stood still, giving the reporters time to get a good look.

The mayor stood almost paralyzed. He was used to such behavior from his opponents. He finally waved his hands. "This is São Paulo, for God's sake. The most important city in the southern hemisphere. There's nothing to fear. We are in control. The best experts in the world told us there was nothing to worry about and, by the way, I'm not going anywhere."

"You're a fucking liar. Tell them about your helicopter. Tell us about your mistress. Did you send her off to Rio? Would you like to talk to her?" The young man lifted his cell phone for everyone to see.

There was a hush as reporters waited for the mayor's response. Most wanted to know who this man was. Who had dared insult the mayor in person? There was a scandal in the air.

"Who do you think you're kidding?" Planter wasn't really expecting an answer from the mayor. Still, he waited for the scumbag to open his mouth.

Planter walked toward the mayor. He was surrounded by his own security detail. Fifteen gang members from the poorest *favela* in São Paulo.

"You piece of shit, *filho da puta*," Planter added calmly.

"Arrest that man," the mayor ordered his police chief.

The cop recognized the young man at once. His name was synonymous with deadly danger.

The police chief knew his story well. Partly because he had had a hand in it, partly because they'd met in secret to discuss how they could get along.

Denis Planter stood his ground.

The press conference was covered live. CNN, the BBC and MSNBC carried the stand-off in living color.

"You leave the building, you die," Planter said as a matter of fact. "You leave São Paulo, you die." Planter was now grinning. "You fly, you ride or you walk out of here, you die. *Filho da Puta*."

"What are you waiting for?" the mayor barked at his chief of police. "Arrest this man."

The chief of police was thinking it over. "I think, Mr. Mayor, the boy may have a good idea. Maybe you should stay here with your constituents. After all, as you said, the city is open for business."

The mayor snorted. "He's a hoodlum. A criminal."

"Try it." Planter walked closer to the podium.

He now smiled at the mayor as the square filled up with hundreds of young men and women. They came together, from different gangs.

United. Angry. Empowered by the mayor's cowardice.

"I don't listen to anyone except the good citizens of São Paulo," Planter added.

The mayor took a step back. The cameras were furiously taking head shots of the mayor. He appeared outraged and afraid. It made for good TV. Even better Internet. Wonderful headlines around the world were already being submitted for future broadcasts. The gangs had gone global and they were using the Net to make their point. The time had come to tell the people the truth about the fate of the city.

"What are your plans to evacuate the city, Mr. Mayor?" Planter asked.

This time, Planter waited for his answer. None came.

"What are you going to do about water, Mr. Mayor?" Planter continued.

Planter clasped his hands together. The gang members followed suit.

There was a rumble. The timing was incredible. God had indeed orchestrated the scene.

There was a queer sensation underfoot. The earth beneath his feet was alive. Planter turned around to see where the hissing was coming from. Was this a trap? Had the mayor planned it all along?

The cameras followed Planter's lead. Planter realized something else was happening. Something everyone feared.

There was a sudden calm. A deafening quiet. Not a sound could be heard. São Paulo was silent at one in the afternoon. Traffic came to a standstill. Not a bird, dog or cat made a sound.

Suddenly, the Altino Arantes Building, completed in 1947,

groaned. The earth beneath its reinforced, concrete foundation gave way. The building was sinking. All thirty-six floors moved as one, downwards.

All eyes were riveted on the sight of a monument to human ingenuity and determination slowly sinking. Plinio Botelho do Amaral's finest achievement. What was once the tallest building in São Paulo was announcing the demise of the brave city.

Another sinkhole, the chief of police said to himself.

"Get the bastard before he skips town," Planter said to his troops.

Planter's Praetorian Guard rushed toward the mayor and snatched him right off the stage. The gangers surrounded him, ensuring a fast getaway. The policemen ran for their lives. The reporters did their best to follow the mob, but to no avail. They were stopped with brute force.

The hissing sound grew louder, emitting sound frequencies never heard before. The mayor couldn't scream loud enough. No one paid attention to Planter or to the mayor they had just kidnapped.

Inspired by the Empire State Building and Frank Lloyd Wright, the Altino Arantes Building had sunk twenty-five meters. The building was screaming for its life as every part of the structure resisted, as best it could, the pull of earth's powerful natural phenomena. The earthquake. Mother Nature's way of saying, "Your time's up!"

Some just stood in place, in the square, not really comprehending what their eyes were trying to tell them. They looked up at the building and wondered what was dropping from it. Most windows were gone by now. The stresses imposed on the building made it rock back and forth, and although the swaying didn't seem like much, men and women were shot out the building to their deaths. Death by gravity. No one could hear their cries as they fell, nor did anyone recognize that the debris falling from the building was actually the city's brightest and best young men and women.

The hissing made it impossible to hear anything. People could barely hear their own voices. Every second was now slowed down to a trickle of time. Journalists in the square had lost interest in their story and were now writing a new one: their own obituaries.

Still, the sky was blue and the sun was radiant.

Planter looked up to the sky while running away with his captive. *How could that be?* he wondered. *How can the world be so beautiful and cruel at the same time?*

Every man, woman and child in the crowd heard or saw something on the Internet about the earthquake. But this, whatever it was, was unlike anything they had read about. In the midst of crashing structures and dying people, many were still in denial.

One journalist turned to his cameraman and asked him what he could make of this. "Who do you believe now, this woman from the U.S. or our own mayor?"

The people ran for their lives. However, one stood paralyzed. Unable to move. An older man was searching through his memories, trying to find meaning. Thinking this would make such a good story for suppertime. *The boys,* he thought to himself, *are really going to love it.*

42

CATEDRAL DA SÉ DE SÃO PAULO

PRAÇA DA SÉ – SÉ

SÃO PAULO

The São Paulo Cathedral, dating back to 1589, was the first place of worship in what was then, a small village. Over the years, the Cathedral was torn down and rebuilt. The last rendering was initiated in 1913 and completed in 1954. It was the largest Catholic church in the city of São Paulo. It was created to impress. It also expressed God's unfaltering love for the people of the city. They had said at the time of its construction in the mid-twenties, that the end of the world would be imminent when the church's spires were no longer. The engineers didn't believe a word of it.

As the people ran for cover from the earthquake, a few hundred could be seen pushing their way through the crowd toward the cathedral for safety. The colossal ramparts of the cathedral would surely withstand the brunt of the earthquake, as they had in 2007, when a 4.9 magnitude earthquake occurred near Minas Gerais in the South Atlantic Ocean some ten kilometers below the ocean's surface. Or so believed those who ventured inside the cathedral.

While city hall was relentlessly sinking into the city's underground, the carillon of sixty-one bells began to ring simultaneously since the cathedral's east steeple began to sway back and forth. Nobody noticed until the bells rang in a cacophony of bongs, brings and ding-dongs.

Inside the cathedral, the priests were preparing to provide the penitents with sacramental confession. All mortal sins would be forgiven. Somehow, someway, the absolution would certainly mutate into the last rites.

The church's dome, some thirty meters high, began showing signs of weakness. At first, dust fell from the structure as well as tiny fragments of paint and marble. The devout looked up for understanding or enlightenment, perhaps both. By that time the bells were swinging helplessly from the rafters, and parts of the structure were breaking off.

First the east steeple collapsed, sending tons of material on the east side of the cathedral's dome. The dome then started to collapse, and within two or three minutes, it disappeared from sight. The sheer weight of materials giving way to earth's gravity sent shock waves throughout the eastern walls of the cathedral. These events generated a harmonic oscillating flow to the foundations which in turn generated more instability to the cathedral. Within minutes, everyone inside or in close proximity to the cathedral was smashed into unrecognizable particles, merely grains of sand.

Outside, São Paulo's traffic ground to a halt as Avenida Paulista, one of the city's most important boulevards stretching over 2.8 kilometers, was the scene of fractures, some the size of a fist, others large enough to engulf a large Mercedes.

Gridlock set in. Traffic snarled to a complete halt for miles in all directions. Thousands of commuters couldn't drive home. Others were stuck in buses or commuter trains. Some twenty thousand were stranded between metro stations as tremors hit power stations and made them fail. Emergency power was also affected because underground power lines were severed by sinkholes. Within minutes, a general collapse of the city's energy grid turned the city into a chaotic nightmare. With traffic lights down and subsequent blocked-off streets, an exodus from the city was no longer an option. Destrey's warnings were no longer relevant.

43

PRAÇA DO RELÓGIO

UNIVERSITY OF SÃO PAULO

The university campus Clock Tower measured over fifty meters high and started to tilt about the same time the cathedral bells began their performance. The largest square in São Paulo was almost deserted save for a few students and a tourist taking video shots of the square with his drone.

The famous tower was built to take on winds of 200 kilometers an hour. Little was known how the structure would fare if an earthquake hit the university campus.

From the drone's perspective, the image later retrieved when it landed on its own, was not only strange but, at the same time, horrifying. The tower tilted forward. When it reached a forty-five-degree angle, the Clock Tower suddenly stopped moving. In fact, from the drone's video feed, it looked like the structure was trying to straighten up. Eventually, it continued its downward path and totally disintegrated before hitting the ground. Some students vanished into a cloud of dust, never to be seen again. A few moments after the Tower went down, a massive sinkhole the size of a baseball field appeared out of nowhere. A hissing sound coming from the ground was an omen that more destruction was to come.

44

OUR LADY OF MOUNT CARMEL

RUA DOUTOR LUÍS DA FONSECA GALVÃO, 18

CAPÃO REDONDO NEIGHBORHOOD

SÃO PAULO

The modest neighborhood church was built with love and secondhand construction material. In fact, the structure was built with anything that was free, scrounged, foraged or borrowed.

As the bells of the cathedral rang the earthquake's overture, the walls and ceiling rattled and swayed as parishioners escaped the building to avoid being crushed by falling debris. Unfortunately, those who found refuge on the streets were greeted by falling walls, bricks and deadly glass from the church's next-door neighbors.

They were killed instantly. Those who didn't find a way out were spared because the church didn't suffer any damage.

The locals believed they were spared by the grace of God. A miracle. A warning from God, not unlike what had happened to the Tower of Babel: the earthquake was taken as God's answer to the pride of São Paulo's elite wanting to reach the heavens and be their own gods. This insignificant building was so poorly constructed that it somehow didn't react to the earthquake's demand to give up and collapse. Once the smoke and dust lifted, the tiny church of Our Lady of Mount Carmel stood defiantly, gently reminding the neighborhood that God would take care of his flock.

Engineers from São Paulo's Escola Politécnica had another idea. They spoke of resonant frequency and a shitload of good luck.

45

EDIFÍCIO ITÁLIA

PIRANGA AVENUE, 344

CENTRE, SÃO PAULO

Parts of the Edifício Itália's forty-five stories of glass and steel tilted slightly before it crashed on its side, smothering all in its wake. The third tallest building in Brazil was no more.

Fires erupted all over downtown São Paulo.

Men and women from all walks of life ran for their lives. Unfortunately, it was too late. Those who hadn't already left the city were sentenced to death. Most of the population of São Paulo had stayed behind, believing the mayor's words and promises.

The ground heaved and groaned. Hissed and sank. Hell on earth. TV network helicopters witnessed the city's final breath.

The earthquake had started a month ago. The final act had begun.

Back in Boston, Destrey also witnessed Armageddon in real time. She was thinking about the boy, Planter.

Unfortunately, Denis Planter died as another building crashed and killed his followers and close friends.

He was nevertheless happy.

Planter carried the mayor's head in his backpack.

A redeeming climax for all.

GLOSSARY

COMPLETE LIST OF CHARACTERS

Amoedo, Cristiane Tarsila. Theoretical physicist. Employed by IPEN - São Paulo Nuclear Research Center at the University of São Paulo, Brazil. Won the Miss Junior Gaia Pageant at the age of thirteen. Obtained her PhD in physics at the California Institute of Technology in 2005. Born in 1980 in Vila Nova de Gaia, Portugal.

Armery, Sir Henry Blake. Ex-MI6 agent, section manager and director. Rumors have it that an order to terminate Armery without prejudice was sanctioned in 1983 by the Director of MI6. No official information regarding his whereabouts or current status is known. Born in Birmingham, in 1945.

Batista, David Costa. Businessman and banker. One of the world's richest bankers. Lives in São Paulo and Geneva. Father of three sons. Owns Manuel Brands International. Born in Rio de Janeiro in 1946.

Bluehawk, Amy. Administrative assistant (summer employment). Canadian Consulate General, São Paulo, Brazil. Born in North Central Regina (urban reserve), Saskatchewan, daughter of William and Mary Bluehawk of the Piapot First Nation, in 1998.

Borges, Ernesto. Captain, São Paulo Metropolitan Police Force. Husband of Nadia Sanchez and father of Pia and Tommy. Born in São Paulo, Brazil, in 1954.

Brothers, Ricardo. Chief of staff to the mayor of São Paulo, Antônio da Silva de Sabóida.

Callender, Willy (Wee Willy). Chemical engineer. Joined MI6 as a British Government analyst. Born in Inverness, Scotland in 1943.

Chagas, Lillyanne. Computer science engineer. PhD in1989 from the California Institute of Technology (Caltech). Born in Campo Grande, capital of the State of Mato Grosso do Sul, Brazil, in 1984.

Cray, Seymour Roger. (1925-1996). American electrical engineer and supercomputer architect. Designed the first supercomputer. Founded Cray Research in 1957.

Da Gama, Vasco. 1st Count of Vidigueira. Portuguese explorer. Born between 1460 and 1469 in Sines, Alentejo, Kingdom of Portugal. Died in Kochi, Portuguese India on December 24, 1524.

da Silva, Hector. Police chief for the city of São Paulo. He was named chief of the police civil force in 1998. He was born in 1965 in São Paulo.

Destrey, Louise Margoe. Consultant. Industrial psychologist. Owner and partner in charge of the Boston Triage Group (BTG) based in Cambridge Massachusetts. Born in Montreal, Canada, in 1957.

Fionnuala, Alexander. Joined MI6 as a British Government analyst. Guest lecturer, journalist and speechwriter. Born in Italy in 1936.

Folmer, Andromaque. Retired Major General in the French armed forces. She had more than twenty-five years of military experience with a strong technological and intelligence background. During the Jerusalem evacuation, she was stationed on the aircraft carrier Charles de Gaulle, the flagship of the French Navy, as a DRM intelligence operative.

Franco, Cesare. Catholic priest. Assistant to Cardinal Hedrick Zimmer. Jerusalem (Cycle) Foundation associate. Son of Ruggero and Adriana Franco. Born in Bologna, Italy, in 1968.

Greco, Constantin. Boston Triage Group (BTG) senior consultant. Created the Lola avatar.

Gutierrez, Carlo. Economist. Son-in-law of David Costa Batista. Married to Joan Batista- Gutierrez. Harvard graduate in economics. Born in Madrid, in 1985.

Harper, John Quincy. Named after John Quincy Adams, 10th President of the United States. White House chief of staff.

Kleinrup, Horace (1942-2011). Former MI6 director. Husband of Lady Jane Elizabeth Sassone, father of John Kleinrup.

Kleinrup, John Thomas. Businessperson. Middleman. Jerusalem (Cycle) Foundation associate. Son of Horace Kleinrup (former MI6 director) and Lady Jane Elizabeth Sassone. Born in Oxshott/Stoke D'abernon (Surrey), UK, in 1957.

Kriekoff, Isaac. Jerusalem (Cycle) Foundation associate. Son of Anatoly and Sophynia (Wirnoff) Kriekoff. Brother of Alexei Kriekoff. Born in Tel Aviv, Israel, in 1991.

Latu, Oswaldo. Catholic priest. Responsible for managing the Holy Trinity Community Center. Friend of Father Franco. Born in Timişoara, Romania, in 1951.

Little, Grant. World-renowned seismologist and the public voice for earthquake science and earthquake safety in California. Retired. Little had been with the U.S. Geological Survey and a visiting research associate at the Seismological Laboratory of Caltech since 1989. He was appointed by the Governor to the California Seismic Safety Commission, which advises the legislature on seismic safety, and served on the California Earthquake Prediction Evaluation Council. Born in McMullen, Alabama, in 1966.

Malfatti, Paulo. Analyst, Paiva Castro Dam, Brazil.

Lima, Janice. São Paulo gang leader. Known by her peers as the jumping knife because she is able to leap like a jaguar ready to attack her opponents with an obsidian knife. Born in São Paulo in 2000.

McGivney, Margaret. Boston Triage Group administrative assistant to Louise Destrey.

Meneghel, Bob. Canadian Consul General, São Paulo.

Menezes, Ruy. First line supervisor, São Paulo Wastewater Treatment Plant.

Moreira, Eduardo Donato. São Paulo gang leader. Known by his peers as the vicious little rat with a God complex. Born in São Paulo in 1999.

Newton, Logan Marion. PhD in 1951 in geophysics at the Imperial College London. Currently working for the Los Alamos National Laboratory as manager of the Earth and Space Exploration department.

Pastor, Joao Pedro. Police Captain of São Paulo R. Paraná. Present posting: Marsilac police station. Married. Born in São Paulo in 1966.

Paulistano. Resident of São Paulo, Brazil.

Planter, Denis (D). Paulistano. Street gang leader in the Jardim Filhos da Terra favela, in São Paulo, Brazil. Planned to marry Maria Estella Flauzarina. Born in São Paulo, Brazil, in 1998.

Precov, Julian Andre Illarion. Jerusalem (Cycle) Foundation associate. Former FSB director, KGB case officer, Ambassador to India, Russian Foreign Minister. Son of Lev Precov. Mother Antonina Precova. Born in Minsk, Belarus, in 1940.

Pritchard, Lucienne (born De Gaspé Beaubien). Schoolteacher, wife and mother of Emmanuelle Pritchard. Born in Ottawa, Canada in 1982. The De Gaspé Beaubien clan goes back to the year 1635. Lucienne Pritchard is presently living in São Paulo, Brazil with her husband Hugh Pritchard.

Pritchard, Emmanuelle. Daughter of Lucienne de Gaspé Beaubien.

Sabóida, Antônio da Silva. Brazilian politician, businessman, former journalist, and the current mayor of São Paulo, Brazil. Former city assembly member. Born in São Paulo in 1956. Known for suggesting feeding the poor with *Farinata* made from expired foodstuffs. Critics had another name for it: human pet food.

Santos, João (1985-2016). Data retrieval technician. Paiva Castro Dam. Mairiporã, State of São Paulo. Born in Itaquaquecetuba, Brazil. Married to Gloria Bracons, father to Maria and Elisabetha, ages 3 and 6.

Silva, Dolores. Private secretary to David Costa Batista. Born in Rio de Janeiro in 1953.

Spinetti, Alexander Francisco. Architect. CEO of Shapeshift SA. Consultant to the Jerusalem (Cycle) Foundation. Son of Dr. Edwin Spinetti and Flora Appia (architect). Born in Bellinzona, Switzerland, in 1971.

Tremblay, Colin. Canadian Minister of Foreign Affairs. Born in Kitchener, Ontario, in 1989.

COMPLETE LIST OF ORGANIZATIONS, PLACES, EXPRESSIONS AND DOCUMENTS

Agora eu entendo o que você quis dizer com especial. Portuguese meaning *Now I understand what you meant by special.*

Airbus NH90 helicopters. Multi-role aircraft designed according to NATO standards.

Altino Arantes Building. Known as the Banespa Building, and, most popularly, by Banespão, is an important skyscraper located in downtown São Paulo, Brazil.

Alto de Pinheiros district. Borough of the city of São Paulo, Brazil.

Bom Dia. Portuguese for *Good morning.*

Book of Deuteronomy. Fifth book of the Torah, a section of the Hebrew Bible and the Christian Old Testament.

Boston Triage Group (BTG). American consultant organization specializing in forecasting geo-political shifts and risk analysis. Based in Cambridge, Massachusetts.

Boston University (BU). Private research university created in 1869, located in Boston, Massachusetts.

Capão Redondo. São Paulo low-income neighborhood as well as metro station.

Capitao. Brazilian (Portuguese) word for *Captain*.

***Chu* pas contente.** Acronym, French Canadian expression for *I'm not happy*.

Corrupto do Brazil. Portuguese for *Brazil the Corrupt*.

Cuzão. Portuguese noun. A vulgar expression unique to São Paulo, meaning *Jerk, nitwit or simpleton*.

Dinheiros. Former currency of Portugal from 1179 until approximately 1502.

DRM intelligence operative. French Directorate of Military Intelligence (Direction du Renseignement Militaire). Created by Socialist Interior Minister Pierre Joxe in 1992, after the Gulf War, to centralize military intelligence information.

Edifício Itália. 46-story skyscraper located in the República district, Central Zone of São Paulo, Brazil. Built from 1956 to 1965.

É este o seu chefe. Portuguese for *This is your boss*.

É fácil para você dizer. Portuguese for *It's easy for you to say*.

É o jeitinho brasileiro. Brazilian expression meaning *It's the Brazilian way*.

EST. Eastern Standard Time. Time zone in use in North America, Caribbean and Central America.

Eu não acredito em você. Por que eu deveria? Portuguese for *I do not believe you. Why should I?*

Eu não preciso do seu dinheiro. Portuguese for *I do not need your money.*

Eu não vou tentar ser agradável ou açúcar casaco qualquer coisa que eu tenho a dizer para você. Você entende isso? Portuguese for *I will not try to be nice or sugarcoat anything I have to say to you. Do you understand this?*

Eu não acredito. Você está aqui. Portugese meaning *I do not believe. You are here.*

eVigill. Developers and deliverers of emergency mass-notification and alert multi-channel solutions for governments, municipalities and businesses. Its world-class, mass notification solutions are field proven and have been tested in real, continuous, life-threatening events. *"Knowing what is happening, when it is happening will save lives, will allow for faster recovery, will save money, and will allow for better control. This is the bedrock of eVigill."*

Filho da puta. Brazilian expression meaning *Son of a bitch.*

Fique tranquilo. Brazilian Portuguese expression meaning *Don't worry.*

Fode-se! Brazilian expression meaning *Fuck it!*

Globo Television Network. Globo is a Brazilian television network. It is the biggest commercial TV network in Latin America.

Hercules, (U.S. Armed Forces). Lockheed C-130 Hercules is a four-engine turboprop military transport aircraft designed and built originally by Lockheed (Lockheed Martin) in the 1950s.

Holy Ghost. Third person of the Holy Trinity: the Triune God manifested as God the Father, God the Son, and Holy Spirit; each person itself being God. Three in one. The Holy Spirit is referred to as the Lord, the Giver of Life.

Holy Trinity Community Center. Hub of parish activities. A special place for all user groups and a place to reinforce a sense of community, from a spiritual, social and health perspective.

Homem. Portuguese noun, meaning *Man.*

Infinity Tower. São Paulo's architectural icon. The tower sets a new standard for Brazilian office market.

Inter-American Development Bank. Financial institution. Largest source of development financing for Latin America and the Caribbean.

Isso é verdade? Portuguese for *Is that true?*

Jardim Filhos da Terra. São Paulo Favela. Permanent slum. The *favela* occurrence in São Paulo begun spontaneously at the beginning of the 1970s.

Limpar como um sino. Portuguese for *Clear as a bell.*

Lola. Avatar. Triage Group's Cray parallel processor supercomputer.

Los Alamos National Laboratory (LANL). U.S. organization created in 1943, responsible for doing classified work in nuclear weaponry and research in such fields as earth and space sciences, renewable energy, medicine, nanotechnology and computer sciences. One of the largest science and technology institutions in the world.

Lutador. Portuguese term for fighter. Also the name of Denis Planter's dagger: a BC-41 combat knife, originally designed for the military.

Ma chérie. French for *My dearest.*

Mairiporã. Brazilian municipality in São Paulo State.

Marsilac. São Paulo's poorest district.

Matarazzo Building. Also known as Palácio do Anhangabaú, São Paulo's city hall.

Milhões? Portuguese for *Millions?*

(Estádio do) Morumbi Stadium. Home of the São Paulo Football Club, the Estádio Cícero Pompeu de Toledo, widely known as Morumbi Stadium, is a football stadium located in the Morumbi district in São Paulo, Brazil.

Muito bonita. Portugese for *Very beautiful.*

Our Lady of Mount Carmel. Catholic Church. Located in the Capão Redondo neighborhood.

Paulistano. Resident of São Paulo, Brazil.

Perrier. French brand of natural, bottled mineral water.

Pilot. A translating earpiece made by Waverly Labs. "An innovative consumer products company created in 2014 at the convergence of wearable technology and speech translation."

Pinheiros subway station. The subway station is part of the São Paulo's public transportation system, commonly called the Metro. On January 15, 2007, the Pinheiros subway station collapsed, taking with it people and vehicles, including a passenger minivan, to the bottom of a 130-foot deep crater. The sinkhole triggered a landslide. Tons of dirt, asphalt and concrete fell into the crater.

Pompeii. Ancient Roman city near Naples. Along with Herculaneum, Pompeii was mostly destroyed and buried under 4 to 6 meters of volcanic ash and pumice in the eruption of Mount Vesuvius in AD 79.

Por favor, sente-se. Tenho notícias importantes. Michel, você poderia traduzir. Portuguese for *Please sit down. I have important news. Michel, could you translate?*

Puta. Brazilian (Portuguese) word for *Lady of the night or prostitute.*

Obsidian (knife). A hard, dark, glass-like volcanic rock formed by the rapid solidification of lava without crystallization. This type of volcanic glass produces a finer blade than steel. Ideal when extremely fine cutting action is required and where trace metals from scalpel blades cannot be tolerated by patients.

Regina. Capital city of the Canadian province of Saskatchewan.

Senhor. Portuguese for *Sir.*

SH-3 Sea King helicopter. American twin-engine anti-submarine warfare helicopter designed and built by Sikorsky Aircraft.

Sinkhole. Also known as a cenote, a depression or hole in the ground caused by some form of collapse of the surface layer. Sinkholes may form gradually or suddenly, and are found worldwide.

Telefónica. Spanish multinational broadband and telecommunications provider with operations in Europe, Asia, and North, Central and South America.

Trésor. French for *Treasure.*

UNICEF. (United Nations Children's Fund). United Nations (UN) program headquartered in New York City. UNICEF provides humanitarian and developmental assistance to children and mothers in developing countries.

Você realmente sente muito? É só isso que tens a dizer? Portuguese for *Are you really sorry? Is that all you have to say?*

Yer bum's oot the windae. Scottish, meaning *You're not making any sense* or *you're talking nonsense.*

World Bank. Financial institution that provides loans to nations of the world for capital programs. It comprises two institutions: the International Bank for Reconstruction and Development (IBRD), and the International Development Association (IDA). The World Bank is a component of the World Bank Group.

Available at all major online book retailers.

WHO WILL SAVE AN ANCIENT CITY FROM NUCLEAR DISASTER?

LOUISE DESTREY LEADS THE FIGHT THAT WILL PREDICT THE FATE OF THE WORLD IN ANDRÉ JOHN HADDAD'S HEART-STOPPING TRILOGY, THE JERUSALEM CYCLE.

ABOUT THE AUTHOR

André John Haddad has spent the past forty years as an industrial psychologist. He graduated from the University of Montreal and has worked in labor relations, strategy, operations, customer service, and marketing. His work has taken him to organizations all over Europe, the Americas, and Asia. His specialty is understanding and predicting the behavior of different components of the organization. He helps businesses develop, change, and grow sustainably.

Haddad was the chairman and president of Suicide Action Montréal and a board member for the Tennis Foundation of Canada. He currently lives with his wife in Sainte-Adèle, Quebec, where he teaches innovation techniques to executives and MBA students. Haddad also remains an active member of the Order of Psychologists of Quebec.